I0742768

BOOK I
THE
PANTHEON

FORGET ME TWICE

E.J. CAMPBELL

To my husband, who never doubts me, no matter how crazy the ride gets. Thank you for always building me back up. I still think you'd look pretty cute in that cheerleading skirt, though.

To my sibling, the actual best of us. Thank you for my endless supply of fresh self-perspective and belly laughs, and the million other ways you help keep me afloat. You're the only reason anything ever gets done around here.

And to all my fellow dark Cliterati—stay unapologetic, ladies. May your books always be thirsty and batteries fully charged.

AUTHOR'S NOTE

The Pantheon series is a dark reverse harem, set primarily in a contemporary fictionalized version of the United States, and is part of the over-arching criminal underworld universe of *Imperium in Imperio*. While care has been taken to keep the writing authentic, the author is Australian, so if you find any inconsistencies or errors of any kind, please send her an email!

Contact information is in the back of the book.

Our heroine is sexually adventurous, and will have more than one love interest #whychoose. Books in this series will contain topics/tropes that some readers may potentially find distressing.

Please be mindful of your triggers before reading.

The Pantheon series as a whole will depict or reference the following (those that appear in Book I are *italicized*):

- *graphic violence*
- *criminal activity*
- *traumatic brain injury, MVA*
- *addiction, risk-seeking behavior (including drugs, unsafe sex)*
- *forced sterilization*
- sexual assault, sexual assault of a minor
- *death,* loss of a loved one
- profanity
- *MF, MM, MMF, MFM & other group sexual scenarios (all 18+)*
- *primal play & CNC, dub-con*
- breath play
- *voyeurism*
- DP
- mild D/s, bondage/restraints, toys
- gentle femdom, pegging

PLAYLIST

I DON'T BELONG HERE · *I Prevail*

DEAD INSIDE · *Younger Hunger*

MAKE IT UP AS I GO · *Mike Shinoda, K.Flay*

DIAL TONE · *Catch Your Breath*

SEROTONIN · *Call Me Karizma*

DOES YOUR BRAIN EVER GET THIS LOUD? · *St. South*

OH MY DEAR LORD · *The Unlikely Candidates*

WORST IN ME · *Unlike Pluto*

BLACKOUT · *AViVA*

BAD LUCK · *Adam Jensen*

BLOOD SUGAR · *Kid Bloom*

MEDICINE · *Syd*

HORNS (ARC NORTH REMIX) · *Arc North, Bryce Fox*

ZEN · *X Ambassadors, K.Flay, grandson*

STUNNING MISSHAPES · *MONJOE, Garden City Movement*

LINE IT UP · *Stephen*

LOVE & WAR · *CHO, Marina City, Ryan Argast*

FEEL IT ALL · *Vinyl Theatre*

VOICES IN MY HEAD · *Falling In Reverse*

PASSIN THROUGH · *Jack and the Other*

OXYTOCIN · *Chandler Leighton*

FRIENDS · *Sixlight*

HEROIN · *Badflower*

BROKENASYOU · *ROMES*

I CAN'T GET HIGH · *Royal & the Serpent*

ANTIDOTE · *NOT A TOY*

THE HILLS · *Archers*

ON THE ROCKS · *Ryan Vera, Letdown.*

SPACESHIP · *Xavier Mayne*

WISH IT WAS LOVE · *Cemetery Sun*

HELL IS EMPTY, AND ALL THE DEVILS ARE HERE.

— THE TEMPEST, WILLIAM SHAKESPEARE

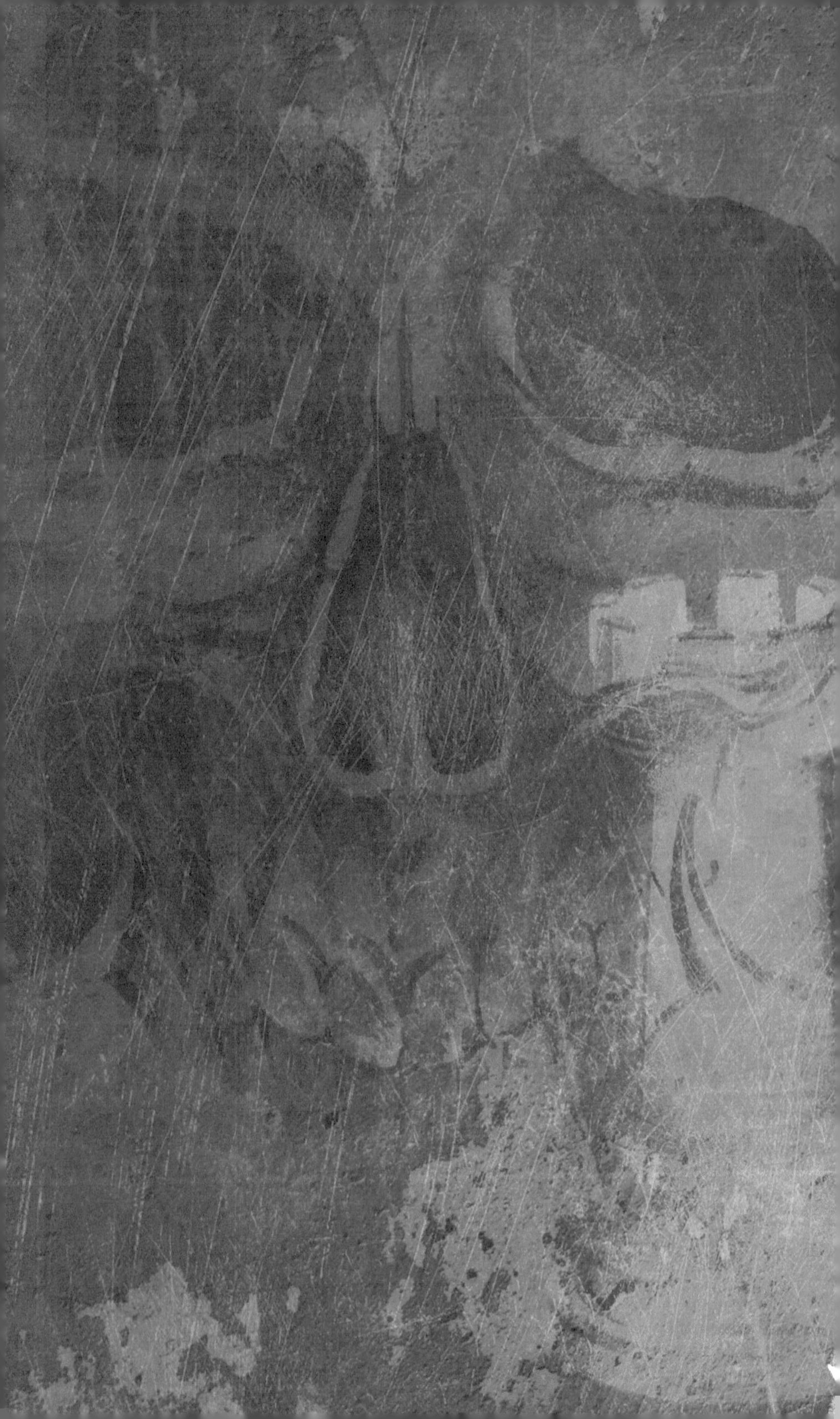

PROLOGUE
SABINE

FIVE YEARS AGO

HE'S BACK.

Again.

Even in my early-morning, pre-breakfast delirium, I could never mistake that finely tailored suit.

That slick, two hundred-dollar haircut.

Or that air of *barely* restrained violence.

Three days in a row he's been here, staking out our neighborhood. No obvious agenda. Just hours spent haunting the street corner like a well-groomed statue.

Unmoving. Observing. Repelling anyone who passes him without the need for so much as a word.

It's confusing as fuck to say the least.

What the hell *is he waiting for?*

Hoping wildly that I haven't already given away my position, I straighten and press my back against the cold bricks of the alleyway. My ratty backpack scrapes softly along the wall behind me, making me wince. It's a rough, narrow passage that smells heavily of overripe fruit and rotting meat cuts, but it's well covered and dry most nights.

The chill now leaching the last of my warmth through the shoulders of my threadbare sweater is a stark reminder that we're on the business end of fall. Winter is firmly creeping in. I'm going to have to magic up some much warmer clothes.

Like, *soon.*

My traitorous stomach decides to gurgle in protest of our pointless loitering. I huff and shift gently against the wall, weighing my options. I decide that for right now, my very real hunger pains trump the overly dramatic hypotheticals of freezing to death.

Unfortunately, taming the hunger beast means *money,* and money means slipping out past our Mystery Man and finding a decent mark.

I blow out an uneasy breath. Hopefully there'll still be a few commuters lingering near the café strip.

Tugging my hood forward, I peer back out to cautiously check the street. When I see he hasn't moved an inch, I laugh quietly under my breath. He really *is* a statue. Reflexively, my eyes zero in and sweep him from head to toe, cataloging what I can from this distance.

Dark hair, coiffed.
Straight, freshly shaven jawline.
Navy suit with crisp, white button down.
Blood-red tie.
Matching pocket square.

Golden tie pin in the shape of something distinct. Too far away to tell.

Gold ring right ring finger. No ring on left hand.

Shoes, expensive, polished.

The handsome stranger is in his usual spot, leaning against the wall of the rundown bodega on the corner with his arms crossed and shoulders loose. He may be trying to sell us *aloof* with that posture, but beneath all that cashed-up arrogance there's a dark undercurrent. Call it street kid intuition. He's oozing ten kinds of *dangerous*, his power uncoiling slowly around him like a python ready to strike.

I can't make out the color of his eyes from here, but if I had to guess, they're probably dark. Black like two lumps of coal. Coals from the pits of hell. Burning and soulless.

Gangster? Gotta be.

This city is certainly *no* stranger to criminal outfits.

No matter who he works for though, it's painfully obvious as he takes in the rush hour tableau unfolding before him, that this *really* isn't his scene. This is a poorer, frost-pinched stretch of South Lexington. It's more of an industrial factory workers with Dad bods, less stockbroker financial bros chasing the latest model of secretary kind of area.

It's like he doesn't even register that his expensive outfit and *fuck off* vibes are attracting him the same sort of unbroken attention that he's giving the street around him. He ignores the young, brunette mother wearing a baby pink sundress—the one who almost steers her kid's stroller into a nearby hydrant while throwing him moon eyes. He barely spares a glance for Mr Giorgio, the mustachioed and balding local grocer so caught up rubbernecking at our phantom, he knocks his entire display of clementines flying. Just a slow, lazy blink for the bright fruits that roll along the sidewalk and spill into the gutter at his feet.

More than likely, he's just too rich to care.

Yeah, definitely some flavor of shady motherfucker.

My head is starting to ache the more I take in, the pain becoming almost as loud as my stomach.

Time to go.

Head down, I finally slip out of the shadows of the alleyway, heading north and away from the strange corner vigil.

HALF A BLOCK DOWN, I spot my mark. A curly-haired professor-type talking loudly on his cell.

Forest green vest. Corduroy trousers. Wallet playing peekaboo in back left pocket.

Gliding past, I angle my body slightly towards the hapless man, shielding both his back and my hand from view. He's clearly upset at whoever is on the other end of the call, sparing no thought for the grubby teen sneaking up behind him. Without breaking momentum, I brush my fingers across the wallet and deftly slip it free. In the same movement, I thrust it safely into my front sweater pocket and continue forward, weaving through the thinning breakfast crowds.

I don't glance back.

Another block and a half from my target, when no angry shouts follow, I stop briefly to do a quick assessment of my takings. If *Karma* hasn't come to bite me in the ass, it'll be enough for a hot drink and something decent to eat. My stomach continues its lament at the thought of a real meal and I roll my eyes. Leaning against the window of a small boutique, shoulders curled forward, I take a quick survey of the adults flowing by.

Young couple. Matching white tees, blue jeans. Yammering about their upcoming getaway.

Woman. Mousy brown hair. Baby blue blouse. Logo of the bank across the street.

Man. Middle-aged. Fit but sweaty. Pre-shift workout?

There's a sudden prickle on the back of my neck, but when I cut my eyes over my shoulder and back down the street, there's no one even remotely paying me attention.

Deciding I'm in the clear, I pull out the creased leather wallet, and thumb through its meager contents with practiced intent. Ignoring the license, library card, ticket stubs and credit cards, I go straight for the cash.

Two twenties, a ten, two fives and four dollars.

I give myself an enthusiastic mental high-five. It's not a huge haul by any means, but less and less people are carrying cash these days, so I'm calling it a win. I'm *absolutely* going to be treating myself today. A freshly cooked white chocolate and raspberry muffin, and some thrifted winter clothes.

I hum happily. *It's the little things, right?*

Sonny's, my favorite eatery in South Lex, is across the street and a few blocks down. I only really get the chance to eat there when I find myself with a little extra money, or when I'm desperate for the pick me up. Otherwise I do my best to save on food by dumpster diving behind the choice restaurants, or cycling through the local soup kitchens.

Plan sorted, I pull my backpack around, shove the cash safely into the largest pocket, and then nonchalantly push off from the window. Stealing a glimpse at my reflection, I can see that I'm still alone, taking the opportunity to slip back easily into the flow of sidewalk traffic.

On the way towards the intersection where I need to cross, I slip the wallet into a half-empty trash can. As I step up to the curb, I check my surroundings and notice a man to my right.

Orange mountain bike. Fluorescent yellow and pink lycra shorts. Matching vest. Water bottle.

Across the street a young girl with strawberry-blonde braids is being led by her Guide dog.

I look away from them just as that little spark of unease tickles between my shoulder blades again. This time I don't risk looking around. If it's the man from the corner, I'll just have to hustle and hope he loses interest in me.

Keeping my hood forward, I'm attempting to relax

my posture as I make my way quickly across and down the block. I try matching my breaths to each step, then distracting myself with thoughts of breakfast, but the growing paranoia and headache doesn't let up. I can't shake the feeling someone is following me, stealing sidelong peeks in the windows of the stores as I march by.

By the time I reach the quaint little building that houses the café, my neck and shoulders are tense and I'm just a little bit hangry. With a frustrated grunt, I push through *Sonny's* charming stained glass door, determined to find somewhere to sit that will allow me to keep one eye on the front windows. I can camp there until all the creeps have cleared out, heading to work for the day.

The bell overhead has barely finished ringing before I'm at the counter and rushing out my order. Snatching my table number, I make a beeline towards the far back corner where I can see my favorite set of battered and mismatched velour wing chairs, each one pushed right up to a scratched, low-rise table.

It's very cozy, and super warm now that I'm out of the wind, but I'm more concerned with the uninterrupted view it gives me of any customers coming in and out of the eatery.

As soon as the bouncy, freckled barista with sun-bleached hair and a wide, friendly grin drops off my muffin and hot cocoa, I fall on them with rabid enthusiasm. It's been at least a month since I've had anything resembling *freshly baked*, rather than *two-day-old leftovers.* My earlier anxiety slowly ebbs away with each to-die-for mouthful.

I'm so caught up in enjoying the whipped cream, dreamy chocolate drizzle, and the fact that my headache has begun to wane, that I totally forget to keep focus on my surroundings. So it's not until I lower my cup on a happy sigh that I realize I'm no longer alone.

Shit.

Across from me now sits the Mystery Man.

With slow, exaggerated movements—like I'm trying my best not to startle a wild animal—I place the mug down in front of me, and just as slowly fold my hands in my lap.

He doesn't say a word. He simply sits, elegant and stony-faced, regarding me from across the small, chipped table. His left leg is folded over his right knee, his hands resting casually along the threadbare arms of the chair.

His posture is languid, but ready. Like a big jungle cat, poised to take down its dinner in one effortless movement.

Shock—and *curiosity?*—root me to my seat.

Under the café's lighting, his golden skin glows, and that shiny, deep brown hair now looks almost black, despite the silver wings I now notice at his temple. It's *immaculate.* He does *not* look like he's been standing outside, braving the South Lex chill for hours. Not a hair out of place, nor a wrinkle on his suit.

I continue to study him. He continues to recline in that big cat way and studies me back. A king on his throne, looking down upon a hungry peasant.

"You are very good at going unseen," he eventually concedes after several minutes of our mutual, silent perusal. His voice is dark, smoky and unhurried. It suits him and the whole *don't cross me if you want to live* danger vibes that float around him like a cloying dust cloud. "It has taken me three days to finally pin you down. My men have been looking for weeks."

He doesn't *look* impressed, despite his words. In fact, he seems…bored. But that gaze is locked on me and it's heavy. His attention leaves the air around us feeling thick. There is no doubt in my mind that the person I am sitting across from is a very powerful man.

The analogue clock ticks loudly away above our heads.

His eyes, to my disappointment, *aren't* blackened embers like a hell demon's, but rather a rich blue. Blue, but still dark enough to give anyone in their line of sight a serious case of the chills.

He hasn't said anything else. Clearly he's expecting me to respond to his compliment.

I'm just wondering what the best course of action here is. If he's here because he wants something from me, perhaps I can use that to my advantage? Solve the *Mystery of the Rich Gangster & the Rundown Street Bodega* once and for all.

I ignore his blunt opener, and ask, rather blithely, "Italian or Russian?"

A subtle crease appears between the dark slashes of his brows, the first crack in his otherwise emotionless mask. "Italian, or Russian?" he echoes slowly, clearly perplexed by this certainly inane line of questioning.

I gesture with both hands in his general, well-groomed direction. "The hair? The suit and shoes? The murder-for-hire aura?"

I lean over and pick my mug back up, just so I can stop talking with my hands. I honestly can't tell if he thinks I'm being serious, so I offer him a small, conciliatory smirk. "It's all very mobster chic. But I don't *hear* an accent. So I was wondering…Mafia? Or Bratva?"

The little line of confusion that had made its appearance with my poor attempt at a joke, now smoothes out, replaced by a smile that spreads slowly across his irritatingly handsome face. It's a very eerie thing to watch. Evil should never smile like that. All bright, white expensive teeth. Sharp canines.

It's a conqueror's smile.

A *predator*'s smile.

I can't look away, my eyes fixed on his mouth. I'm imagining him ripping out throats with those teeth.

"Sabine," he drawls, "What was your server's name?" The smile is gone, and an intense look—something *expectant*—is now in its place.

My eyes drag up from his mouth only to collide with that all-seeing gaze. I blink, the realization that *he knows my name* sluicing over me like an ice-cold bucket of *what the fuck.*

"How di—"

"There are no real *loyalties* on the streets, Sabine. You should know this by now. Every man, woman and child will talk for the right pressure. It's a fact of life." His expression is so cool and knowing, like he can see every cog and gear inside me, and exactly what makes me tick. "Be careful with whom you share these pieces of yourself."

I don't miss that he says *pressure* instead of *price*.

Jesus. Who the fuck is this guy?

But I know exactly where he's applied his so-called *pressure*. The middle-aged librarians at the County Library are the only adults who know me in any capacity these days. The library had been a safe haven; warm, open long hours and full of free books for a bored, homeless teen to devour.

"Nobody cares about my secrets," I say, somewhat bewildered.

He doesn't move, but his eyes flash dangerously. That choking presence of his is somehow becoming even *more* oppressive. It's like he's sucking the remainder of the air out from the small space between us, just by virtue of being here.

"Ah, yes. Because you are nothing more than a traumatized, orphaned, street urchin. A runaway princess with a tragic sob story." Those eyes burn with derision. The blue is darkening dangerously, making them look more and more like the Marina's Trench by the second.

"Couldn't cope with foster care, so you decided what? To brave it on your own?" Each word hits like a slice across my skin.

For the first time since he sat down, his eyes slip away

from mine, scanning up and to the left side of my face. He makes no effort to hide that he's openly eyeballing the brutal scar that cuts back jaggedly from my temple and under my blonde hair.

He doesn't say anything else. He doesn't need to. That succinct call-out already has me at a solid disadvantage. The tops of my ears feel hot and my skin feels tight.

I stare back at him, sullenly. "And who are *you?*"

I go to sip the drink clutched in a death grip between my palms, only to find the whipped cream has long since given up on life and started its slow descent into the lukewarm cocoa.

What a waste.

The mug returns to the table with a resentful *thunk.*

"Sebastian Grayson." He watches my face carefully, like he's looking for even the smallest hint of recognition.

I raise my eyebrows slowly. "Freshly re-elected Mayor of Lexington, Sebastian Grayson?"

His own eyebrows inch up at the disbelief in my voice.

Everyone knows the name of the man in charge of our City, but the truth is I've never *actually* laid eyes on a member of City Council before. I've spent all my time and energy since I landed on the streets, trying to navigate and survive South Lex. I was never intrigued enough to pick up a newspaper.

Why would I care about what the suits and their pearl-clutching wives were up to on the other side of town?

The enraptured attention earlier this morning makes a

lot more sense. *The Mayor, here? In our shabby, low-income slice of Lexington?* No wonder everyone was staring at him; fresh-pressed and polished, he does cut a striking figure.

But how do they not see how dangerous this guy is?

When he speaks again, it's to repeat his earlier question, albeit more forcefully. "Sabine. What was the server's name?" It's a tone that says I should not even contemplate disobeying. My shoulders pull up a fraction. I must make a move like I am going to look towards the counter, to lay eyes on the bubbly blond that was my barista.

"Without looking at him, Sabine. What was his name?" Sebastian's eyes are boring into me now, like he wants to trap my whole body in place with the sheer potency of his glare.

"Evan?" I finally answer, with a hint of uncertainty. I have no idea what he's after. *Is this a test?*

"Is that a question? Or was his name *Evan*, Sabine?" His brows are drawn down now, as he continues his scrutiny of my face. His scowl is intense. His tone is *more* intense.

"Not a question. His name was Evan. Is Evan," I correct myself quickly, like a confused afterthought.

He lifts his left wrist, touching his right index finger to the cufflink there. It seems like an absent gesture. *Irritation?* Something out of habit, perhaps. My eyes dart to the movement. The button is a golden bird. The same as his tie pin, I note now that I am close enough to see the details. *A crow, maybe?*

"Today's menu. Recite it for me."

I glance away from where he continues to press into the cufflink.

Menu? I shift slightly in my seat.

I can't see today's list of food and drinks from where we sit. It's on the wall behind the counter, and the angle is all wrong. But I begin to recite the items anyway. *"Espresso / Americano $2.50. Macchiato $2.50. Latte $3.50. Cappuccino $3.50. Mocha $4.00. Chai—"*

He cuts me off with a curt wave of his hand.

"The bike rider, waiting at the lights. What color was the water bottle he was drinking from?"

The...biker? Why does he care about the biker?

"It was a fluorescent yellow. Stainless steel. Had a logo down the side that said Lexington Razorbacks."

Sebastian nods slowly. "The girl with the seeing eye dog. What color vest was the animal wearing?"

Understanding dawns, and I want to shrug, throw him off his game. But I know the answer. I couldn't forget the details if I wanted to.

It's my curse.

And this man knows that.

"It was royal blue, with white stitching that said *In Training*. It had a patch but I didn't pay attention to what it was for," I fake-grimace, hoping that's the end of the interrogation.

I should have known better.

He quirks one of those dark eyebrows and I huff out a breath.

"It said *Don't Pat Me - I'm Working*," I continue, my voice sounding flat and resigned to my ears.

That eyebrow is still quirked. *What an asshole.*

"Interesting. Still, seems little more than a neat party trick, wouldn't you say?" He's trying to goad me. "One might even suggest you are merely a very *observant* young girl."

When I don't rise to his bait, he leans forward, reaching for an expensive-looking, leather messenger bag that the table had previously hidden from view. He reaches under the flap to retrieve a piece of white letter paper from inside. In a smooth motion, he slides it across the small table, past my abandoned cocoa.

I pick it up and glance down at the words. It appears to be the first page in a consulting contract between the Mayor's office and a construction firm. I look back up expectantly, but Sebastian just nods curtly towards the paper in my hands.

He wants me to read it. So I do, scanning as quickly through the document as I can without skipping any of the details. As soon as my eyes hit the words *Page One of Twelve* I look up. He doesn't say a word to me, just reaches over and grabs the paper from my loose grip.

"Now, recite it back to me."

I try my best to school my features, but my eyebrows are starting to pinch a little. This is the beginning of the end, I can feel it. The noise in my head that the food was working to quash is getting louder, but I can see the page clearly in my mind's eye. As clearly as if I still held it up before my face.

"Consulting Agreement as pertaining to City Construction Management Services," I begin. *"This consulting agreement is made and entered into between the City and County of Lexington, acting by and through its Board of Council Directors, whose address is—"* I pause when he holds up a hand.

"Now, two paragraphs down."

I shift my inner focus to where I can picture the bottom half of the contract perfectly.

"In terms of Consultant responsibility, the Council shall not oversee the work of the Consultant or instruct the Consultant on how to perform the agreed upon works. Consultant shall remain solely responsible for the professional quality, technical accuracy, timely completion and co-ordination of all studies, reports and other works rendered during the agreed time period of the project. Consultant is responsible for—" Again, I am pulled up by the motion of his hand.

I'm sure my expression looks petulant. I'm cornered and trapped. Only this isn't something I can gnaw a limb off to escape.

Sebastian on the other hand, looks *triumphant*. It's the most emotion I've seen on his face thus far.

I close my eyes. I know what's coming next.

It's his *gotcha*.

Sebastian knew *exactly* who I was and what I could do before he ever sat down. Before he ever turned up on that street corner. I can't even fathom *how*, but at this point, it doesn't matter. Only that I know my days of anonymity and independence are numbered. *Endangered.*

"Sabine Ingrid Winters. 14 years, 2 months of age. Severe trauma to the left anterior temporal lobe following motor vehicle accident at 12 years, 3 months of age. Accident also responsible for the deaths of father Quinton and mother Andrea Winters. Eleven months of rehabilitative physical and occupational therapy before being removed from emergency foster placement."

I slowly open my eyes. His voice sounds smug. It's as self-satisfied as his stupid, devilishly handsome face. I want to say I wasn't *removed,* but rather was *run off,* but I'm not giving him any more *pieces* of myself today.

I also don't want to admit that everything I know about myself—my name, my parents' names, how old I am—I learnt for the first time during my recovery. I can only remember the days I've lived since I woke up in that hospital bed.

Everything prior to that is one big blank.

The filthy clothes and irreverent mouth are thanks to living and surviving alongside the esteemed homeless community of South Lex for the last year. The head full of useless knowledge and stories is from the daylight hours spent curled up in the comforting warmth of the municipal library.

Were my parents loving? Was I polite and well-spoken? Did I do well in school?

Was I happy?

I look away, my eyes following a couple as they make their way towards the door. I don't feel all emotions as strongly as a result of the brain injury he's so gleefully dissecting, but it doesn't mean I appreciate the very public post-mortem I'm receiving in the corner of this cutesy hipster cafe.

"Acquired Savant Syndrome. Photographic memory, with *perfect* recall abilities."

Now I roll my eyes towards the ceiling. At this moment, I feel distinctly less like a teenage girl, and more like a circus sideshow. He's having me perform his tricks like a show pony and all I want is to put as much space between Mayor Grayson and myself as physically possible.

I half expect him to keep throwing inane memory tests at me, now that he's dropped all pretenses. Instead, he looks me dead in the eye and says, "I want you to come work for me."

I don't stop the half scoff-laugh that falls from my lips. "Come work for you? What, for the Mayor's office? No thanks."

I throw a last, doleful glance towards my mug of disappointment, then smack my hands on the arms of the chair, ready to push up and make tracks. I haven't even managed to lift myself out of the armchair when he drops his next metaphorical bomb.

"Sabine, sweetheart. Surely a street-wise girl like you has heard of the *Gray Man*?" The question is so slippery and chilled in its delivery, his tone practically *arctic*.

As the horror his words brings starts to set in, I can feel a sharp little kick of adrenaline up under my ribs. Any other time, that sweet zing of fear would be welcome, the rush of it working to calm the storm that's been growing day by day in my head.

Instead, my hands slip off the arms of the chair and land back gracelessly in my lap. I feel boneless and disoriented. No doubt my complexion now resembles something akin to the color of his infamous *nom de guerre*.

Have I heard of the Gray Man?

Have I. Heard…?

I'm not sure what this feeling bubbling in my guts now is. I want to say it's hysteria. It's doing a good job of drowning out the chaotic thrumming in my skull though.

Everyone in Lexington—hell, probably everyone in the state—has heard tales of the Gray Man.

Yes, even urchins hear the things whispered about the sinister crime lord, at all times flanked by several of his notorious army of henchmen. The Gray Men. Known colloquially as 'The Suits'. One of our first lessons out here on the streets is to avoid them at all costs. Don't see. Don't hear. Don't interfere.

They have a well-dressed stranglehold on near goddamn everything in this city—guns, drugs, gambling, clubs, protection.

And obviously, politics.

I have no doubt they're the puppet masters behind Lexington's many misdeeds and scandals; the rumors of which always seem to hit the street without fail. Newspapers be damned.

Now—now it makes sense.

That pure *malice* I can feel emanating from this man. It's so potent you can almost *feel* it, like a physical brush across your skin. For three days it's been tripping my inbuilt Bogeyman danger-sense. The set of instincts that all street kids have, the ones loudly telling me to *stay the fuck away*!

Only the Gray Man *is* our Bogeyman. The reason my earlier mafioso jest was just that—a joke. Because there *are* no Russian or Italian mob families left in power in Lexington—there are only The Suits and their clandestine gangland bullshit.

And the Gray Man is our *fucking Mayor?!*

My mind is buzzing with this bizarre revelation, but one thought is clear. Working for Sebastian Grayson? I'd wager it's a matter of damned if I do, dead if I don't.

A cell pings in his pocket, and I hold my breath. Hopefully there are some baby cheeks that need kissing —or more likely, some kneecaps that need breaking—and he will leave me in peace.

He doesn't glance at the phone as he stands to pull it out. He just slides it across the table, much like he did the contract. "Yours," he says simply. "Instructions for the commencement of your employment have been sent via text." He looks down his nose at me. Those cavernous, deep-sea eyes are harsh, and that commanding tone is back in full force. "Don't disappoint me."

Then he picks up his bag and strides away, disappearing out the front door like he was never even here; like he didn't just bulldoze my whole goddamn life into a fresh pile of rubble.

As soon as the navy suit and dark hair are no longer in my line of sight, I take a big, gulping breath. Snapping my eyes shut, I slump down miserably in the seat until my chin hits my chest. Then I contemplate the very probable end of my life, while absently pressing two fingers against my scar.

He knows my name, what I look like and where to find me. Somehow, I don't think the word *no* is in this man's vocabulary.

Guess that means I'm now working for Sebastian Grayson.

The Mayor of Lexington.

The goddamn Gray Man.

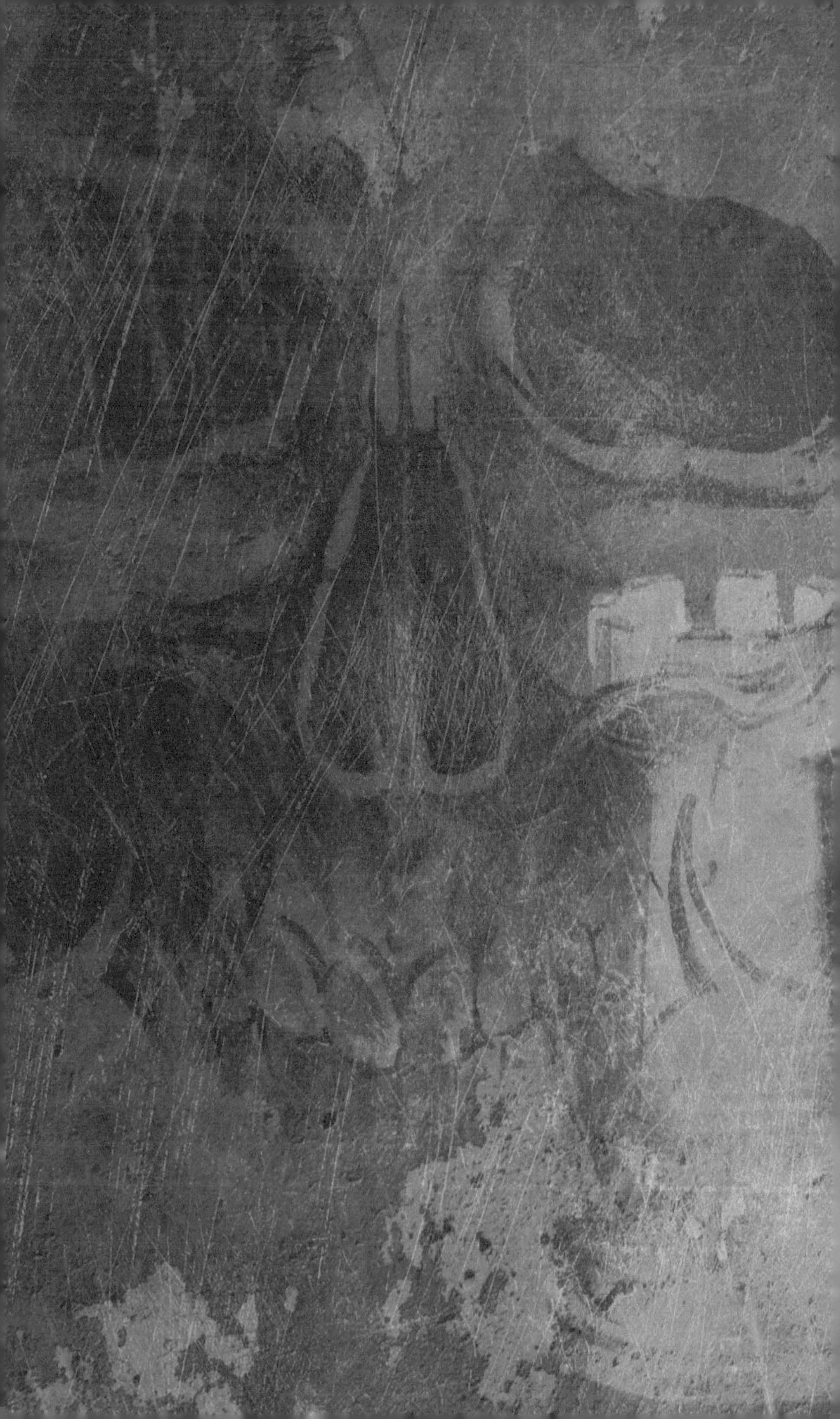

CHAPTER I

SABINE

PRESENT DAY

THIS WEEK'S war council is barely in session and already I'm praying silently for the sweet release of death.

Tilting my phone screen towards me, I flick bleary eyes down to check the time. *Fuck.* I barely manage to conceal a pained groan as my vision blurs and the back-lit numbers begin to swim lazily. I blink dumbly at the display until they slowly start to make sense.

Still twenty-five minutes to go.

As a ranking member of the Junior Council, I am required to physically attend all levels and nature of Gray Men meetings. As our organization's Librarian, I'm also expected to make observations and read and commit to memory the complete minutes of each and every one.

Right now? Just the *thought* of reading words is making my scalp contract painfully. Everything above my neck is currently throbbing with the steady beat of my post-bender headache, and there is a very real possibility I might just straight up perish from this hangover.

In fact, I am *this* fucking close to diving across the conference table and liberating that ballpoint pen from Foster's white-knuckled grip. I'm imagining with a clean shot straight past the orbital bone, I could silence the thumping baseline that's made itself at home in my skull ever since I woke up this morning.

I squeeze my lids tightly shut, leaning my head back against the wall, whose valiant effort is solely responsible for my current vertical position. It's a vague hope that a moment without the bright lights of the conference room might grant me some reprieve.

A low scoff sounds from my left. Cracking my eyes slowly, I slide my red-rimmed gaze away from where our junior crew's Security Officer still sits rigidly, and over to where I find Rhett standing shoulder-to-shoulder with Jax like an unbroken wall of delicious muscle and bad ideas.

Bastard.

My intention is to shoot my drinking partner-in-crime a well-deserved scowl, but thanks to the incessant pounding between my temples, I'm almost positive the careful movements of my face resemble more of a wince.

Rhett, our Enforcer, is definitely still wearing last night's outfit of a black, long-sleeved Henley and all-black tactical cargo pants. He appears *entirely* too sober, considering the amount of whiskey I *know* he was putting away. Did he even go to sleep?

The normally cheeky and easy-going bastard gives

me a subdued grin. *Hmm.* That's odd. He never hesitates to heap on the shit when he sees me the morning after a big night and a little worse for wear.

Jax, always the consummate professional, is freshly showered; dark hair wet, beard neatly trimmed, brooding posture in place. He's dressed and looking devastating in his usual business casual. Today is a white button up shirt, a dark charcoal tailored vest and matching slacks.

After years of practice, my mind is much more proficient at cataloging scenes or documents with a quick but thorough sweep. Theoretically, it *should* be causing less strain for my overworked brain, but it seems I'm not that lucky. I guess the issue is the sheer size of the sprawling cerebral storage system my mind adds to whenever it sees something, *not* the processing speed.

Both men have their arms crossed now as they watch me, a matching tension across their chest and shoulders. Judging by the muscle jumping along Rhett's jawline, and the pulse hammering away on Jax's corded neck, I'd almost say they seem…worried?

I don't have a chance to study that further however, because Sebastian's eternally cold voice cuts straight through my distracted musings. *Shit.* I haven't been paying *nearly* enough attention to this meeting, and if his tone as he addresses Faceless Henchman #86 is anything to go by, our Boss is in a *mood*.

The Low Man in question is actually a middle-aged Accountant named George Higgins, 41. He's kneeling in his eponymous attire, trembling like a leaf at The Gray Man's feet. Sebastian's Second-in-command, Dominic, looms from behind, his handgun trained casually at the back of the unfortunate man's head.

From where I'm standing, I can only see the side of the Suit's gaunt face and the back of a pock-marked neck, but I'm close enough to see that his skin is flushed a deep red. He's also covered with an unbroken sheen of flop sweat.

A clear sign of guilt.

This will be one for the Cleaners.

With Dominic's broad back still blocking most of my view, and the Tequila drummer in my head knocking out a brand new solo, I completely miss what the man stammers out next. But from the sudden hush that falls over the gathering, it's clearly *not* the answer Bossman was looking for.

A sharp gunshot follows—and *yep*—that's a fine spray of backspatter across my left forearm. The accompanying ringing that starts up in my ears just serves to amplify the already near-deafening noise in my head.

I sigh internally. *This* fucking *morning*.

Although the room is packed to the brim with Gray Men of all ranks, the nervous silence continues. All eyes are firmly fixed anywhere but on Sebastian. Nobody dares breathe, just in case he's still on the warpath and looking for more patsies. Today is definitely *not* the day to find yourself on The Gray Man's shit-list. Or any day, if we're being honest.

Glancing back at the Anxiety Twins, I'm suddenly struck with the distinct impression that maybe I should *also* be feeling some level of concern here. Instead, I check the time again. Only a few minutes have elapsed, and there is still a whole slew of mindless bullshit left on today's agenda.

Yippee.

So imagine my surprise when Sebastian grinds out a glacial, *"Adjourned."*

There is no mistaking the venom in his voice, and for Gray Men, keeping one's ass intact firmly wins over morbid curiosity any day of the week. Two jittery lackeys, eager to please, scurry over to remove the body of their fallen fellow. The rest of the lower rank members scatter like cockroaches after the lights come on.

The meeting has almost completely emptied out when I hear his angry hiss.

"Librarian."

The hair on my nape prickles and now I really do wince. Not that my guardian is the kind of man who regularly bestows me with great displays of affection— but *fuck*—that particular sobriquet was delivered devoid of *any* warmth.

I turn my head slowly, hoping my wide-eyed expression is serving guileless as I mentally prepare to face one of only three people on the planet who possess the ability to set me on edge. "Boss?"

Sebastian's dark blue eyes are locked firmly on me, their study of my rumpled, bleary-eyed appearance just as chilly as that summons. The dark, expensively tailored suit is perfectly fitted and pressed as always. His hair is immaculate, his tie a rich red, like a dark swathe of blood.

He looks every inch the politician that the public sees and fawns over every day.

The rest of the Junior Council—who also happen to make up my Crew for day-to-day operations—are still standing stiffly nearby. I know they'll stay behind out of team solidarity, but I don't blame them for not being eager to face down a pissed off Sebastian Grayson. It's fucking terrifying, and if he's not wanting an audience for this, you just know it's gonna be *A Really Bad Time*.

I wonder briefly if one of the spineless Suits from last night ratted me out for leaving the Compound again. Instinctively, I start to run through my memory of last night's duty roster so I have a list of names to give Rhett and Knox to play with. Someone's definitely snitched and I'm going to find out who.

When I hear a quiet throat clear, I blink to refocus. I then realize that the bottleneck at the door has finished clearing, and only my Crew and Dominic remain behind as potential witnesses to my incoming verbal scourging.

At least I *hope* it's only verbal.

During my first few years under Sebastian's *tutelage*, I was made to participate in what my new guardian liked to refer to as a 'conditioning program'. But let's call a spade a spade—it was months and months of both carefully scripted physical and psychological torture.

When I'd been plucked off the streets, I'd already been having trouble processing certain things thanks to the head injury. The training's purpose was to sever those remaining connections and reflexes. The end result, of course, being the forging of an unbreakable, untraceable, and hack-proof biological database of all organizational resources and information. A shell of a girl, only able to experience echoes of anger, fear and embarrassment. Disconnected from true feelings of affection and joy.

A vital asset that belonged solely to *him*.

The visible marks I cover up with tattoos. The rest is carefully concealed beneath a fucked up sense of humor and a borderline death wish.

So yeah, I'll straight up volunteer for one of Sebastian's soul-crushing monologues over what I know is the alternative.

No hesitation.

His wrathful gaze is still very cold and very fixed on me. I may as well be the only subordinate still in the room. He gestures towards me. "Care to explain *this*, Sabine?" His tone is firm and deadly calm. I almost find that worse than shouting.

A vague question, but he rarely ever uses my name these days, and I fixate on that. I haven't exactly been giving him many reasons to be proud of me lately. Perhaps there's a chance I can come out of this relatively unscathed.

I go to swallow, but my tongue is thick and my throat feels as rough and dry as sandpaper. *God, I am so dehydrated.* My head gives another vicious throb.

For once, I'm unsure what exactly he's referring to, so instead I clasp my hands together and attempt a demure smile.

"Explain what, Boss?"

I swear I'm not *trying* to sound flippant, but I'm really *not* a good actress.

The answering dark shift in his mood is an almost tangible thing.

I really should have known better than to hazard a gamble like that, knowing Sebastian can read me like a fucking book. The expression now taking over his face is no longer ice cold—no, he's positively *glowering*.

Even granite-faced Dominic, who has worked for The Gray Man for almost a decade, subtly leans away as if he can somehow physically dodge the anger now rolling off his boss. The disgruntled glance the older man shoots me says it all: *You've really fucked up this time, kid.*

I'm not surprised. It's been a long time since my superiors have looked at me with anything other than sheer disappointment.

In addition to being an ill-adjusted, unfeeling mess, the jagged scar I wear across the left side of my skull means that over the years my headspace has become an increasingly dangerous place to cohabitate.

Each waking minute brings with it the misery of my accident's curse. What started out as infrequent headaches when I was younger have since devolved into a chaotic jumble of constantly firing synapses. It's become a daily struggle for my brain to perform even the most simple of chemical reactions without pain and overstimulation.

Finding a way to deal with my training *and* my trauma-given gift has birthed a steady routine of risk-taking behaviors. After much experimenting, I found that a mixture of recreational, prescription drugs, and alcohol, somewhat muted the mayhem inside my head. Well, temporarily. Like most vices, it's not perfect, but it gets me through the day.

If I'm careful not to overdo it, I can usually pass myself off as a version of a functioning human being. And not the barely concealed substance abuser I actually am.

It's the best I can do when I can't find myself a healthy shot of adrenaline. Uppers. Racing. Fighting. Fucking. Killing.

The call of the void.

It seems that my brain gets especially drunk off of those small boosts of serotonin and dopamine, enough that it forgets it's supposed to be making any extra noise. For a time at least.

The only thing that doesn't work is seeing my own skin bleed. The Belgian took care of that.

But I have *no* doubts that if I wasn't Sebastian's ward and asset—my constant thrill-seeking stunts and shaky semblance of self-control would have earned me permanent accommodation at the bottom of the Lexington Canals a dozen times over by now.

As if to remind me of my legacy of poor self-preservation skills, someone settles a large hand on my shoulder, squeezing gently. The whiff of subtle, spicy cologne tells me the hand belongs to Jax. He never leaves me alone to deal with his father's displeasure. Not if he can help it. He's still fiercely supportive; even now while I've been off busy self-destructing.

As I continue to stand there, realization of just how little I actually remember of last night's exploits begins to creep in. It's not a welcome feeling. There's a few memories of the initial binge drinking with Rhett, and then…*nothing*.

I'm now trying not to think about Sebastian's long list of favorite corpse disposal methods as he stares me down.

He gestures towards me a second time, his brows pulled low and suspicious. "*This*, Sabine. Your head injury." The way he says it makes it sound like he's talking to an unruly child. If I didn't know better I'd say he was almost exasperated. Right now though, I'm just so thoroughly confused.

Head injury? Does he mean the car accident?

I'm about to question his sanity, or perhaps my own, when I'm interrupted by the large, warm hand sliding off my shoulder and down past my wrist to grip my own. Jax gently guides my fingers up and to the—*what the fuck!*—dressing that's tapped in place, high on my right temple. *Not* my left.

"This head injury, Sabe," he says quietly, his warm breath feathering across my cheek as he leans in to speak against my ear. I want to close my eyes at the electric feeling of having him so near, his domineering presence never suffocating like Sebastian's.

He's been my rock; steady and safe despite the hellish storm of the past five years.

I can't even enjoy the rare dose of comfort from his proximity; the air is still too thick with his sire's displeasure. So thick you could stick out your tongue and taste it. Suffocate on it.

Jax can obviously sense it as well. His lips thin as he drops the hold he has on my hand, his strong fingers slipping gently over mine. He takes a small step forward, angling so he's standing slightly in front of me. I'm almost touched that he's trying to shield me, but then he shoots me a sidelong glance that's full of regret.

Fuck, this can't be good.

I suck in a breath and brace myself.

"I don't believe she has any recollection of it, Father. She was inebriated prior to…the *incident*, and was given some pretty strong sedatives to sleep."

Sebastian's eyes are now almost black as they flit between Jax and I. A muscle tics along his jaw. It's like he can't decide exactly where he wants to focus his ire more: his fuckup Librarian or his disappointment of an heir.

"*Incident?*" he practically spits. "Has she crashed another one of your cars? Why wasn't she being supervised?"

Jax looks down at me again, a dark curl falling forward and an apologetic look still staining his mythically handsome face. There's no point trying to lie or downplay this. Sebastian *always finds out.*

He looks back to his father, and I can tell that this time I've gone too far. There's a line, and during my alcohol-fueled antics last night, I've somehow crossed it. His Adam's apple bobs once as he swallows and then answers in a flat tone, "No, not racing. *Russian Roulette.*"

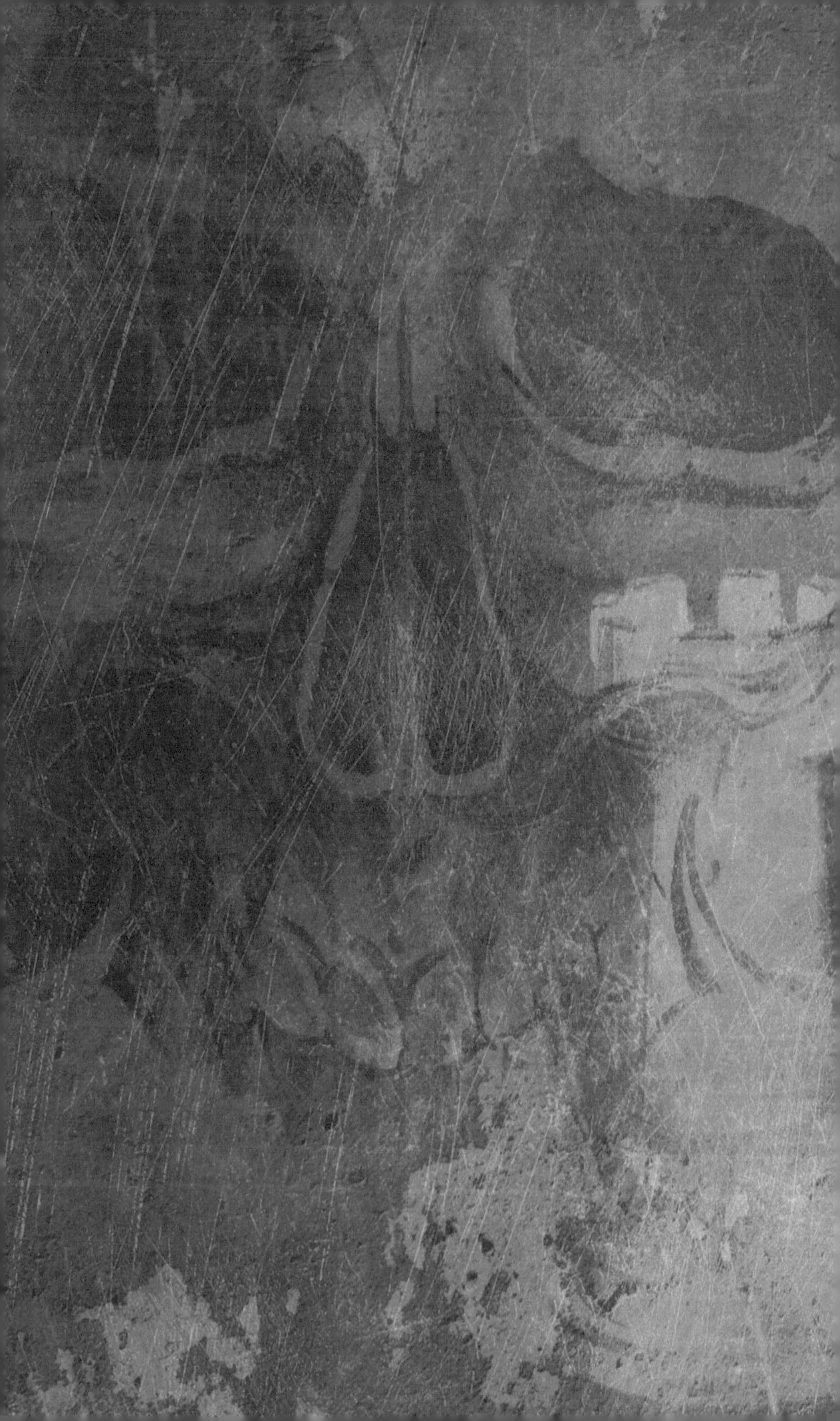

CHAPTER II

SABINE

I FEEL my eyebrows hit my hairline, the dressing on my new wound pulling tight.

"I shot myself in the fucking *head*?"

I have to clap a hand over my mouth as laughter threatens to bubble up and spill over. I feel off-balance and giddy, even just the *thought* of doing something so monumentally stupid lighting up the pleasure centers of my brain. Already I can feel the haze-like tendrils of happiness starting to creep in at the edges like I'm not actually awake, but standing inside a lucid dream.

What a trip.

Jax's expression doesn't change, not even so much as a twitch. Always the stoic and competent team leader. He deliberately ignores the jibe about supervision.

A quick peek over my shoulder and I can see the rest of our Crew's gamut of reactions. Foster, our Security Officer and resident wet blanket is looking pointedly at his boots, sullen as ever. Our deputy Enforcer Knox's dark brown eyes are pained. He's a round-the-clock worrier and hates when anyone on our team purposely puts themselves on the line.

Rhett, always the Devil on my shoulder, is fighting and failing to contain an amused smile. "Just a graze. You were too drunk to hold the handgun steady," he chuckles before roughly coughing into his fist. Even the chaotic prankster realizes how fucking bad that sounds out loud.

I quickly glance back towards Sebastian and Dominic and immediately wish I hadn't. I can now see visions of my team's very painful demise written across both older men's faces.

"Four overdoses, nine cases of alcohol poisoning, two hairline fractures, two concussions, and three cars completely written off." His voice is still pitched low, tone murderous. "That's just this year to date, Sabine." He doesn't curse. Instead he clenches his jaw and presses a finger to his cufflink in that old habit; the only outward sign he's agitated. I know now that his insignia shows a rook, not a crow. It's an homage to his favorite chess piece and the symbol for his organization. *"Thin. Ice."*

Someone on the outside looking in might mistake that agitation as fatherly concern for my well-being. But I know he's simply terrified I'm going to cause irreparable harm to his most priceless asset—the keeper of his secrets. The amount my life is insured for would make your fucking toes curl.

I watch as he visibly collects himself.

"As Junior Council, you represent the future of our empire. I can't say I'm still entirely confident that said future is a bright one." His meaning is crystal clear as he looks between Jax and I. I represent the ongoing financial and structural foundation of The Gray Men. Jackson, despite being a talented tactician and natural born leader, doesn't have his father's stomach for indiscriminate anarchy. That makes him an unsuitable heir and a current source of great disdain for Sebastian.

He leans forward, his hands clasped together over the table. The aching in my skull has spread to my eyes now that little spike of excitement has ebbed. What I wouldn't give for a horizontal surface right now. The strain of his stony silence doesn't help.

Finally he announces, "I have decided to offer you one last chance to redeem yourselves."

Like a benevolent overlord and not like we weren't all just silently waiting for him to share exactly how he was planning to dispose of our bodies.

I can feel my team move a little closer, stand a little straighter. What utter bullshit has The Gray Man cooked up for us this time?

He ignores the men at my side, his focus solely on me now.

Interesting.

Unsettling.

"As you are well aware," he continues. "Control of Roxborough's city limits would solidify our hold over the State. This, along with my successful run for Governor, would free up the resources and manpower necessary for me to finish moving the other Southern pieces into place."

I nod along. Every Suit alive knows dominion over

Rox City has been Sebastian's white whale since he maneuvered himself into power. Lexington's less industrialized sister-city is located straight across the Tethys River, but remains firmly in the clutches of our organization's number one rival—one-percenter MC, the Strange Aces.

In times of peace, the criminal Underworld in this country stays firmly divided into two distinct empires—the Northern and Southern Sovereignties.

The two normally coexist without too much extra bloodshed, but with the recent death of The Green Knight, The South has been left in total disarray. Multiple contenders for the throne have obviously stepped up, including Sebastian Grayson.

In fact, spread across the conference table between us is a topographical view of the two Sovereignties, drawn up and divided like a battle map. If the Suits can flip Roxborough, they can finish weeding out the remaining dozen Southern chapters of the Aces, leaving the rest of the disorganized bottom States to topple like dominoes.

The Gray Man would be unmatched in his bid for the Southern throne, his power and reach only equalled by the sitting leader of the North—a similarly dangerous and confident tyrant that styles himself simply as Midas.

The problem is, it's only so long before all this infighting amongst the contending syndicates turns into an outright civil war. If The Gray Men don't manage to secure the South soon, the Underworld's Arbiter is going to step in and the issue will be settled for us.

"We already have recruiters working on Lexington

Prep. Roxborough Academy's graduating class, however, holds another source of untapped potential we'd be remiss to ignore."

I know every last one of the file details of the Lex Prep upperclassman that Sebastian's Front Men have recruited so far. But this is the first I've heard of any plans to expand into the Roxborough student population. I can't say I'm surprised. As he said, we'd be stupid to ignore their existence just because it still falls under enemy territory.

The Aces have their claws in close to everything down there, including many of the disenfranchised youth. There will be tons of impressionable and ambitious thugs greedy for a better offer, as well as a plethora of academic kids on the fast track with marketable skills that we can potentially tap into. I begrudgingly admit that it makes the most sense to hit them now; making sure the tendrils of influence can creep through one convenient location, taking root *before* they disperse out into the world of universities, internships and the greater workplace.

I groan inwardly at the thought of the amount of information associated with profiling an entire Academy of students and staff. We can't have our Front Men going in without leverage on every single person associated with the place. I'm calculating roughly how much data that's likely to involve when I realize that Sebastian's still speaking.

"This obviously requires more preparation and finesse than was needed for Lex Prep. The local rhetoric there was already firmly in our favor." He pauses, and there is now a hint of smug malice in his expression. I just know that this is the second chance he promised, and I am going to fucking hate whatever words he utters next.

"That's why I am sending you in personally on this one, Sabine. You will head recruitment as an attending senior student at Roxborough Academy this coming academic year."

My stomach does a little wobble.

I couldn't care less about the fact I have to go back to school, even though I thought I was firmly done with it. I've been privately tutored since I was scooped up off the streets, and I'd already finished out enough credits to 'graduate' quietly months ago.

Seeing no real future outside of my role as The Librarian, I honestly gave up on the idea of higher education. Despite my ability to store visual data indefinitely, I don't really believe I'm all that *smart*. It's difficult to measure genius when you can memorize all the textbooks and reading materials, and just regurgitate them as needed for written exams. I can speak dozens of languages because I can suck up facts and knowledge like a sponge, but I'm not logical, or strategic. I'm not inventive, progressive, or a pioneer of ideas.

And I'm definitely not clever or charming enough to manipulate teenagers into throwing their future lots in with a crime lord.

That's something Jax would excel at though.

As if he could hear my thoughts, Sebastian's attention moves back to Jax. "Your face and name are too recognizable as my son, so you will remain in Lexington by my side. Sabine will be the *only* one enrolling at, or attending the Academy in any capacity. The rest of the Junior Council may station themselves in Roxborough, and offer their skills *off* campus, as needed."

Out of the corner of my eye, I watch my Junior leader's shoulders roll back and his posture stiffen. I can feel the indignation and anger bristling from him like spines.

I don't risk a glance at him. We can all hear the unspoken implication of Sebastian's words.

He's effectively neutering his son's ability to lead and protect his team, and he's throwing me in the deep end as an inexperienced Front Man, laying the responsibility of success or failure firmly at *my* feet. I can't even have the rest of the Council as back up during school hours, carefully placed as staff members.

Sink or swim.

He suddenly lifts a folder from below the table, presumably from his signature, polished leather bag. Flicking it open, he runs his eyes quickly down the front page.

"This is a preliminary gathering of numbers. There are currently 871 students, and 217 primary and ancillary staff for you to cultivate intel from over the year. There is also a small but prominent group who seems to have established a power vacuum amongst the student body. The students call them the Rox Boys." He taps almost absentmindedly at the numbers in front of him, but I know him too well. The movement is anything but.

"I do, however, expect a recruitment rate of at least 30% from the student body and 50% from the staff by graduation."

Ah, there it is. There's that rare pang of fear I was waiting for. It's now skating down my spine as my already dry tongue sticks to the top of my mouth. That's almost 300 lives I need to personally invade and 300 souls I need to bargain away in the name of expanding Sebastian's gruesome empire.

"Sabine, you will be required to live on campus to maintain the facade. The rest of you will have restricted access to your legacy fund in order to secure housing and vehicles, as well as to cover appropriate living expenses during the school year. Foster, you will send Dominic monthly statements of your team's spending, not the Accountants. Include with it a copy of all remittance of funds."

His chair moves silently back as he unfurls, like a Leviathan rising from the Deep. He smoothes down his tie and swiftly buttons the jacket on his perfectly pressed suit. "Consider yourselves on strict probation. I expect your behavior going forward to reflect positively on your positions as Councilors at all times." He flips the folio closed, leaving it on the table between us.

That one gesture felt weirdly significant, if not a little ominous. Almost like he closed a metaphorical door on a chapter of our lives at the same time.

Nobody on my Crew moves as he strides towards the door, his Second two steps behind him.

As he reaches the doorway, he pauses but doesn't

turn. "Let me be clear, Sabine, *do not* leave the Rox Boys under the influence of the Aces. They *must* belong to us by the end of the year, or do not return to Lexington expecting a warm welcome home."

And then he's gone, disappearing from the room like smoke.

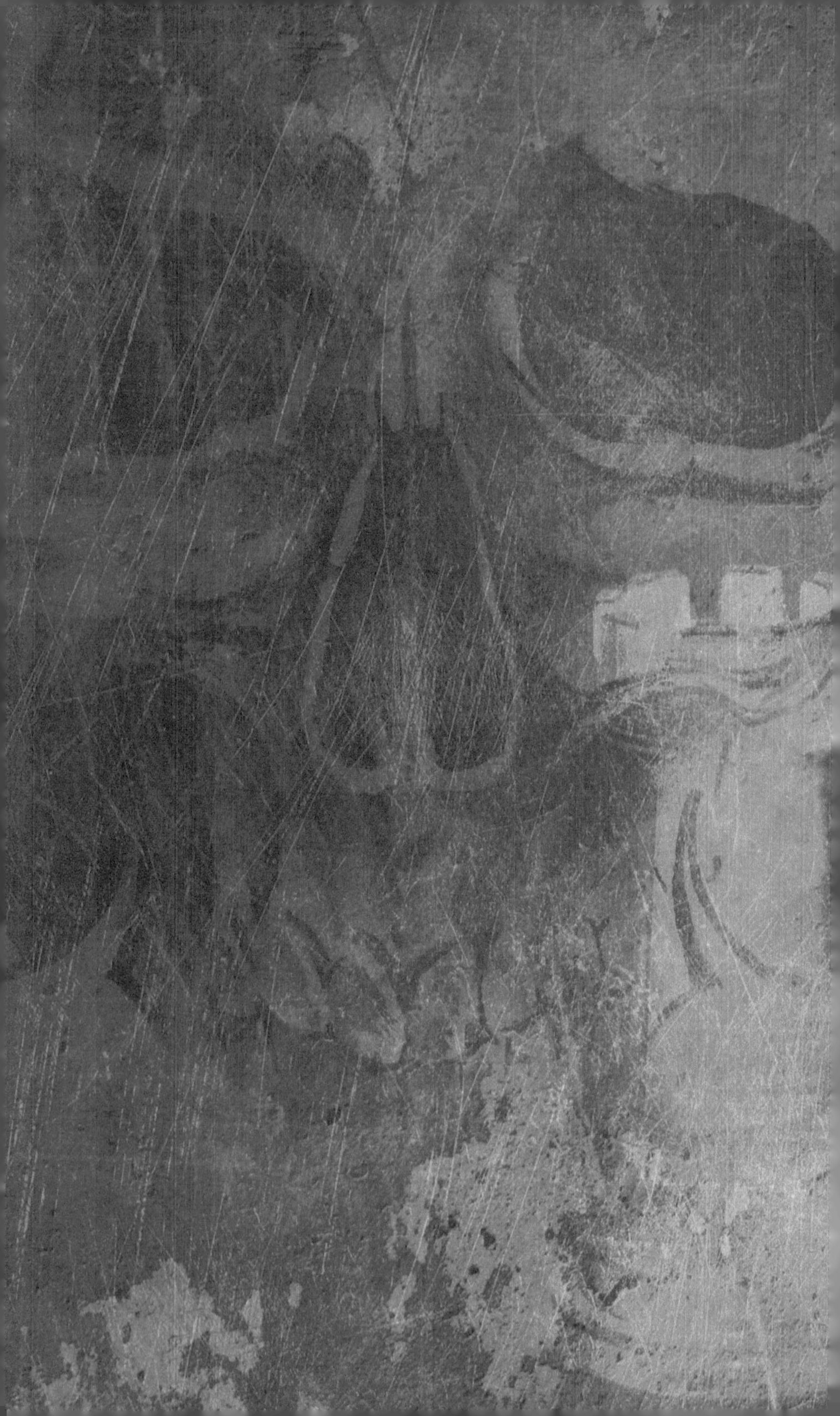

CHAPTER III
SABINE

THE ROOM ERUPTS around me with raised, defensive voices.

Fuck. My eyes start watering as my headache ratchets up to new, higher proportions with the din. My scalp feels like it could split and start peeling back at this point, the tension is that high in my neck.

If only I had a baggie or a flask in the pocket of this dress. I could really use some hair of the dog.

I tip my head back and blink my bleary eyes at the ceiling, as if searching for the strength to move forward and wade into this shitshow of my own making. Sober. Yuck.

Here we go.

Dropping my chin, I take quick stock of where each member of my Crew is in their heads right now.

Foster Andrew Brannons, 24 years old, and our newest member, slides down into the chair he was using during the meeting, as if he no longer possesses bones. He doesn't say a word, just fixes the opposite wall with the haunting, thousand-yard stare of his dark brown eyes.

His auburn hair is lank. I don't expect much else from him right now, if I'm being totally honest. He's a half-empty kind of guy on the best of days, and always has a dozen emotional brick walls erected between himself and the rest of the team. It's been impossible to get close to him.

Jax is across the table, growling and posturing sharply at Knox, who despite being almost twice as wide and several inches taller, is still doing his utmost to quietly talk him down. *Knox Levi Morales, 22*, our gentle brunet giant and second Enforcer will only use violence in the line of duty, and usually as an absolute last resort. You'd think that would make him an awful bodyguard, but just his size and presence is usually enough to make opponents shit their pants.

Despite Knox's calm intervention, I can see that our captain is close to breaking point. It's not often we see such a display of emotion from Jax—his usual, unwavering composure is probably the only personal trait he does share with his father, aside from his dark, brooding looks.

Jackson Sebastian Grayson, 26. His lips are pressed together tightly and his sculpted jaw grinds, agitation clear. All composure has just boiled completely off at this point. The calm and collected team leader now nowhere in sight.

I anticipate a few airborne chairs in our near future.

I lean over and swipe up the offending folder before the table gets flipped as well.

My arm feels like it weighs a metric fuck load, and I

drop it back to my side, the file hanging loosely against my thigh. Everything pulses with the beat inside my skull as I do my best to focus. My tired gaze slides up and collides with Rhett's.

The most wild, most carefree member of our group is now staring back at me with his full mouth pulled tightly into a grimace. *Rhett Matthew Orbison, 22,* is our emotional barometer. He routinely rolls with any and all of the punches, always giving exactly *zero fucks*. It takes an almost world-ending event to knock the head Enforcer off-kilter. His cheeky smile from earlier has completely disappeared, and his dirty-blond hair is standing up at all angles like he's been tugging on it in distress.

It's clear to anybody that Sebastian's ultimatum has left us all in a tailspin.

"Guys," I say quietly. Foster continues to stare blankly and Knox now has his large hands wrapped around Jax's shoulders. Their foreheads are pressed together as they speak quietly. Only Rhett seems to have heard me, his shoulders dropping a fraction at the sound of my voice.

"Guys. Listen to me," I say, a little more firmly, and I can *hear* just how exhausted I am. I lift my hand and distractedly rub my fingers back and forth along my scar. It's a force of habit whenever I'm close to hitting the wall. I'm not sure how long I've got until this hangover-slash-head-injury combo completely does me in for the day.

I let out a long sigh, letting my gaze run over the four of them now that I have their attention. They know I'm usually never this serious, but I feel like this particular mess warrants at least some kind of sincerity on my part.

"Look, we knew this day was coming. We haven't been blindly following orders like good little Low Men for quite some time now. Sooner or later, he was going to make a move designed to bring his wayward sheep back into the fold."

Jax huffs out a cynical breath and swipes his hand angrily across his bearded jaw. "Darling, he's separated *you and I* for a reason," he says, emphasizing bitterly and gesturing wildly between us.

I try to ignore the small ripple of pleasure the term of endearment sends through my gut. He's still almost vibrating with anger. There's so much power coiled in his rigid stance, it's like a dark, furious aura.

He's not wrong. This is not *just* the fallout of our quiet rebellion, or my own behavior. While it's true that the Gray Man *is* concerned that he's losing more and more control over his Librarian and her Crew with each passing day, he's also starting to obsess over his so-called legacy and the cost of leaving Jax the keys to his criminal kingdom. He firmly believes his adult son has amounted to nothing in the eyes of the Underworld.

If only he knew the truth of Jax's ambition and loyalty to his Crew. We've been dutifully preparing for the day Sebastian decided he was no longer worth the investment needed to fulfill his twisted vision. We have contingencies for everything short of complete and total anarchy. Whether that's in a battle of us *vs* The Strange Aces or us *vs* The Crown.

Or us *vs* Sebastian.

The problem is the rest of the team aren't nearly as indispensable as Jax and I.

"Yeah, of course he did. He wants to knock you down a peg. Send you home with your tail between your legs. Make you look like a complete pussy in front of the rest of the Suits," I toss back drily, throwing with my arms wide in a helpless gesture. "He's either going to have you sit back at headquarters for the next year with your thumb up your ass, or he's going to ship you off somewhere far away, probably under the guise of territory expansion as an Ambassador."

And to the real heart of the matter.

"All so you won't be there to yank *my* ass out of the fire," I add.

Everyone our rank or higher knows that I'm not Front Man material—that I can't be trusted with a solo mission. Without Jax there to compensate for my impulse control issues, or to clean up my messes, this whole endeavor has failure written all over it from the start.

As badly as Sebastian wants fresh blood and the city of Roxborough under his control, I suspect he wants us humbled and back under his thumb even more.

For him, this is a win-win.

My hands drop back to my sides, the file slapping lightly against my thigh. I'm so fucking tired, all the way down to my bones, and all the political hoops of bullshit that we need to be jump through in order to navigate this mess suddenly seem so goddamn overwhelming.

Jax narrows his eyes and pulls away from Knox's

gentle grip on his shoulder to stride towards me. The tension and frustration we're all feeling at this moment is reflected across his tight, broad shoulders and clenched fists.

After all these years I like to think I know him pretty damn well. I can see the guilt in every flicker of the muscles beneath his neatly trimmed beard as he grits his teeth. In the tight lines around his eyes. He's the one in charge and yet he's effectively been cut off from his whole team.

I know he believes *he's* failed us even though this all starts and ends with me.

A token apology sits right there on my tongue as I watch him move around the table. There are no feelings of genuine remorse however—my stupid gray matter so hard-wired to crave danger, that this latest turn of events is starting to excite me way more than it frightens me.

And the way he's stalking towards me? His sharp, crystal blue eyes locked on my blue-grays? My lizard brain is receiving an obvious *predator* signal and instead of the proper *fight or flight* response, it's flooding my system with dopamine. I do my darnedest to ignore the expectant *zip* of adrenaline racing up and down my spine, and to school my features as I watch him approach.

A quick glance at Rhett's small, knowing smirk lets me know I wasn't as smooth as I thought.

Shit.

Jax comes to a stop directly in front of me, so close

we're practically toe to toe. He stands a few inches over me at 6'1, but I'm tall enough that I don't need to crane my neck to meet his gaze. His bright eyes dart between mine, like he's trying to get a quick read on how seriously I'm taking our new set of circumstances.

The blatant crowding of my personal space is decidedly *not* helping my horny bitch self, and my heart rate picks up in what it thinks is sexual anticipation.

But his dark brows only pull together in a frown as he mistakes the reason for my racing pulse. "This isn't a fucking *joke*, Sabine! For once, can you please just take something fucking *seriously!*" His voice is a low growl, and again I have to reign in my gutter thoughts.

Despite a very close and physically affectionate relationship, I'm relatively sure Jax has only ever viewed me as the annoying little sister and asset he's obligated to protect.

I, however, can't simply turn off years of my lady parts' unrequited crush on a whim. Jax is not a hulking, ripped and tattooed specimen like Rhett or Knox. He's tall, broad and athletic, with golden skin, a neatly trimmed beard covering a sharp jawline, and stylishly cut hair that's dark and wavy like Sebastian's. He's always immaculately dressed, more along the lines of *CEO mafia prince* than *TAC team operative* like the rest of the boys. While his father's eyes are a deep, oceanic blue, Jax's are bright and clear like the summer sky.

He's breathtaking to look at.

Not to mention his dominant, no-nonsense, alpha-boss vibes are just...*swoon.*

"I am taking this seriously, Jax, I promise." I gesture at my bandage. "Between this hangover and my failed suicide attempt I'm feeling a lot like roadkill and not so much up to Gray Man reindeer games." He doesn't smile at my lame attempt at brevity, instead he simply bristles further at my attitude.

Double shit.

I hold up the folder between us as a peace offering. "Look, I only need leverage on the staff and the most promising students. We don't need a full deep dive on every single person on this list. A quick background will be enough for most of them."

I look over at Foster who is now staring morosely at Jax and I instead of the wall. I could really use his help on this. "Hey man, we got this, right?" I waggle the folder in his direction and am rewarded with a strained smile and slow nod. Eh, that's enough for now. I might have to promise him a few games of *Counterstrike* later to butter him up. Maybe a few episodes of *Death Note.*

Jax flicks his eyes down to the file. "I'm not worried about your *intel*, Sabine. I'm worried about your *people skills*," he says, completely deadpan and with not a single hint of his usual affection.

Rhett barks out a laugh. Knox makes a quiet noise of distress.

"*Ouch*, Cap. Straight for the fucking kill shot," I laugh weakly. He's not wrong though. I'm not exactly Miss Congeniality and this mission is going to require a certain bag of social party tricks I'm not currently in possession of, thanks to my general daily outlook of *chaos and orgasms.* I think it's why Rhett and I have such easy chemistry.

Jax swipes a troubled hand over his beard again, holding my gaze for a moment longer before stepping away from me. He takes a further beat to study the other members of our Crew, and I feel an odd sort of loss as he moves away, knowing our time left together is already limited.

I hold my breath until he straightens, watching the mantle of leadership settling back across his shoulders with practiced ease. When he starts barking orders I feel the sag of my own under the familiar, reassuring weight of his dominance.

He's a natural at this authority figure business, and I can't imagine how we are going to fill the veritable crater his absence will leave behind.

"I'm going to work on finding out exactly what else my father is up to. He definitely wants us to learn a lesson, but he also wants us out from under foot and occupied." *Nice.* That Jackson Grayson self-possession and command is *firmly* back in place.

It's a beautiful thing to behold.

"Knox, you handle locking down a place for the three of you in Rox City. Someplace modern, location need-to-know, easy enough for Foster to outfit for surveillance and close to the school. I want eyes on Sabine's dorm as well."

I smirk at Rhett, before saying, "I'm sure there will be more than enough eyes in the dorm without needing cameras." I look back at Jax just in time to catch a hot flash of *something* cross his striking gaze. There and gone.

Was that...*jealousy*?

No. That would definitely classify as *wishful thinking* on my pussy-drunk behalf.

Jax doesn't respond, just turns to our resident motorhead, barking, "Rhett, you find some wheels. Can't risk taking any of ours down there, even with new plates."

My eyes go wide at the thought of car shopping, only for Jax's voice to slice straight through my excitement like a newly sharpened knife.

"Nothing for Sabine."

My jaw drops. *"Jax!* I'll be the only fucking senior in a sea of rich kids without a car!" My indignation is clear and it definitely slips out with something resembling a whine.

I can't help it though, my head is about to burst. I press harshly against my scar again as I give him my best scowl.

"You'll be living on campus and won't need a car. Besides, I'm not having you wrap yourself around some random fucking utility pole while you're down there in the middle of an Ace-controlled viper's nest, Sabe. No, nope, *no fucking pouting.*"

I roll my lips inwards instead. The concern is heartwarming, but c'mon, he's being a tad melodramatic, isn't he? "It was one time!"

"Twice," Rhett chimes in happily over Jax's shoulder like a goddamn traitor. As easy-going as the man is, he's also a world class shit-stirrer. He finds equal satisfaction in sowing the seeds of discord as he does giving and receiving pleasure.

"Twice, Sabe," Jax reiterates. "And if it's not a pole, it's another fucking car. *So. No. Driving!*" The tough mask he so painstakingly reconstructed almost cracks again.

I groan and look at the ceiling once again, deflating a little with the spark of frustration my shitty brain allows me. They all know I'm a bit of a prima donna when it comes to my vices, and a sleek set of adrenaline-on-wheels is one of them. I just happened to enjoy mixing racing with some of my other indulgences.

Namely drugs and booze.

It doesn't always end well.

Okay. Perhaps I can sort of see his point.

"Fiiiine," I concede, impishly.

Rhett is shaking his head at me, that wide grin making its decadent appearance again. Now I *know* the asshole's going to pick *him*self up the sexiest ride, just to rub it in. I'll have to bide my time and snag the keys.

A flicker of a smile tugs at the side of Jax's lips as well, the hard look in his eyes slowly taken over by something more affectionate the longer he stares me down. "What am I going to do with you," he admonishes under his breath, exasperation clear as day.

It makes my heart kick for an entirely different reason. I don't know how we're going to do this without him.

How *I'm* going to do this without him.

I give him a small smile that I hope looks reassuring. I'm dead on my fucking feet but I need to start forming a game plan for the little time we have before the semester starts at Roxborough Academy in September.

Six weeks to profile over a thousand people?

One school year to recruit 300-odd new Suits, including a handful of baby Aces?

The lives of my team and I on the metaphorical line?

Piece of fucking cake.

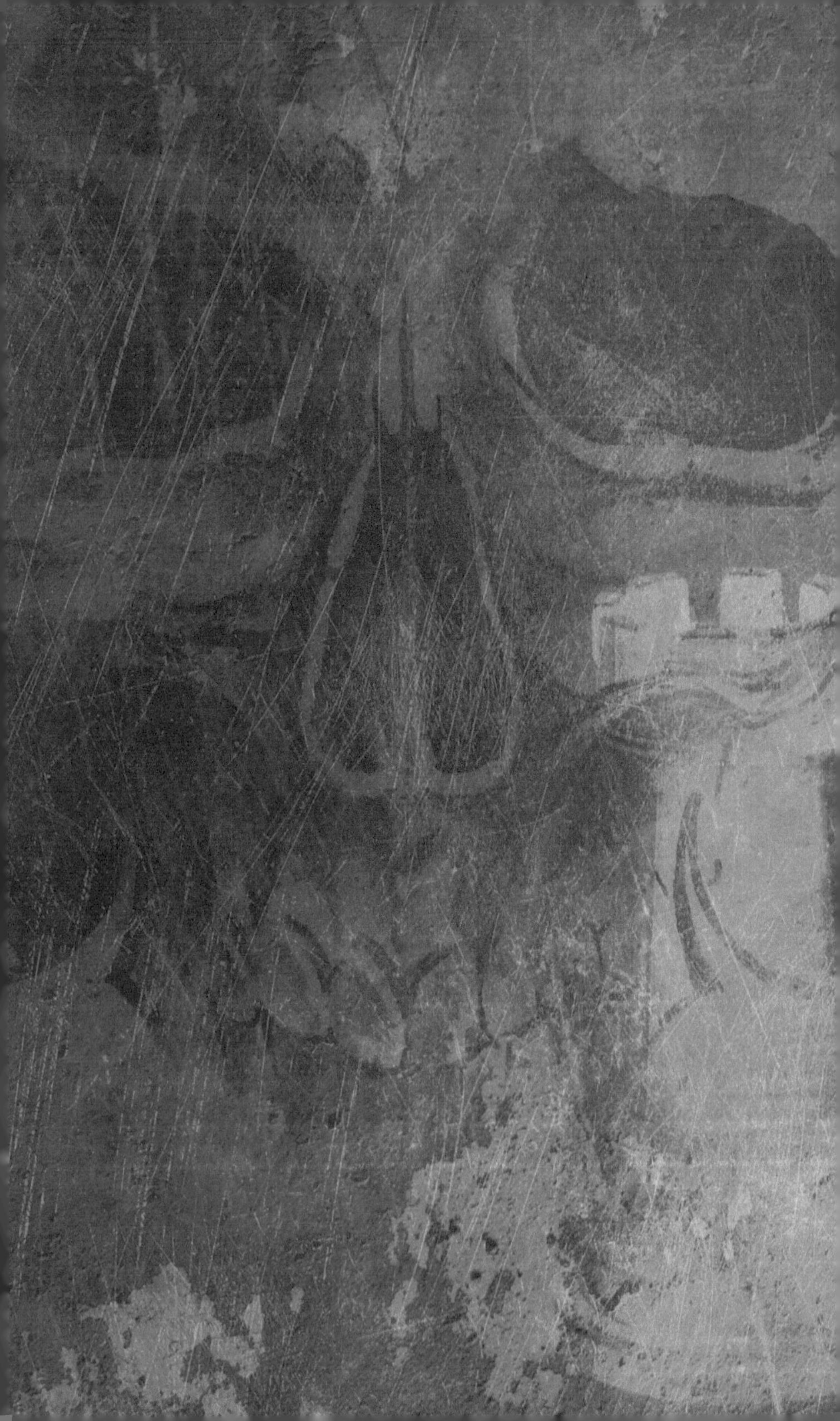

CHAPTER IV

SABINE

"GIVE US A SPIN, MS. WINTERS."

I let out an amused huff at the sultry tones, though it's not enough to interrupt my close inspection of the full-length reflection before me.

"No, *Mr.* Orbison, I look cute as fuck right now, and I'm not having you mess up my shit just to indulge your school-girl fantasy."

Despite still enjoying his post-coital bliss, the man is *always* up for another round. I swear, his refractory period is practically non-existent. I blow him a flirty little kiss instead, shooting a graceful middle finger over the shoulder as I do.

There's no need to turn around in order to catch his reaction. Thanks to the mirror, I have an uninterrupted view of all six feet of sin incarnate, stretched out as he is behind me.

Rhett is lazily propped against the pile of pillows on my new dorm's king-size bed, watching me with heavy-lidded eyes as I check over my finished outfit. The muscles in his arms look obscene with the way he has them casually folded behind his head, and his dirty-blond hair is still adorably sex-mussed. He's wearing nothing but a pair of gray sweatpants and his trademark playboy grin.

He gives me a husky chuckle in return, one beautifully tattooed bicep flexing as he catches my air-kiss. That grin is all self-satisfaction, his perusal of my tailored Academy uniform blatant and heated. When he catches me looking back at him, he just slips a hand down the front of his sweats and squeezes the growing bulge there.

"Mmm, is your homework ready for hand-in, Ms. Winters?" he purrs. "Don't make me have to give you detention."

I can't help the laugh that bubbles out at his teasing. I really needed his levity this morning. The ogle-worthy view that's currently on offer as he reclines on my bed ain't half bad either.

"Nice try, but you so much as *touch* a hair on this head, and I will key the Lambo," I warn him, only half joking, but trying to keep my lips from breaking out into a full smirk all the same. Rhett's lime green Lamborghini Aventador is one of the only things he enjoys about living down here. To him it was worth the tongue-lashing he received from the Senior Council for *misappropriation of funds during a field tenure*. He wouldn't hesitate to maim a man if they so much as looked sideways at his new baby.

In fact, I'm pretty sure he has.

"Oh, *sweetcheeks*," Rhett growls. "You'd be staying after class for an entire month for that one." He sits up, abdomen rippling, his forearms coming to rest on his knees. His gaze is now anything but easy-going or playful. Now, it's promising me some form of corporal punishment.

"Don't give me those bedroom eyes, Orbison, I'm serious. Hands off." I focus back on my outfit, twisting to one side. Today's impression has to be perfect. It's my first day as both Front Man and Roxborough senior.

Six weeks, two dozen cartons of energy drinks, 1000-odd personnel researched and vetted, and I am now officially ready to kick off *Operation: Rox Academy.*

I run a French-tipped hand down one crisp lapel as I turn back towards the mirror. The gold-trimmed, navy blue blazer fits well, sitting nicely over the standard-issue white blouse and matching navy pleated skirt. Both blazer and blouse are embroidered with the Academy's trident logo. The uniform also includes a set of dark knee-high socks paired with black pumps.

It's no wonder Rhett's drooling. I wasn't lying when I said I thought the whole outfit was cute as fuck, so I've polished off the look by pinning up my chest-length hair with a retro flair. The sweeping hairstyle shows off my prominent scar, but the thing is impossible to hide even with makeup, so I'm just rolling with it.

My lips are ruby red, my nails are a midnight blue, and my winged eyeliner is sharp enough to draw blood.

I've got my warpaint on. I'm ready for the inevitable stares, glares and strange looks that being the new kid brings. My piercings and tattoos aren't immediately visible, so I'm confident I can pass as an average Academy student.

Yeah. I think I'm finally ready to press play on this whole ordeal. Oops, correction—*campaign.*

When I look back up, Rhett is no longer lying across my pillows. He's standing directly behind me, his olive-green eyes following a searing path up my legs in the reflection before us. "Don't you—" I start to say before his large, tattooed fingers land on the backs of my thighs, tracing the hem of my skirt.

His voice is low and raspy. "Shh, baby girl. You said don't touch a hair on your *head.* I won't mess up this sexy as fuck school-girl look you've got going on, I promise." His gaze drags up past my hips, to my small tits and finally locks onto my own. "I just need a moment under this fucking skirt," he groans. "Please."

And then he's on his knees.

All I can see now are his thick, muscular thighs straining his gray joggers as he spreads them, sliding a knee to either side of my ankles. He must be close to eye level with the bottom of my short skirt, which is definitely *not* at regulation length. His hot breath skitters across my skin and a fizz of excitement runs up the backs of my legs to the base of my spine. It simmers delightfully low and tight in my pelvis.

Rhett gently grabs my hem between two fingers and slides it slowly up and over my ass, dragging my blazer with it.

I hiss at him, "No wrinkles, asshole."

"I'll be good," he laughs against my ass, a reminder

that Rhett and I are much darker and way more primal in the way we normally come together than we've been on this lazy Monday morning.

Rhett Orbison is a purely sexual being, and so far the only one of my string of lovers who hasn't questioned my need to continually explore limits in a bid to chase a higher, more prolonged pleasure effect. It's not always a sure thing for a guy in a club to drunkenly agree to depraved sex acts with some girl they've just met. I find it's easier just to keep those particular encounters contained to good ol' regular railings.

But with Rhett—I don't know. It just feels easy. Uncomplicated.

Next time, it will *have* to be off-campus. That thought sends another tingle up the inside of my thighs.

Two fingers on his other hand trace lightly down the line of the lacy thong he's just revealed. "A definite uniform violation," he muses, his voice still low and rough. He loves his roleplay. "Seems detention is not enough of a deterrent for you, Ms. Winters. I might have to think up a more fitting punishment."

I don't say anything as he slips those two fingers under the string and begins to stroke up and down. I can't see what he's doing, but the movement feels almost hypnotic. Instead, I focus on his groin in the reflection, his lap spread wide as he kneels behind me.

I watch as the bulge in his sweats really begins to tent, running my tongue slowly over my bottom lip.

It's a magnificent sight.

Suddenly those two fingers are joined by Rhett's nose.

My hands shoot out to grip the wide mirror in front of me, fingers curling around the gold frame. He presses the tip firmly into the dampening crotch of my panties, and I instinctively tilt my hips back to meet him, a low groan escaping us both.

Inhaling deeply, he pushes up further into my pussy, still wet and waiting in anticipation of his oral ministrations.

He places a gentle kiss before those teasing fingers push the scrap of material aside. "Christ, darlin' girl, walking those prissy Academy halls with all this hiding under your fucking skirt," he whispers against my slit, before his tongue starts a slow, torturous circle around my entrance, caressing and nuzzling, but without delving too deeply. "Those high school boys won't know what hit 'em."

I rock forward onto my toes, my breaths becoming shorter the longer he teases. He's still holding my skirt up with one hand, but soon the fingers of his free hand slide back in next to his wicked mouth to trace in further, infuriating patterns.

He runs them up and around my swollen lips, but never directly over my clit and only ever penetrating me for a moment at a time.

"Rhett, you fucking tease," I cry breathlessly, but without real heat. The front of my skirt still shields everything from my view in the mirror, heightening every touch. I'm so turned on and anxious for relief, that I can feel myself beginning to drip slowly down the inside of my thigh.

Rhett's face must be a mess. The image of my juices flowing down his chin and neck has the beginning whispers of an orgasm starting to form, gathering like a mist. A dreamy smile creeps over my lips, replaced quickly by a defeated groan surging up my throat as the feeling ebbs away.

"I told you, Ms. Winters, you need to be brought to task," he says as he pulls his mouth away, leaving just one thick finger to roll sensually through the mess he's made, over and over. He dips inside, hooking it lazily towards the front so that he can now add torturing my G-spot to his growing list of punishable crimes.

My head rolls back in mock frustration, because I can't bring myself to be mad that the fucker is edging me. Even just the promise of release has pushed enough happy chemicals into my bloodstream to start shutting my brain down.

I start to lose track of how long he continues this epic taunt, prolonging the way my senses drift and ride those fleeting crests of euphoria.

It's such an indescribable thing to be able to switch off, even if only for a brief moment.

So freeing to relinquish all control.

And just…*let go.*

I breathe out, rolling my neck forward to face the mirror again. My muscles might be tense, desperately waiting for release, but my mind is still loose and untethered. That breath turns into an audible moan as Rhett finally goes in for the kill. He bends and sweeps that lone teasing finger up, a knuckle pressing abruptly against my overwrought clit.

A hair trigger could have sent me over the brink after being tortured so expertly. So it's no surprise when the sudden pressure sends an intense shock of pleasure up through my pelvis and into my abdomen.

Rhett, bless him, quickly replaces the finger with his tongue, wrapping two big hands around my thighs, and gripping tightly right before my knees give out.

My moan this time is long and almost pained, my vision whiting out as the waves roll and pulse over my entire body. My forehead falls forward to press against the cool glass of the mirror, and my sweaty palms slip down the frame.

Rhett's answering noises as I ride out the orgasm and fill his mouth are almost as obscene. He doesn't break contact with my pussy though, just sucks and sips and laps like a death row inmate devouring his last meal.

For a precious, uninterrupted moment, I'm boneless and sated, floating in a thick lust fog. Then, still in a daze, I remember Rhett's erection—no doubt painfully hard. I twist on wobbly legs, my eyes drifting back down to his lap, but it's obvious I'm too late to the party.

Some time between burying his nose between my cheeks, and my intense, knee-buckling release, Rhett has abandoned my skirt and pulled out his magnificent cock. He's still gripping the shaft, cum already dripping over the top of his clenched fist as he continues stroking it slowly.

With another purely seductive Orbison grin, he runs

his tongue over his bottom lip, his whole mouth and chin still glistening with *me*. He then holds my matching lustful gaze and licks his hand clean.

All before tucking himself back in.

Jesus.

"Better get moving, love button. Don't want to be late for your first day," he murmurs jovially as he stands up, using his clean hand to pull my skirt and blazer back down over buttocks which are still covered in erotic gooseflesh. Then he slaps my ass before disappearing into the attached bathroom.

Rolling my eyes, at the back of his stupid, sexy head, I then test my post-orgasm jelly legs by taking a small side-step. I think they'll hold me up.

A quick check in the mirror behind me shows my makeup and hair are still untouched.

The cheeky bastard kept his promise.

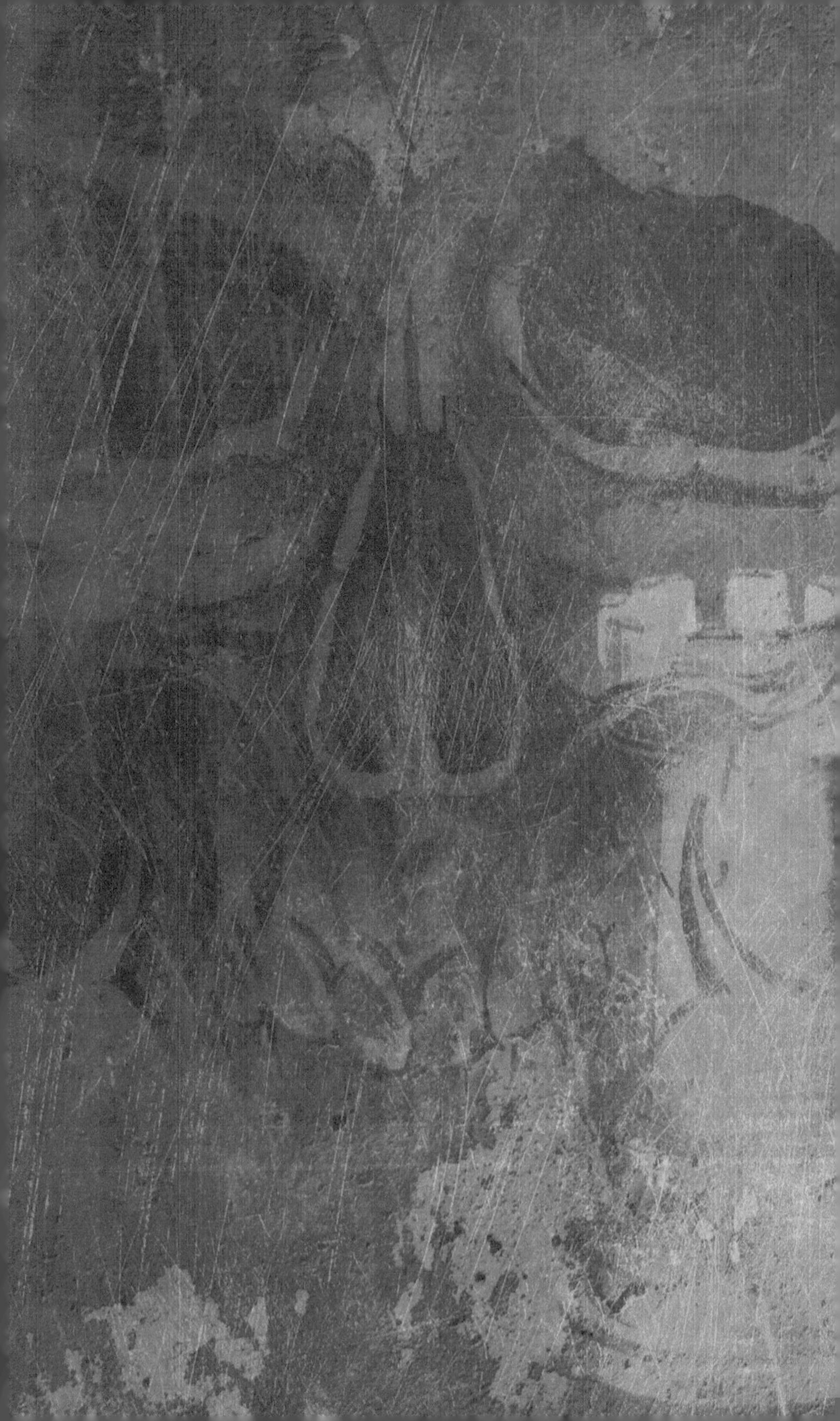

CHAPTER V

SABINE

WHEN I'M confident said legs really won't give out on me, I change my saturated underwear, pop two Xannies in the hopes of prolonging my sex-high a little longer, and then grab my book bag, ready to head down to the Academy food hall to find some breakfast.

I wait near the front door, taking in my new home for the next academic year. I was a little disappointed to find there had been no vacancies in any of the historical dorms, and that I would be staying in one of the newer buildings on campus.

Thanks to Foster's interference however, I did end up in one of the more ritzy and private suites still available —an exposed brick, loft-style apartment with the equivalent of a master bedroom, private bathroom, kitchenette, and combined living and dining area. It's sparsely furnished in a modern, industrial-style design, with decor in shades of black and white. It's simple, but the overall effect is comfortable and most importantly, easy on my eyes.

I'm now starving and eager to leave when Rhett

finally emerges, hair wet and slicked back from his forehead. My wretched libido weeps when I see he's swapped his gray sweatpants and bare chest out for his habitual outfit of TAC cargo pants and Henley.

They do cling delightfully to every muscle though, so I'm still very much being optically blessed.

It's been a rewarding morning.

As he makes a beeline towards the front door, he tosses my cellphone at me. I catch it with my free hand as I follow after him. "Thanks," I offer. I must have left it by the bed.

Rhett winks and nods towards the phone. "Daddy Jax texted you for your first day."

My cold, shriveled heart gives a tiny thump inside my chest. The last several weeks have been just short of grueling—endless hours of research and reading, learning to navigate our new team dynamics, and establishing a safe foothold in unfamiliar, enemy-controlled territory.

Despite the new and intense workload, Rhett has stepped up and filled our team leader's rather large shoes without issue. But I never anticipated how hard it would be not to be greeted every morning by Jax's darkly handsome face, gruff commanding voice and strict routines.

He's always been my safe place, and without him, I feel more and more adrift. Less and less in control. The noise is louder and sporadic texts sent when he can dodge both his new handlers and his father just don't hit quite the same.

I miss him fiercely.

Rhett's irreverent nickname for him forces out a smile though, and I swiftly unlock the phone, opening to a message sent about the time Rhett was still buried under my skirt.

JAX

Sabine.

ME

Oh Captain, my Captain

His reply comes through straight away.

JAX

Are you ready for today? It's okay to ask for help. I don't know when, but I'll do what I can.

A breathy laugh escapes me. Poor Jax. This is some Knox-level worrying.

ME

Do you doubt me, Capitano?

ME

Give me until winter break

ME

And I'll have Rox Academy on its knees
;)

There's a short pause before he's typing again.

JAX

That's the part I'm afraid of.

When the three dots don't appear again, I lock the screen and slip it into the inner pocket of my blazer. His faith in me despite the sarcasm wraps around my chest like a hug. Sebastian is not the only Grayson I really don't want to disappoint by fucking up this assignment.

Taking a step forward, I almost run into the back of Rhett. A surprised but happy yelp escapes me as he spins in the open doorway, scooping me up and kissing my neck and jaw, careful to avoid my lips. He drops me back to my feet just as quickly, giving my ass cheeks a firm squeeze before he turns and saunters away without a word.

I watch his own fine set of glutes as they disappear down the hallway before pulling the door shut behind me. A satisfied smile lingers on my lips as I adjust my heavy-ass book bag, ready to finally hunt down some food.

My mind is firmly occupied by thoughts of pancakes and bacon and Rhett in sweatpants, so it's very jarring when my gaze accidentally locks with a figure reclining against the entrance to a room just a few doors down, and on the opposite side of the hallway.

Fuck.

I was hoping to have at least made it through until lunch before encountering one of the four head-bad-boys-in-charge of Roxborough Academy. My plan had been to try and get more of an organic feel for the school and its citizens than what my clinically written files could give me. Get a read on the social tapestry and vibe of the place before diving headfirst into a tête-à-tête with one of the main reasons that I'm here at all.

Instead, slouching directly against a doorframe, arms crossed and glaring at me like a disdainful god, is Tristan Sinclair—unofficial head of the Rox Boys.

Standing before me in living color.

At least now I've pegged the reason for my Enforcer's passionate goodbye display.

I quickly shut my expression down, hoping wildly that there hadn't been an obvious flash of recognition when we made eye contact.

As far as he knows, I have exactly zero idea who he is.

While that couldn't be further from the truth.

Tristan Marcus Sinclair, 18. Wealthy. Parents still married despite infidelity. Academy Prefect-Captain. Captain of the Roxborough Krakens basketball team. Plays four instruments. Speaks three languages. Slated for Valedictorian and early acceptance for Pre-Med at Rox U.

According to his file, at his full height, he stands at 6'2. His broad shoulders and golden-toned, muscular body—currently wrapped up like a present in a neatly pressed, academic uniform—speak to his obvious athletic ability. Dark, almost black hair sits artfully tousled atop his head like a crown. His sharp, clean-shaven jaw is set firmly, his ocean-blue eyes tight.

Weeks of making my acquaintance with his photo have not done the actual Tristan Sinclair an iota of justice.

He looks way too good to be an actual real life boy.

I'm cautiously reminded that even the Devil himself was once an angel, and a pretty face is the perfect trap for intrepid travelers.

A pretty face doesn't always mean pure of heart.

But it's not just his stupidly good looks. Even relaxed as his posture appears, there is a dark *vibration* of power that emanates from him; a *magnetism*. It's in his bearing.

He's evidently a person who considers himself unquestionably in charge. Somebody who wields significant influence over those around him. Our recon had shown that the Rox Boys have a curious but unshakeable grip on the student population here. That their word is *law* and that if they pointed to a bridge and said jump, their classmates would be shoving each other out of the way to be the first to show their loyalty.

In other words, they are used to enjoying an unchallenged and easy reign.

I concentrate on keeping my features neutral, but he's staring me down like someone just whispered in his ear that I've personally arrived at Roxborough solely to shit in *his* cereal.

I suppose I am the quote unquote new kid moving into *their* undisputed territory.

Guess I need to set the tone from the start. *This ought to be fun.*

As I near his doorway, he straightens subtly, his presence expanding slowly until he's positively *looming*. The light overhead glints off the Prefect-Captain badge on his lapel. His expression is dark and frigid.

"Overnight guests are a direct violation of the

Academy dorm rules," he says dispassionately, when he's sure he has my attention.

His voice is low, sinful, sliding down my spine like a caress. *Exactly* how I imagined him to sound, conjured by my fantasies after hours studying his file. I bet he has a singing voice to die for. I've come across no evidence of it, but I know he has a significant interest in music.

Fuck, it really does pack a punch. A punch straight to my nether regions.

Christ, my poor libido has taken some serious hits this morning.

Tristan doesn't so much as blink, seemingly oblivious to my internal lustful musings. His focus is intense though as he tracks my movements, watching as I stride towards him without stopping.

Hmm. He likes to keep tabs. Noted.

I throw him a jaunty salute just as I pass him. "Good thing he was only an *early morning* guest, then," I drawl with an added, sarcastic tip of my lips.

When there's no response, I'm tempted to risk a look back over my shoulder, just to see if I managed to put even a small dent in that contemptuous mask of his. But I don't. It's clear from my intel gathering that Tristan Sinclair and his gang are social predators and predators like that can *always* sense weakness.

So instead, I concentrate on putting one heeled foot in front of the other.

And maybe I put a little extra swing in my hips. Maybe.

Game on, boys.

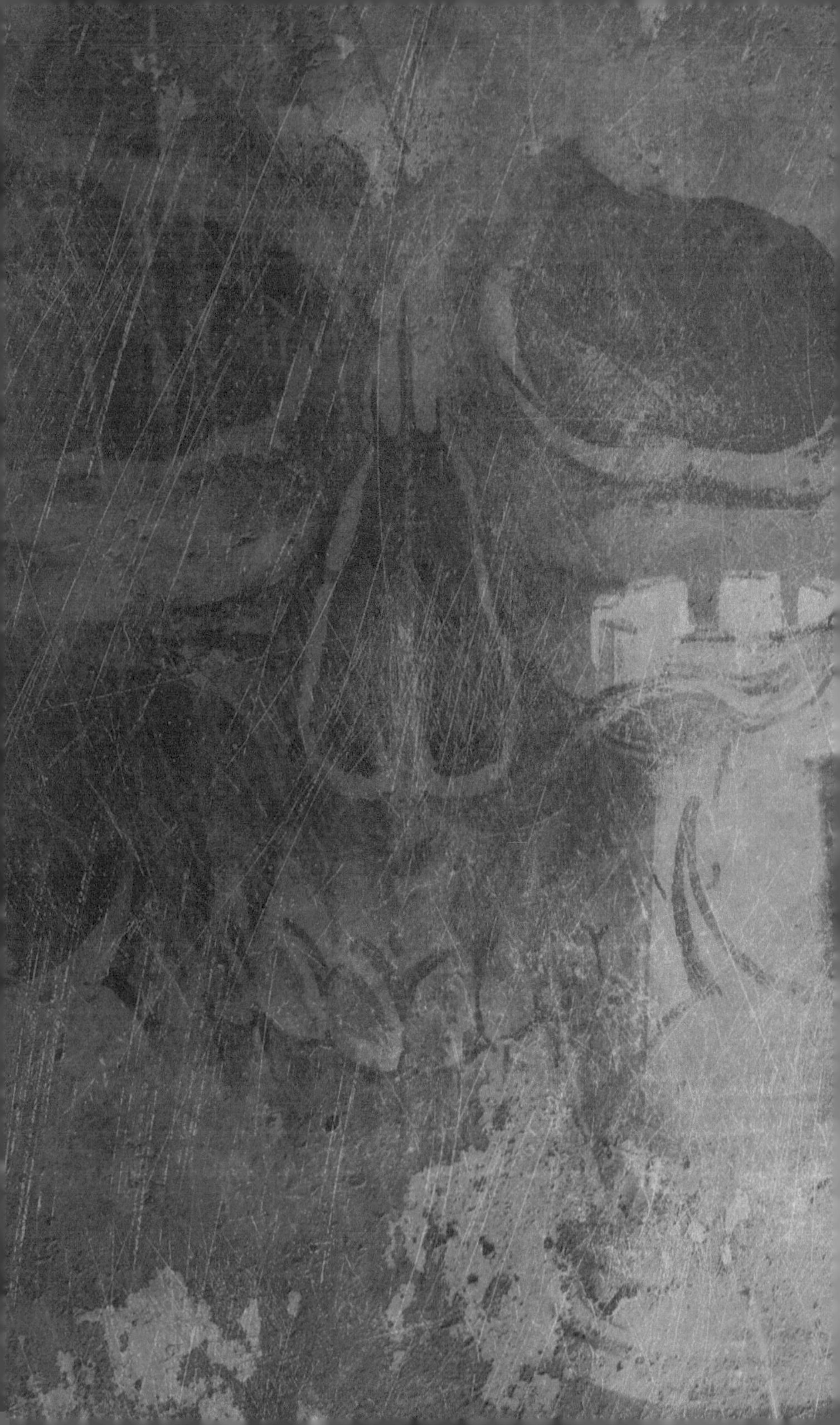

CHAPTER VI

SABINE

"WELL, I THINK THAT'S EVERYTHING," Principal Brunswick says brusquely, her hands slapping down on the desk in front of her. Despite the fact that I'm insisting on a transfer to her Academy in my final year of schooling, she's barely given my flawlessly doctored transcripts a second glance.

She's evidently keen to wrap up my enrollment and move on with her day. I politely mirror her movements, smoothing down my blazer as I stand to grasp her outstretched hand.

Her handshake is dry and firm, as no-nonsense as the woman herself. *Anita Helene Brunswick, 59. Principal of Roxborough Academy for 11 years. Divorced. No children. No known connections to the Strange Aces.*

Our weeks of heavy research into the faculty have not produced even a sliver of evidence that the graying, tight-lipped, but efficient headmaster has been compromised in any way. In fact, her bank records going back for the last decade show that she seems especially immune to bribery and coercion. Her leadership style is decidedly a little hands-off when it comes to the student body, but there have been no major complaints or life-altering scandals.

What I need to work out is if that's because we've uncovered an actual, honest-to-God academic official with an intact moral compass, or if it's simply that no one has managed to find the correct leverage on cat-loving, two-time Open League Bowling Champion Anita Brunswick?

"Thank you, Principal Brunswick. I look forward to my time here at Roxborough," I manage through a forced smile. My tenure as charming Front Man has begun, and practice makes perfect.

She gives me a bored hand flick in return. "If there's anything else, be sure to book an appointment with Vice Principal Cressel." In other words, her task as the glorified Welcome Wagon has concluded.

Thoroughly dismissed, I leave her suite of offices—an enrollment package, textbooks, and schedule in hand—and head on out past reception.

The young receptionist, pretty with chestnut curls but dull blue eyes, shoots me a friendly smile as I pass. *Single mom, kicked out by her fiancé and living hand to mouth in her great Aunt's spare room.* She can barely afford formula and child care, let alone the anti-depressants she's supposed to be taking. She could definitely use the money being a Gray Man lackey would bring. Perhaps she could be a steady source of staff lunchroom gossip.

I give a small nod in return and mentally file her onto my *Maybe* list.

Stepping out into the main hall, I'm surprised to find it still swarming with students. I'd just made the assumption my orientation spiel would run me late for my first period, but it seems as though I may have a little time to spare before classes begin for the morning.

All grades seem to have congregated out in the vaulted halls of this two hundred year old gothic Academy; laughing and shoving and hollering greetings, catching up after the long break and establishing cliques for the new year.

My mind wants to reel as I take in all their faces, each of their files blooming to life in my head like an impromptu and unwanted PowerPoint presentation. Luckily for me, the extra Xanax I took after breakfast is still doing its job, working to keep the rising chatter between my ears to a dull static and the edges of my mood smoothed out.

I fondly pat my pocket where I know my beloved flask is also sitting. I'll inevitably need *that* later.

Eager to dump these textbooks and paperwork before my English Lit class, I allow one long, slow blink to reorient myself. I then hoist my bag up onto my shoulder and stride off down the long hallway, heels clicking sharply.

My line of sight stays fixed to chins and shoulders so as not to continue overloading my poor brain by taking in all their profiles one by one. Thanks to my schedule and a set of Academy blueprints that I memorized earlier, I could navigate my way around these halls blindfolded.

What greets me at the bank of my assigned locker,

however, only validates my suspicions that I used up what meager stores of cosmic luck I might have had by trying to shoot myself in the head. Blocking access is a group of drop-dead gorgeous boys and girls, busy holding court before the crowd of simpering seniors. The rabble are each taking turns sneaking adoring glances at their leaders and swapping summer rumors with their neighbors.

My *Karma* gauge must really be sitting on *Empty*.

The Rox Boys.

When it doesn't seem as though anyone has noticed my arrival, however, I take a few precious seconds to hastily compartmentalize my thoughts. It's the first time I've been able to see the Boys out in the wild together, and not just as a wall of mugshots.

The problem is, while I'm not exactly short, they're being partially obscured by the press of gossiping students. Experimentally, I try to move in through the excited crowd, but the mass of bodies simply continue to push and undulate, not giving way at all.

I grunt in frustration. I can *not* catch a fucking break.

Not wanting to spend my morning in a locker bay mosh pit, I place my thumb and finger in my mouth and let out a sharp whistle.

The chatter of the excited group in front of me dies abruptly as all attention instantly swings to me.

If I was someone prone to feelings of embarrassment, I'm sure my face would be lava-hot right now. I suppose I can thank the repeated scrambling and reprogramming of my brain for *that* small miracle, even as I feel the dull beginnings of a headache pressing in.

As it is, I just feel mildly annoyed that my nuanced undercover operation is already in damage control. Before the first bell of the day has even rung. Rhett would be on the floor in a fit of laughter at my piss poor spy efforts right now.

Eyes wide at the audacity of my intrusion, the crowd parts violently and shuffles back, as if just being in my general proximity might infect them with a fatal dose of *Social Outcast*.

I'm now in the direct path of the narrowed, frosty blue-eyed gaze of their leader. Leaning directly against *my* locker, and surveying his gathering of minions coolly, is the subject of my previous Rox Boy encounter.

He still looks like he just stepped off a photoshoot.

Sexy, sporty *and* academic. Yes, Tristan Sinclair is deadly hot. He reminds me a little bit of Jax. A goddamn wet dream, and only one amongst a veritable bouquet of Rox Boy eye candy.

"Hey Adonis, you're blocking my locker," I say as I tip my chin, indicating where I want to be. "Much obliged if you'd just slide to your left there for me."

The silence that answers me is *absolute* in its shock.

Then a loud scoff. Pushing forward from Tristan's side is a tall, fiery-haired bombshell.

Fuuuuck. Lady Fortuna is really getting her licks in this morning.

Sloane Imogen Walker, 18. Head cheerleader, track star and

Queen Bee of Roxborough Academy. On again, off again girlfriend of Tristan.

Now *here* is a prime example of one of a few surprises we uncovered during our clandestine deep dive into the Academy. I wonder blithely how many of her lemmings know that their perfect teen idol is actually one *Sloane Imogen O'Sullivan,* daughter of Michael 'Smiley' O'Sullivan—all around bastard and head of a prominent Irish mob family with significant holdings across parts of the Southern Underworld.

Pretty, poised pep rally Sloane is actually a bonafide mobster princess.

That, of course, makes her nearly impossible to turn as an asset. I have a strong feeling I'll be needing to find a different way to cross her off my list by the end of the year.

Permanently.

"Desperate's not a good look on you," she scowls at me, her plump lips turned down tightly. Crossing her arms up tightly beneath her breasts, she tilts her head at me.

She's gone straight into mean girl mode. I wonder if she saw my encounter with Tristan this morning and has concluded I must be on the prowl for a Rox Boy.

If only she knew.

Amusingly, she looks and sounds just like Cheryl Blossom.

"Only desperate to drop off my books, *Riverdale.*" I say with an artificially wide smile and a light shrug of my book bag. "Your boy here is blocking my locker."

This time my snark isn't met with silence, but gasps and low jeers as the crowd ripples around us, excitable with bloodlust. There's fresh meat, and it doesn't know its place.

What did I say? I guess that means they're...off again?

Sloane's eyes darken. "What's with the cutesy fucking nicknames?" she asks with a sneer.

What the hell? Cutesy fucking nicknames are my love language, *thankyouverymuch.*

I wonder vaguely if playing the part of the new student 'properly' means that I should at least *try* to appear upset. But like always, it's a matter of I probably *should*, but I *won't*. So instead, I let a sharp grin slip out.

A genuine look of discomfort begins to smooth over the derision on the redhead's features. "You're a cold bitch, aren't you?" she says, giving me a calculating look up and down.

Shit. I never really did learn how to smile with my whole face.

I tilt my head so there's no way she can't see my jagged scar. "That's one way to put it," I say, a hint of my amusement leaking into my tone.

She steps forward, eyes flicking over my temple, before two perfectly manicured hands move up to grab my lapels. She opens my blazer for a closer inspection, and then gestures her chin towards my chest and narrow hips, pointedly ignoring the scar.

"You wouldn't even know what to do with someone like him," she murmurs, just skipping ahead and straight to the body shaming.

My eyebrows jump to my hairline. *Hey, I'm a proud card-carrying member of the Itty Bitty Titty Committee, sister.*

Several girls have peeled away from the faceless crowd and are now pressing into Sloane's back and shoulders, giggling. I recognize them as part of her cheerleading slash bully girl posse—Dakota, Parker and Reid.

Guess friendship bracelets are off the table, then.

I hum and before I can stop myself, "You're absolutely right, Regina George. I *wouldn't* know what to do with him because I don't normally fuck high school boys." Then with a conspiratorial smile, I lean in and whisper loudly from behind my hand, "Bit…*vanilla* for my tastes, you see."

Sloane releases her grip on my blazer and drops her hands like I've burned her. The matching confused looks that blossom across all four girls' faces are positively delightful. So is the choked laughter that comes from somewhere behind them.

Oops.

"Jesus, what the fuck is your damage?" Doe-eyed Dakota curls her hand protectively around Sloane's shoulder.

"Hundred says she's still a virgin," Blonde Parker chimes in, acidly. Reid, Dakota's twin, looks like she's ready to start collecting bets. The crowd titters. Sloane smiles wickedly again.

C'mon girls, now we're virgin shaming, too?

My eyes roll to the ceiling, one hand subconsciously stroking down the pocket holding my hidden flask.

It's still too early for these social gymnastics. Thank Christ for Xanax.

Okay, okay. My cold shoulder wasn't enough and we're doing this. They want to throw down gauntlets? I'm in. I've already fumbled my advantage and if I start off on the back foot here, I'll never be able to cultivate targets. They'll slot me in at the bottom of the totem pole and I'll never get a look in again. So I'll have to see these girls now and raise them.

I just have to hope that the hostility might actually play out in my favor for once, and help keep the gossip mills in motion.

Between these Queen Bees and the Rox Boys, I'm going to have my hands full.

Eat or be eaten.

The shrill sound of my phone ringing out on speakerphone cuts through the laughter. Everyone's focus is now locked on my cell, lit up and held aloft between Sloane and I. Within seconds, Rhett's sultry, disembodied voice is floating out across the hushed crowd.

"Bored already?" Then, more seriously, "Has something happened, doll?"

I watch the mocking smile start to slide slowly off Sloane's beautiful face at the husky, masculine voice. My own grin is back and still full of teeth.

"No, no, nothing's happened. Yet." An exaggerated sigh. "But all I've got is study hall this afternoon. So much free time," I huff, idly inspecting the nails of my other hand. "Feel like grabbing me early for lunch, and then picking up where we left off this morning?"

I look past Sloane's shoulder, searching for and locking eyes with Tristan. Just my luck that he's my one and only witness. He can verify the existence of my visitor, or he can pull this rug out from under me right now. I silently dare him to try and contradict me.

His eyes narrow further, aggressively boring into me with the weight of an afterlife judgment. He doesn't move, but there's an audible chuckle through the phone.

"Fucking insatiable, baby girl," Rhett teases. "Yeah. I know what you need. I'll pick you up after I've finished training with Knox. Be ready," he adds just before he hangs up.

I slip my phone back into my blazer, my attention back on Sloane. She's quiet, lips pursed and her dark amber eyes simmering hotly with the beginnings of a year long vendetta.

"So, thanks for the concern, but as you can see, I'm doing okay in that department." I raise my eyebrows as if to say *your move*. And wait for a catty retort that doesn't come. It seems she realizes her little stunt has fallen short and she's refusing to double down.

Smart girl.

There was no question I was going to land myself on her blacklist at some point, but this may be a record, even for me. What I really need to do now is a one-two-punch; give her a reason to think twice about how she retaliates. She needs a *warning*. A warning that I know *exactly* who she is, and if she wants to keep her identity secure, she's going to have to bring her A-game.

I bring my face close to hers, gently brushing a fiery lock back over her shoulder as I erase the small space between us. This time my words are for her and her alone. "Cat got your tongue, *mo rós fiáin?*" I breathe against her ear.

I lean back so I can catch the moment the color spills from Sloane's face like a kicked paint bucket.

It's a thing of beauty. Truly.

There's my confirmation—her true roots *are* a well-kept secret, and by the look of horror now crowding her features, it seems Daddy wouldn't appreciate that kind of information getting out.

Jackpot.

Then the warning bell for the first period finally sounds out from above. The upperclassman who had previously been standing frozen, watching our arch-nemesis origin story play out, now thaw out and quickly disperse.

I shoulder Sloane's little squad aside and I move towards my locker with a sigh. My skull gives one tight, vicious squeeze, heralding an oncoming headache. *Great.* I'm going to have to visit a bathroom so I can medicate again before first period.

Not a great start at all.

I've barely finished putting in my combination when I hear an exaggerated, masculine groan from somewhere behind me.

"Be still my beating groin."

Knowing the owner of the flirty curveball is most likely one of the remaining three Rox Boys, I stop myself from turning and engaging directly. It's a fucking struggle though—I *really* want to lay eyes on them, and that voice is arguably as playful and honeyed as Rhett's.

It's the voice of someone you could find yourself in a lot of trouble with.

But I have to set the tone here. They aren't going to be calling all the shots this year. I won't let them. I can't.

So instead, I continue opening my locker door, effectively creating a barrier between me and their avid attention. "High school boys, remember?" I call out in a sing-song voice.

I have to bite down on my lip to tame the treacherous smile that's trying to make a break for it. Damn it, I love flirting.

The answering chuckle is just as musical, and in the same bedroom voice I hear, "*Meow.* New girl's got some claws."

There's a blur of movement to my left and then Mr Beating Groin is there, slumping one shoulder noisily against my neighbor's locker door. I snap my own door shut in surprise, turning and raising my eyebrows at his theatrics.

The demigod I'm greeted with shoots me a heartbreaker of a grin, his teeth a shock of bright white against tanned skin. His eyes are equally as bright with mischief, sparkling as he rolls his head of wild bronzed curls dramatically back and forth against the metal door behind him.

There's an air of barely repressed, frenetic energy—no, *chaos*—that surrounds him like a messy aura of sorts.

Lake.

I should have guessed.

Lake Ezekiel Miller, 17. Adoptive parents still married. Three younger siblings; youngest sister, deceased. Bipolar I disorder, diagnosed at age 15. Avid surfer. Proficient in computer sciences and information technologies.

A jokester with limited boundaries and the ability to procure intelligence from just about any source.

Makes for a dangerous foe.

Something akin to excitement bubbles in my chest. From this close, I can see the dark freckle in his right eye, the color of the irises otherwise a mesmerizing hazel.

"Maybe you just need to get in some practice time with said *high school boys*, Wifey."

I hear a sharp *snick* and glance down to see that he's idly flipping a Zippo open and shut, running his other hand suggestively over his crotch as he does.

"Wifey?" I ask with a snort.

"Don't play with your food, Lake," Tristan drawls, appearing just behind his best friend's shoulder like a sexy ghost. He'd been leaning directly against my assigned locker earlier. I didn't even see him move.

"Yeah Lake, I already have *lunch plans*," I say pointedly and suggestively.

Lake's grin just grows wider.

"Sharing is caring, ya know? Who's your squeeze? I'm sure he agreed that three's *always* better than two."

The funny thing is he's not far off the mark. Rhett would not even *hesitate* to take Lake Miller to bed.

So tempting. So very tempting.

"He'd ruin you, pretty boy," I smirk back instead, shaking my head wryly, like there's *no way* I'm even contemplating the idea of a ménage with the two disgustingly attractive blonds.

He leans in and without skipping a beat, purrs, "And who says I don't *want* to be ruined?" His warm breath skitters across my cheek. He smells like board wax and sunshine.

Fuck. I'm going to have to really keep my wits around this one.

Before I can even formulate a response, he darts in, licking a hot trail from under my jaw, across my cheek and up over my temple. "I licked it, now it's mine," he growls playfully and then he's shoving off the locker and sauntering away.

"See you around, Wifey." The incessant click of the Zippo follows him down the hall.

I blink, and with something akin to shock, reach up and gingerly touch my temple.

There's a fine tremor in my finger.

He licked my scar.

He licked my scar?

Jesus Christ.

Why was that so oddly…erotic?

Then, as my headache madly rushes back in, I realize that my head had not hurt at all during that entire encounter. I guess just the stress of having to be so *on* around one of the Rox Boys was enough for a quick dump of nonsense adrenaline. Maybe having to constantly deal with them during school hours won't be such a horrible thing if it means more sporadic bouts of drug-free reprieves?

With another blink to clear my sudden hot boy-induced stupor, I finally notice that I'm the only one left in the hallway, and I *still* haven't dropped off my textbooks.

I also never even managed to catch more than a glimpse of the rest of Tristan's ruling cohorts.

Something tells me that encounter didn't exactly come out *entirely* in my favor.

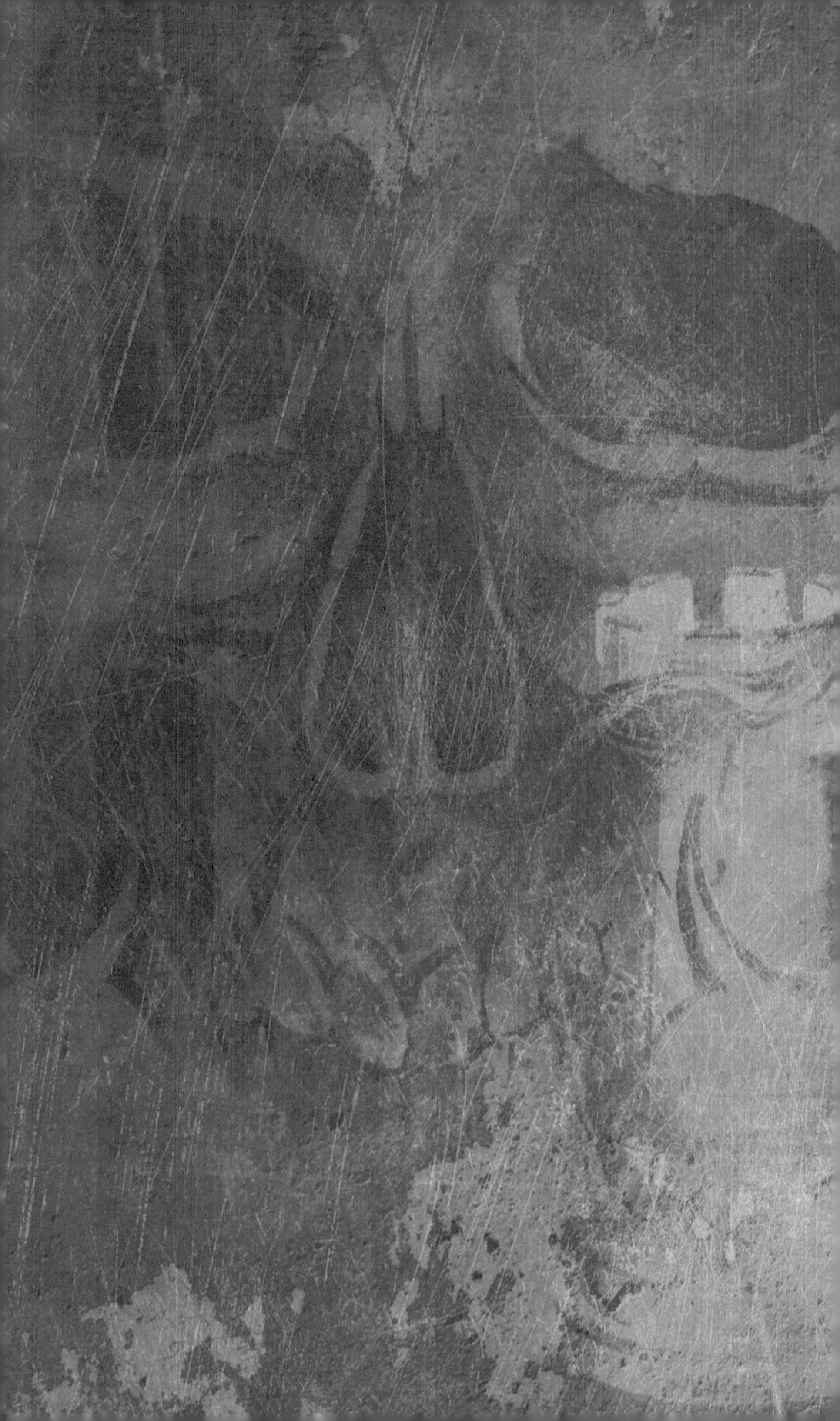

CHAPTER VII

I MANAGE to slip into English Lit right as the final bell reverberates overhead. I'm early enough that I barely register on Mr Moorebrook's radar as he writes out his lesson plan—but too late to get a decent seat.

Taking in the short, harried teacher, I do a quick pull from my mental rolodex. *Peter Moorebrook, 42. Married, two children. Penchant for horse racing. No known affiliations.*

He's not exactly a priority of mine, but I haven't completely written off his usefulness just yet. Family men with gambling predilections are notoriously easy to bribe.

With a surreptitious glance over the rest of the assembled students, I also file away the seating plan, before sliding into the only vacant chair in the room.

According to the class roster I memorized beforehand, and as confirmed by my quick sweep, there are no Rox Boys or their girls in this particular period. What's unfortunate however, is that my seat is closest to the door, which means I don't have a great viewpoint for observing the rest of my fellow classmates during the lesson.

I'm only disappointed for a moment, and then I manage to get a good look at my desk neighbor.

A small, victorious smile cracks my lips. *Finally,* something is going my way this morning.

The desk directly to my right is occupied by a slight figure, currently hunched over his books, his face hidden by a swath of platinum blond hair so light it's practically white. Elegant neck, broad shoulders, long fingers.

From the little skin I can see showing at the end of his blazer sleeves, his forearms are wrapped in heavy, swirling patterns of ink.

He's tense, tapping a pen aggressively across the back of the knuckles of one hand.

Wren Michael Jacobs, 17. Born and raised in Roxborough, eldest of four children, academic scholarship student.

But the part that really fascinates me?

Budding forger.

Wren's counterfeits have been popping up all over the state in the last twelve months. And they are good. *Really* good. In fact, if wasn't for my stupid brain's hyperfixation with cataloguing details, I would never have been able to track and trace his work.

He'd be a major boon for The Gray Men.

Or to us, I think slyly. There was always going to be some potential assets that I'd be loath to share with Sebastian, knowing that Jax will need every advantage in the days and months to come.

This kid's one of them.

Suddenly, I now have the attention of a glittering set of brown eyes so dark and intense they're almost black. His face is unreadable as he takes his time to openly scrutinize mine. I gaze back, noticing he has an adorable smattering of freckles across the bridge of his nose that wasn't as apparent in his photo.

A frown tugs briefly at his brow as he takes in my scar, before his expression smoothes back over. Eventually his eyes lift to my hair. A strained smirk pulls at the corner of his mouth. "Nice victory curls," he says in a throaty but detached sort of voice, before directing his attention back to the front.

His pen continues tapping.

"You have a good eye," I chuckle with a soft, impressed laugh. His mother is a hard-working, middle-class woman who trained in hairdressing before becoming a stay at home mother full-time. I wonder if that's where he got his random knowledge of 1940s pin up hairdos.

I can't outright ask him that, of course. Instead, I pass my hand over for a friendly handshake. "Sabine."

He blinks when he hears my name and again that frown appears. He looks down at my offering for a solid three seconds before sliding a cold hand into my palm. "You're on Sloane Walker's shit-list, you know," he informs me bluntly in reply.

I retrieve my hand on a sigh and blow a raspberry. "Is that the hot, angry red-head? Yeah, I was kind of hoping to make it a full week before incurring the wrath of any of the head BICs. But guess I'm kind of an overachiever when it comes to pissing people off."

I cover the small inward cringe that always follows thoughts of Sebastian with a casual shoulder lift. Turning more fully towards him, I prop one elbow on my desk so I can rest a cheek on one fist. "So."

"So." He's still not giving me much of anything with his body language. Just a lot of tension.

"You gonna tell me your name?" I wave a hand between us. "That's usually how these sorts of social exchanges tend to go. Me Sabine and you…?"

He side-eyes me. "Wren," he says slowly, almost as if he's wondering if he should be guarding against my small-talk slash distraction tactics.

Baby, you have no idea.

His defensiveness makes me wonder where in the Academy totem pole Wren Jacobs fits. Is he a victim of these same girls? Or does he prefer to fly under the radar? Is he worried being seen with me might garner him unwanted attention?

"Nice to meet you, *Wren*," I drawl. "No need to get your back up, I'm just trying to scope out some potentially friendly faces before I go out there and get eaten alive by the Roxborough elite."

He's quiet for a beat before he asks, "Where are you from?"

"Lexington. Moved here over the summer."

His mouth pulls down at the corners. "So…you're *not* from Rox City?" He almost sounds confused with the way his voice rises on the question. Hesitant.

"Nope, why?" He must have assumed I was transferring over from one of the public high schools.

Those dark eyes search my face again before he shakes his head. "Never mind, I just thought—" He doesn't finish that sentence though.

Okay, I'm a little weirded out, but more intrigued than anything. "Thought what?" I probe.

"Nothing. So you don't know how it works around here," he states like it's a foregone conclusion.

I perk up. Shit. I didn't even have to needle him for leads. I try not to look too enthusiastic.

"Well, obviously *Sloane* and her twat brigade run things around here. So I guess there goes my lifelong cheerleading aspirations." I purse my lips in a mock pout.

He's the opposite of impressed. Jesus, he's going be a tough nut to crack.

"Yes and no. Sloane, Parker Hall, and Dakota and Reid Adams have a lot of pull. But they're not in charge. They're popular, but just as firmly under the Rox Boys' thumbs as anyone else around here," he explains, rather darkly I might add.

His affect before had been flat and bored, but now there's a subtle hint of anger laced in his voice. *Ooh,* someone who is *not* a fan of the school's bad boys? Any information will be unfiltered and uninfluenced by his distinct lack of hero worship.

Perfect.

"Rox Boys?" I ask sweetly, feigning complete and

utter ignorance. Man, my acting chops are improving. I could join the Theater kids at this rate.

He grunts and looks around, checking the nearest desks. Nobody is paying us any attention though. In fact they seem to be pointedly *not* acknowledging my existence. Instead, they're all busy chatting in groups or flicking through their texts while the teacher continues to write on the chalkboard half of the interactive wall that each of the classrooms here seem to have.

Nonetheless, he lowers his voice as he continues. "Tristan Sinclair. Callum Jameson. Lake Miller. Atlas Rhodes. They've got the whole damn school, including the teachers, in their thrall. It's like a fucking wolf pack around here with the way things are. They bark, they growl, everyone bares their throat. Everyone wants to fuck them or be their best friend. Rumor has it they are into some shady shit, and that reputation is how I guess they keep everyone in line."

I didn't expect to get that much out of him. Wren seemed so reluctant to even talk to me, let alone gossip. I almost have to giggle at the disgust on his face. He's into some shady stuff too, but the difference is he doesn't have the fan club. What I can't tell is if he directly resents their popularity, or if he just doesn't tolerate the bizarre hierarchy he finds himself subjected to.

I mean, it *is* pretty fucking weird.

Four high school seniors with an entire school community at their beck and call. My research so far has failed to uncover any tangible links, but there is *no way* they aren't tied up with the Strange Aces. Tristan does have access to a sizable trust fund, but they still could not have manufactured this kind of pull on their own without a sponsor. They must have a connection to the MC, still hidden well enough so as to not leave a paper trail.

I wonder if Sebastian knows something we don't, and that's why he's so adamant on me turning them into Gray Men. Seems surveillance and cyber deep dives aren't going to be enough. This is going to require boots on the ground.

I also still need to get close enough to check them over for hidden Ace tats.

Such a hardship.

"So, how do the girls fit into the picture?"

Wren is still utterly unimpressed with me, if his continuing glares are anything to go by. "The girls help keep the sheep herded in exchange for scraps of affection. They're all Prefects. The eight of them *are* the Student Council."

I snort. The Student Council information I already knew; it's the social drama and tidbits I'm after. Saves me hours scrolling through Instagram, trying to read the nuance in filtered photos taken by a bunch of drunk teenagers.

"Scraps of affection? I thought Sloane and the dark-haired one must have been a thing, the way she was pissing all over the dude's leg at the lockers."

"Oh Tristan fucks her, but they aren't *together*. The Rox Boys fuck indiscriminately, but none of them *date*."

Oh she must love *that.* It was easy to tell Sloane thought Tristan was hers and hers alone.

I go to open my mouth, eager for more intel, but Wren cuts me off sharply. "I don't know what Sloane has planned for you, but just keep your head down and stay away from them." He turns towards the front again.

Dismissed.

Alrighty then.

With that, I let Wren get back to the lesson. I know full well he has a grade point average to maintain in order to keep his scholarship. I'm not that heartless.

I, on the other hand, do not, as I'm not *actually* graduating. I just have to play the part of the dutiful senior student. I already have the syllabus and texts read and memorized so I can better spend my school hours observing the animals in their natural habitats—the classroom, the dining hall, sporting events.

Since I'm looking for targets with marketable academic, sporting and social skills, the best way will be to watch them interacting during their normal daily routines—when they don't realize they still need to be performing for their peers.

It will give me a much clearer picture than if I only networked during parties or mixers. It's common for people to swap out a series of masks during gatherings, which obviously skews my intel. Doesn't matter whether it's for business, friendship, or sex.

At Roxborough Academy, I'm going to assume most seniors are horndogs like me, and that it's usually for the latter.

DESPITE MY BEST EFFORTS, however, my spot by the door doesn't afford me much in the way of eavesdropping, and lip reading only gets me so far.

It's in the following period, during Calculus, that I at last catch wind of a conversation worth listening into.

Dakota and Parker are one row ahead of me, their beautifully groomed heads together as they chat animatedly. Like most of the class, they are happily ignoring the droning voice of Mr Lomack.

I glance up, taking in *Cresley Lomack, 41. Single. Living with his elderly mother. Enthusiastic Hummel collector.* He's about as interesting to watch and listen to as drying paint. The human equivalent of the color beige. He's been firmly on my *Probably Not* list since I first looked into him.

His tall, rigid form is still facing away from the room as he furiously chalks out the semester's syllabus on the board.

I fix my eyes and ears back on the cheerleaders in front of me.

"Looks like Tristan finally decided. It's this Saturday night, at the Guardhouse," Parker is saying in a forcibly bored tone, scrolling idly through an open group chat on her phone.

Dakota pulls her own phone out, sliding it open to her messages and typing. "The Welcome Back party is *always* at the Guardhouse. What was all the hush-hush and the suspense about?"

Parker shrugs, flicking a mass of blonde hair back over one shoulder as she does. "I think Sloane was hoping Tristan would move it to his Dad's place. You know how big the guest wing is. And it's got that massive pool."

"Looks like we're stuck near campus again, then," Dakota sighs.

"I don't really care where it is, so long as I get a chance to take Callum for a ride again. He's even bigger and hotter than he was at the beginning of the summer."

Interesting.

So at least one of the Rox Boys has beefed up. I wonder if that's intentional. They would need an Enforcer if they are serious about stepping out as a proper crew. Callum is a big guy. He would definitely suit such a role.

Parker has her camera open now, checking out her makeup.

Shit.

I quickly drop my focus back down to the page of notes I've been pretending to take, but because I'm such a lucky motherfucker, she catches a glimpse of me sitting behind them, regardless.

She spins, a sour look taking over her pretty face as she deliberately looks me up and down. Sloane would be so very proud, she's nailed that organic condescending look *down.*

"The fuck do you want, New Girl? Or should I say

Dead Girl Walking?" Both girls now have matching smirks, so confident that my little showdown this morning was the signature on my social death warrant.

Plastering a serene smile on my own face, I shoot Parker a wink and a finger gun. As if she's sharing the joke *with* me, and *not* that I'm the butt of it. "Clever, Minion #1."

It's obvious Parker doesn't know what to do with my aggressive nonchalance, so she rewards me with an epic scowl instead. Her blue eyes darken with disdain as she sneers, "Sloane's right, you *are* crazy."

I place my hand on my chest like a smitten lover, pulling my brows together in a hopeful look. "Aww, she said that about me?"

Dakota blinks once before exchanging a confused look with Parker. "Psycho," she says under her breath before they both turn their backs on me. Their shoulders are tense as they both hunch over their phones, fingers flying across their keyboards.

Well, today is going *swimmingly*.

Not sure how many times I can fuck this Front Man thing up in one day, but I am off to a solid fucking start. Really setting down the gold standard.

Sigh.

Some days I wish they'd burnt out the sarcasm part of my brain when they were taking me apart.

I slump back into my seat, careful to keep the outward smile in place, because inside, my wretched brain is starting up its usual internal cacophony.

Lomack's dry ramblings, so easy to tune out before, now send a wave of prickles cascading over my scalp.

The clock ticking away on the wall begins to echo like a drum snare.

The scratching of pens against paper scrape in my head like metal on metal.

I squint painfully at the time, relieved to find that there's only a few minutes left in the lesson. It's the lunch break next. I'll be able to take care of my growing headache by spending a few sordid moments alone with my flask, and follow that up with a good dose of Rhett.

I breathe out slowly.

Yes. Solid plan.

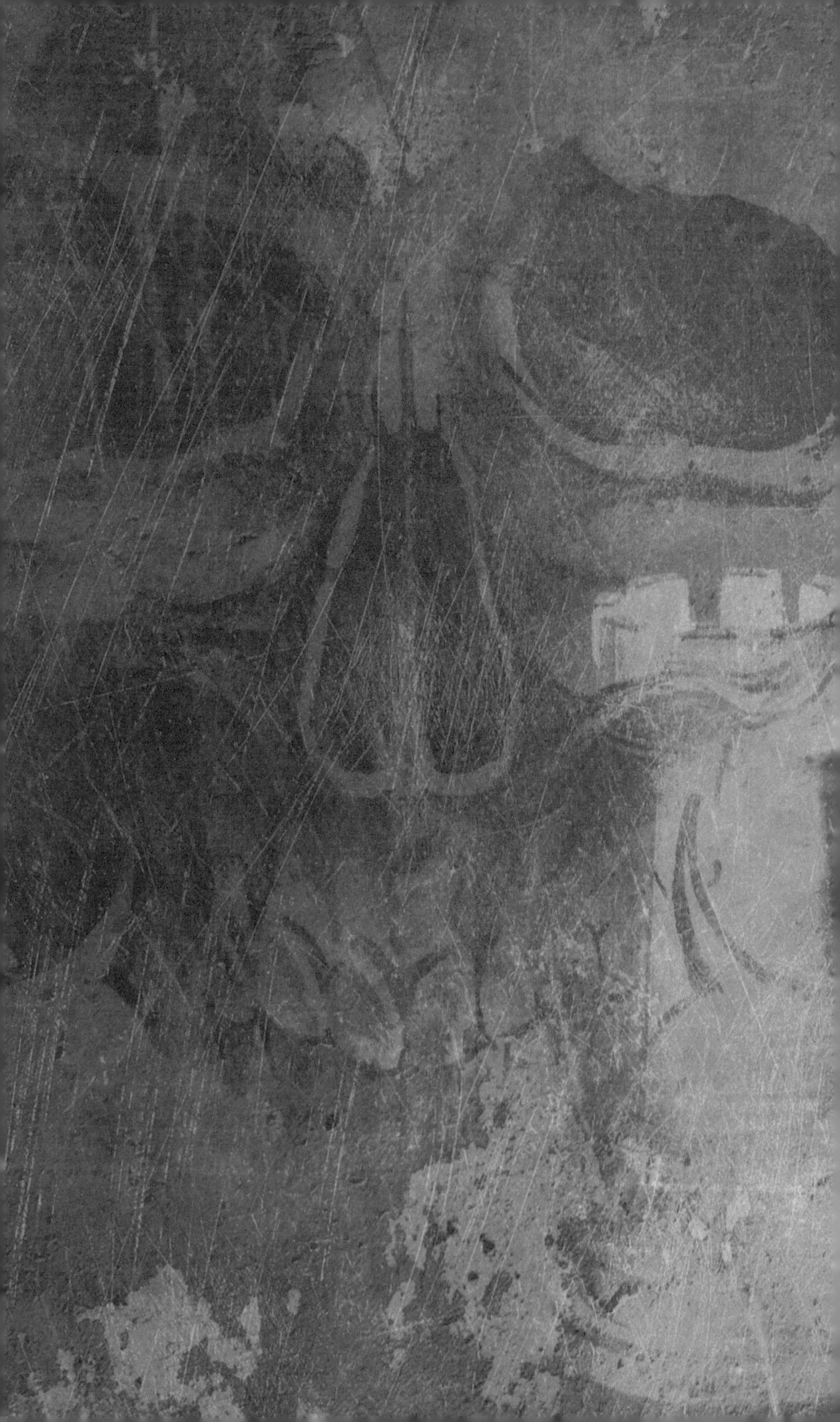

CHAPTER VIII
SABINE

I GLARE down at my phone screen.

RHETT

Be there in 30. Had to shake some Suits.

Fucking Sebastian. Figures he would be having us tailed. His paranoia knows no bounds these days.

Pivoting on my heel, I decide to head to the dining hall to wait. There's no reason to waste the most optimal time slot of the school day for me to head out on safari and observe the wildlife.

I'll just have to be careful about how I use my focus when in a crowd that large. The last thing I want is a recall cascade of hundreds of names and profiles—and the inevitable migraine that will follow.

Marching down the mostly empty hallways, I take a moment to admire the classic, dark academia vibes the Academy is serving. Impossibly high ceilings with massive, ribbed vaults. Clustered columns pitted by time and greenery. Windows with hundreds of stories hidden amongst their delicate patterns of frosted glass work and lead cames.

It's only outshone in both size and grandeur by its more prominent counterpart, the Roxborough University.

I've long thought this preservation of gothic architecture is what truly separates the rival Twin Cities at heart.

Lexington crashed headlong into the new century by committing what I consider a veritable architectural massacre. With the exception of the poorer districts like South Lex, there's barely a heritage building left in the place. It's now an industrial marvel of glass and steel and concrete.

Lex City may be nice to look out, but beneath the glitzy surface, Sebastian's influence has filled its core with rot. It's a wonder Roxborough is nicknamed the City of Sin, when Lexington is arguably a hundred times worse.

Pushing through the heavy double doors of the crowded dining hall, I'm not in the least bit surprised when a dramatic hush follows my entrance, the silence rushing in like the rapids of a river.

Like most common areas in the school, the large space boasts a vaulted ceiling and walls punctuated by a series of tall leadlight windows. The long space is filled to capacity by clusters of dark wooden tables with comfortable-looking bench seats. At the opposite end of the room, another set of double doors sits open, showing a glimpse of a courtyard ringed by trees whose leaves are just about ready to turn.

I keep my sweep of the room light, trying not to look at any one particular student. I just need to get my bearings and a rough idea of the layout of the room before I can move. Then I can spend the next twenty minutes or so working my way through the crowd and hope like hell that most of them keep a regular table so I won't have to re-do this every day. If I have a mental map of where every person usually sits, I can find or avoid targets as I need to without looking directly at faces.

Low titters and a flash of Sloane's red locks tells me that the Prefects and their whitelist minions are occupying prime real estate in the very middle of the hall. It's marked by a six-feet deep buffer of empty tables that surrounds their group, almost like a force field.

I haven't been here nearly long enough to get a full picture of the Rox Academy hierarchy, but if I had to guess—and judging by the weird void of bodies nearest the center tables—I'd say the further out you go, the lower your notch on the popularity pole.

I also catch a glimpse of Wren's shock of white hair not far from the open doors, but I don't linger too long on him. I only have a few minutes and this is the first time I've had an actual, unobstructed view of the Rox Boys as a unit. So I allow myself to focus solely on their table, only to find them as equally focused on me.

And what a view it is.

Directly in the center of the room, the four kings of Rox Academy are lounging; comfortable and untouched in their lunchtime domain.

In fact, one of them is literally lounging. Propped

lazily on muscled forearms, Lake is sprawled across the top of their table, one that looks like it would normally seat around eight. Both his blazer and shirt are completely unbuttoned, giving the room a seductive display of one very tanned chest and one very muscular abdomen.

A silver, cuban-link necklace is currently being dragged between his front teeth by his tongue.

He tilts his head to the side, sliding his attention down my body with a look so blatant and seductive I feel it *everywhere*. Those unruly blond curls fall across his forehead with the movement, and he bites down on the chain, grinning.

There's a small tattoo high on his chest, right above his heart, but I can't make it out from this distance.

His hard, flat stomach flexes as he sits up slowly, emphasizing the prominent lines of his Adonis belt as they disappear into his dark gray slacks. His eyes are gleaming and he almost looks half-feral.

Jesus wept.

Look, I'm not colorblind. Despite having by far the best home life of the four, the boy's got red flags for fucking *days*.

I have a very raw memory of his tongue slashing a heated path along the length of my scar. Two minutes after we met.

So, I'm absolutely sure his warning label comes with words like *fuckboy, poor impulse control* and *boundary issues*.

But I also really, *really* want to lick him back.

I wonder what the flavor *The One Your Mother Always Warned You About* tastes like? My money's on long, sweaty nights and stolen orgasms.

Seated to his immediate left is Tristan, his uniform still immaculate. The embodiment of a Prefect-Captain. His face is once again masked with an expression of cool superiority.

Those eyes are something else though.

Intense and blazing with an emotion I can't quite read, I'm pinned to the spot as he stares me down. Blue and dangerously alluring, like the hottest part of a flame. He leans forward, hands clasped on the table next to Lake's hip. A muscle pops along his jaw.

What's got his boxers in a twist?

For now though, I'm more interested in the table's other two occupants. My last two primary targets.

Looming behind Tristan like a guard dog, is *Callum Patrick Jameson, 18. Former foster child. Mother deceased. Father not listed on birth certificate. Works part time in local garage. Interests in health and physical sciences. On scholarship, sponsored by the Sinclairs.*

According to the records we pulled, his mother OD'd three years ago on a dirty batch of coke. We don't *think* it was any of our shit, but we can't be sure. She had loose ties to the Aces when she was younger, with some time spent as a hardbody living in one of their clubhouses.

Callum then had a year bouncing around group homes and couch surfing before Tristan convinced his father to pull some strings and secure Callum a spot in the Academy. Evidently all four boys have been close since childhood. The underlying connection seems to be some rec center that they all met at.

Now if Tristan has perfected the look of icy disdain, Callum is 100% glower and rage. Topping out at 6'3, he is a broad, tense, hulking beast of a man. Rippling, olive-skinned muscles and acres of tattoos. Passion and violence given form.

Colorful ink covers every surface of skin visible below his harsh, defined jawline. His straight, auburn hair is shaved in a fade around the sides and back, left long on top and swept back away from his forehead. I know from his files that those eyes are honey-brown. A silver ring glints from his left nostril.

His poor shirt truly has its work cut out for it, struggling to contain a set of massive shoulders and arms. It looks like he must have abandoned all ideas of wearing a blazer. He's even larger than Rhett, though not as big as Knox. I can definitely see him as Tristan's Enforcer. I swear those biceps must be the size of my head.

And finally, sitting directly across from Callum is the fourth member of their crew.

Atlas Orion Rhodes, 18. Single mother, father unknown. Only child. Interests include economics and political sciences. Stock market prodigy.

His mother, who evidently has a love for mythology, has only lived in this country for a little over two decades. There is zero record of Atlas's father—he wasn't even listed on the birth certificate.

Like both his mother and closest friends, Atlas is

strikingly beautiful. Warm, bronzed skin like caramel. Full pouty lips and darkly lashed, slightly upturned eyes that I know will be a dark blue-gray. An elegant neck with a prominent Adam's apple. Long, unruly hair in a brown so dark it's almost black, and swept back into a high, messy bun.

Gathered together in one place, it'd be hard for anyone not to recognize the popularity and influence they wield; the haze of it surrounds their group like a living entity.

Their leader, Tristan, exudes an easy fog of dominance. Callum radiates waves of strength and violence. Lake pulses with a spiky aura of mayhem. Atlas, on the other hand, seems to fold his aura around himself like a blast shield—one crafted from pure, undiluted hostility.

His knee is bouncing rapidly, his hands fisted tightly on his thighs. It's like his discomfort and obvious desire for personal space is so intense, it's damn near becoming a tangible thing.

He also has a dark look on his face that's putting Callum's scowl to shame. That dead zone around the popular tables is making a lot more sense now.

The last thing I need is to be caught staring, however, so I slide my gaze away from the middle, pretending to cast my interest out elsewhere like a net.

It's hard to concentrate, however. I can still feel the weight of their full, unerring focus, no matter where I'm looking. It's heavy, like a pair of hands pressing down on my shoulders.

It doesn't help that the rest of the senior class is also still silently staring, waiting for my next move.

The smallest tingle of adrenaline sweeps up my spine, gently caressing the base of my skull. Coupled with the quarter flask of gin I just downed in the bathroom, and I'm left with a pleasant warmth in my stomach and a small but welcome reduction in brain noise.

At this rate, I'm just going to have to scrap my plans to profile the lunch crowd today. It's not exactly a conducive environment for spy work when I'm the one still being given the petri dish treatment.

Smiling tightly, I make the final decision to just abort my recon mission. I'll make a beeline for the courtyard and wait for Rhett to do his thing from there. But *of course*, the most direct path will take me straight through the middle of the tables and past the upper echelon that's currently still burning holes in the side of my head.

I don't really have time for a confrontation right now, but I will definitely look like a coward if I choose to deliberately skirt around them.

I can't show weakness. Not this early in the game.

I focus on the open doorway leading outside, keeping my gaze fixed just above the sea of heads. I'm oddly grateful at this moment for my hard-earned alcohol tolerance; I don't think my reflexes should be fuzzed-out too badly. I do have to stay on guard though—I don't trust anyone in this hall yet, and I can't shake a feeling like I'm wading into battle.

At the table directly next to the Rox Boys, sits Sloane and her best gal pals. I cast them a quick glance. Each one of them is watching me intently, pouty lips twisted with amusement. That alone sends my alarm bells ringing.

One more table down, and coming up on my right, is a large portion of Tristan's basketball team. Some of them are perched on the tabletop, some lounge across the benches. Each of them have some version of an excited smirk or leering grin across their faces, mirroring the girls.

A player sits astride the bench closest to me. Jasper Lennon, Tristan's starting power forward. He's tall and broad and cocky; a consummate ball player. His mousey, brown hair flops across his forehead as he leans back and shoots a smug look in my direction.

Right as I close in, I sense it in my peripheral—a tensing of muscles, a subtle stretch of a leg.

The anticipation squeezes my chest.

I'd expected cat calls, or maybe even food, but I suppose a nice public date with the floor is always a solid fall-back plan for these brain-dead jocks.

Bullying 101: Tripping.

My mind is sprinting now, frantically trying to visually catalog every guilty tell before they can put their plan into action. Then I see it, right there—*part two*—a bowl of *something*, chunky and putrid, on the table right near where his elbow rests. With those two puzzle pieces clicking into place, I *just* manage to clock the moment his large, sneakered foot shoots out, looking to connect violently with my ankles.

One important fact that you should know about Sabine Winters, is that I am not physically strong in *any* sense of the word. Dominic likes to call me 'a scrap of a thing'. Not fondly, mind you. So to compensate, my many years of offensive and defensive training have been primarily focused on agility, precision, and flexibility.

It's a very close thing, but I do manage to side-step Jasper's foot trap—rather deftly I might add. Only to realize my *rookie fucking mistake* as I pivot to face my would be attackers.

CHAPTER IX

SABINE

YES, I'm sure the plan did originally involve getting me down on my knees. It would have made their little show just that touch more entertaining for the restless masses.

But in endgame terms? Jasper's foot was merely the misdirection.

The sound of congealed, mystery meat leftovers splattering across my chest is obscene.

I don't dare glance down, because my gaze is locked with Sloane's, but I can feel exactly *everywhere* the alien concoction is now soaking through my blouse. It's clinging in coarse, freezing patches against my skin, a matching chill skittering down my spine. I grit my teeth in revulsion. Sloane's face remains poised but her eyes are fucking sparkling with glee.

I let out a slow, steadying breath and push down the very real urge to put my hands around her slender neck. Feelings of true anger consistently elude me on the regular, but I *definitely* still experience the urge to punish if wronged. Like a callous, avenging Angel—so detached from humanity that their righteous wrath becomes something sharp and clinical.

But, I digress. It would be poor form to murder someone on the *first* day of school, though wouldn't it? That's *at least* a Week Two endeavor.

The hall hangs on its collective intake of breath. A wet plop sounds out as the first chunks begin to slide off and hit the floor at my feet.

I flick my attention down to where Jasper still sits, determined to come away from this shitshow with *something.* I bend my knees slightly and lean over so I can speak directly against the shell of his ear. "Your father has quite the taste for high class cocaine. Shame he's such a shitty customer. Consider this your family's first warning. Next time little Rebecca becomes the payment."

I straighten, watching as my message sinks in and his slackening face goes chalk white. There is no love lost between father and son, which is why I had to resort to using the sister as leverage. Younger siblings are always much more effective as threats than the pressure of the debts themselves.

He doesn't notice the chunk of meat that's fallen off my shirt and onto his lap. *Jasper Gregory Lennon, 18,* is now officially my first recruit.

I slip out my phone, pulling up his contact details. I'd programmed every student and teacher's number into my phone before ever stepping foot on campus. For times exactly like these.

SABINE: I'll be in touch. You're spoken for now.

A cruel smirk blossoms across my mouth as I hear the

distinct ding of a message go off in his pocket. Satisfied that I've got him on the hook, I look back up and lock eyes again with Sloane. Leaning over to grab a fistful of napkins, I say, "You're lucky we didn't decide on first blood, Red. But I guess that's a strike to you. Best of five?"

The raucous laughter that had started the moment their buddy had made his move now falters. I suppose they still aren't used to receiving any pushback.

Sloane's lovely face is now tight with fury. At least that smug fucking look is gone.

I finish scraping off what slimy mess I can and then drop the now soaked napkins in the middle of their table. I don't wait for any further retorts, turning on my heel and stalking towards the open courtyard. I've got a playdate with my Crew mate, and I don't want to be stuck in this hall playing their childish games any longer than necessary.

Breaching the doorway at last has me sucking in a long, steadying breath. The cooling September air is a crisp kiss against the sharp planes of my cheeks, and an even colder caress against my wet chest.

I honestly thought I'd feel more relieved having just ripped off the bandaid and taken the first step to fulfilling my mission.

But all it does is remind me that I'm essentially trapped here by Sebastian's machinations and I have no control over my life for the next 180 or so days.

I'm tempted to lean on my flask again, but decide I'll kill some time with a quick blunt instead. I slip on a pair of oversized sunglasses against the harsh midday glare and give the courtyard around me a once-over. It's quaint. Behind a low-lying retaining wall I spy a grassy incline, clear of debris and shaded well by one of the huge oaks that line the space.

I pluck at my blouse, and groan with disgust. The wet, gravy-stained material is almost translucent now and determined to suction itself to my breasts. But knowing there's not much I can do until my ride's here, I stretch out beneath the tree, using my neatly folded blazer as a makeshift pillow. I cross my legs at the ankles and light up.

I'm heavily invested in watching the plume of smoke that's curling seductively around the leaves above me, when movement at the retaining wall steals my focus.

Dropping my chin, I spy Lake now perched gracefully atop the knee-high barrier in his best impersonation of a gargoyle, curls wild as ever and eyes shining. His shirt and blazer are still hanging open like heavy theater drapes, giving me a solid view of the cut abs right there on center stage. His focus bounces between my face and my now see-through shirt.

The remaining three Rox Boys are arranged behind him like marble sentinels, arms crossed and chiseled faces giving nothing away.

There is something extremely eerie about how well they fit together, how cohesive they present when gathered as a group. In fact, I'm struck by an odd compulsion to observe them working as a team in a combat situation. I bet they'd move seamlessly, like cogs in a well-oiled machine.

I'm expecting a confrontation after the cafeteria, but they haven't said a word. They just continue to stare me down. And like inside, the weight of their combined focus sends a small pulse of adrenaline through my system.

Great. Now I feel like a zoo exhibit. *Again.*

"No tapping on the glass, and no flash photography," I drawl, tipping my head back and blowing out an unhurried smoke ring.

Wow. Not even a hint of a smirk.

Tough crowd.

After what feels like an eternity, it's Lake who finally breaks the silence. "What's your name, Wifey?" he asks, playful, but guarded. He's still balancing on his toes in that crouched position.

"Nobody's wife, Goliath," I respond drily, puffing out another lazy circle of smoke.

"Just a matter of time before I put a ring on it. You'll see."

I try to ignore the little fireworks *that* sets off in my stomach. Why would he say something so…possessive?

And hot. Why is that so fucking attractive? I don't even *do* commitment.

But it's like a smutty novella meet-cute playing out before my eyes.

Enemies-to-lovers. Am I here for it?

There is no way these four wield the power they do around here without having access to the administrator's office. I'd even wager a tidy sum that Tristan already knew who I was when he spoke to me outside my dorm this morning.

Had he been standing there, waiting for me?

"You guys already know who I am."

"*Sabine Winters,*" he hisses, confirming that they do, in fact, know exactly who I am. So what's with the ambush? The subterfuge?

I dip my chin and smirk over my sunglasses at Tristan's glare. "Reporting for duty."

That muscle along his jaw jumps again. I'm surprised he hasn't cracked a tooth yet. "I don't know who the *fuck* you *think* you are, but I know for a fact that you are. *Not.* Sabine. Winters." He almost grinds out those last words.

The vitriol I can hear in his normally unruffled tenor is *potent.*

As potent as my genuine confusion.

I sit up, glasses sliding down my nose as I empty my lungs with a surprised, smoke-filled laugh. "Excuse me?"

My eyes flick between the four of them, looking for tells. There's no humor on any of the handsome faces before me. No smirks, no giddiness. Not even from Lake. Each one of them is tense, muscles taut and on guard. I recognize that familiar way they pull their emotional shields into place. There's no shared joke here. They are deadly serious.

"Sabine Winters? Sabine Winters is *dead.* So who the fuck are you?" Callum's voice, while angry, is pure sin; deep and roughened. I feel it behind my ribs and between my legs.

My mouth drops open just a little bit. I'm…almost at a loss as to how to respond to that.

Dead?!

"I assure you, I am very, very much alive," I say, after a breath, my tone incredulous.

There's no relief on their faces or relaxing of postures.

"Sabine *Ingrid* Winters?" Tristan continues, posing it as a question, but he sounds so skeptical that it may as well be rhetorical. He's obviously had access to my full file and transcript; all the information about who I am *supposedly* claiming to be.

"Yes."

"*Liar.*"

If I thought Tristan or Callum's voice gave me a kick in the guts, I was *not* prepared to hear Atlas speak. His voice is dark and gritty as if it regularly goes unused. Like he only speaks when absolutely necessary. That one word is all he needs though, and it's dripping with venom.

I'm so disoriented now, both by the heady effects of their combined presence, as well as the batshit words coming out of their dumb, handsome faces. That combination is *lethal.* My own shoulders tense, and I can't help the tremor that shudders up my spine. Blood pulses in my ears.

What the fuck is going on?

I fucking hate being on the back foot. I hate not having all the information.

It's literally my fucking *job* to have the information.

No. No. Fuck. Now is not the time for a fucking

headache to kick back in. I squint my eyes as the pounding begins, royally irked that my reprieve was so short lived.

I need control. I need to maintain control here. With some degree of difficulty, I grab onto that semblance of annoyance with both hands and use it to pull myself back together. I stand, hauling my blazer up with me and draping it over my arm.

"I don't know what to tell you. You must have me confused with some other Sabine Ingrid Winters," I say coldly, dropping my joint to the ground and crushing the cherry under foot.

Sabine Winters is dead.

Nope. I'm not engaging them further. I need to wrestle back the command of the narrative before I do. I can't let them be blind-siding me with this crazy sort of shit. Here I thought my work was going to be cut out for me just trying to uncover their secret Ace connections. Now I need to figure out why they think I'm walking around with the name of some dead girl.

An emergency ripcord comes in the form of my cell phone vibrating inside one of the pockets now tucked under my arm. Retrieving it, I grin as Rhett's name lights up the screen. *Finally.*

He's going to have his work cut out for him, because I don't think a quick fuck in the back seat of his car is going to be enough.

I hold it up and shake it. "Excuse me, but I have a lunch date I need to keep."

I spin around and with my back to them, carefully

pick my way down the other side of the incline. I know I'm off my game right now, and I'm *not* about to trip and ruin my exit.

My shoulders drop as I see it—up ahead is the gate which leads directly to the parking lot.

To my awaiting ride.

And some well-deserved stress relief.

CHAPTER X

CALLUM

FOR A MOMENT, nobody moves; each of us transfixed by the retreating form of a ghost that has haunted us since our teens.

Sabine motherfucking *Winters.*

No.

It's *not* her. It can't be.

"Someone's fucking with us," I seethe. "Someone must have found out about our plans, sent a plant here on purpose."

I'm only met by silence. My brothers don't bother to point out how insane that sounds. But this *is* insane. "Do you think it's *him*?" I hate how shaky my voice sounds, the panic skittering across my skin like the buzzing of a wasp.

"Callum. Lake. Follow her."

The cool delivery of Tristan's command doesn't fool us for a second.

Not when the bonds between this group run so fucking deep, they're practically etched right into the fucking bones themselves. Not when the four of us are closer than any blood tie, reading each other like human decoder rings.

Just a single glance is all it takes to betray the cracks running down the middle of that legendary Sinclair composure. Cracks that appeared the moment Lake lifted the new girl's file.

Atlas says nothing. His face is a dark storm, still glaring at the wrought-iron gate she just disappeared through. Not unusual. I'm actually surprised he spoke to her at all. I love the guy, but he's been carrying around this damage for *years*.

Damage with gnarled, tangled roots that all lead their way back to our sass-mouthed specter.

My neck and shoulders are killing me. The tension trembling through my traps leaves me feeling like a recurve bow that's been strung with strings too goddamned short.

What a fucking nightmare.

I pull in a long, labored breath, my lungs wrestling oxygen up and in through my nose. I flex my fingers and clench them back into tight fists. Once. Twice.

It can't be *her*.

Sabine. Motherfucking. *Winters.*

"*Go,*" Tristan barks.

This time, Lake and I don't hesitate, heading quickly in the same direction as our imposter did.

The new girl with a smile that doesn't quite reach her eyes.

What color are those eyes?

Does she have *Sabine's* eyes?

No, don't go there. There's no way it's her.

I can't lie though; she's a new, wild kind of beautiful. I was there for both her little stunts—in the dining hall and this morning. My eyes had trouble leaving her.

There's something about the way she carries herself that pulls at me.

All those hard, spiny edges and that attitude. A sharp, elfin face with nose and cheekbones to match. Expressive eyebrows and bold makeup. A generous mouth with a deep cupid's bow. When she bared her teeth at Sloane, I swear I saw a goddamn smiley piercing.

She kinda has this larger-than-life, punk-rocker thing going on. But then she's got that blonde hair and face done up like one of the girls from the faded pin-up posters down at the garage. It's a lot, but, *fuck*. It works.

Sabine had blonde hair, a small, cloying voice whispers in the back of my mind.

My stomach clenches and I push the thought away.

What I do know is that she's confident, bold as hell, and she stood her ground against Sloane and her sharks. Sharks that'd smell a drop of blood in the water a mile off. Hell, some days it feels like they've got the angle on any and all bullshit before it even fucking happens.

But she stood there and took it, didn't she? Took their jokes, and a chest full of old stew and turned the other cheek. Immune to their mind games. Smiling like a lunatic, like she was above it all. It was fake and hollow and I felt the chill of it in my bones, but she didn't cry when they pushed her.

And the mouth *on her. Fuck.*

What kind of fucked up shit has she been through that's got her so goddamn fearless? The way she moves like she's counting out each three moves in advance.

And then that gnarly as fuck scar running across her temple and disappearing into her hairline.

How in the fuck *did she get that scar?*

I cut Lake an uneasy side-eye as we slip through the gate, following the path she's most likely to take if she's meeting someone with a car. His eyes are glowing; mouth in a wide, sadistic grin.

He's practically skipping along at this point, so worked up by the excitement of tracking down this mystery girl. His Zippo flips open and shut in time to his uneven steps.

Fuck. Even if it's *not* her, I already see the telltale signs of obsession slipping its vile claws in, moving deep under his skin like an infection. Either that, or he's toeing the line of one of his manic episodes.

I'm going to have to check up on his meds.

See? She's already causing fucking trouble.

"Are we going to kill him?"

Until now, I figured it had all just been a clever bluff to save her ass. But she really *is* leaving to meet up with whoever was on the other end of that phone call this morning, isn't she?

Something unnamed and acidic bubbles high in my guts. It simmers up underneath my rib cage and leaks into my chest.

I don't like it.

Wait. *No.* I don't give a flying fuck what she does.

I let out a low, frustrated growl. *Because. It's. Not. Her.*

"No, we're just going to follow her. *Them*," I grit out. "We're not going to do shit. Just watch and wait them out."

Just as Lake's about to burst forth into the lot, I grab him by the nape of the neck and haul him back behind the corner of the admin building. He hisses like a cat, but he's no match for my sheer strength.

"Fuck, big guy. I was just making sure we don't lose them."

Lake is normally stealthy as fuck when it comes to surveillance and scoping out rendezvous points. It's why he's our in-and-out guy. But he's not usually this worked up or chasing tail when he's staking out a drop off.

I give him a sharp shake before I let him go. "She's going to see us and know she's being followed if you don't settle the fuck down."

He hums low under his breath, entire frame taut with his impatience. "I still think we should cut him up, at least a little bit. Then he won't be so pretty. She won't want him. Do you think he's as pretty as me?"

I groan under my breath, not bothering to point out that a scarred beauty like her would probably just find that shit hot. Instead I nudge him hard, tipping my head as I spot her blonde hair right by the curb, directly in front of the building we're sheltering behind.

Right before a bright green, *goddamned Aventador* rolls up.

That car's worth some fucking cash.

Who is *this guy?*

I feel Lake draw himself up to his full height, coiled and ready to spring as we watch her slide into the passenger seat with a natural grace. The car door closes behind her but the window tint's too dark for us to see inside.

Great. So we still don't know who she's actually meeting.

As they pull away from the curb, I shove Lake ahead of me, moving us out from our hiding spot and towards the front of the Academy. Where my formerly boosted 1967 Ford Mustang GT390 is also parked.

"And no, you can't drive," I snap out, knowing that's exactly what my wide-eyed, jittery brother is about to ask me. He doesn't respond as we sprint towards my car, just throws me a pout before flinging himself into the passenger seat like the drama queen he is.

"Focus, man. Do you still see them?" I shouldn't be barking at Lake like he's an unruly puppy who's pissed on my shoes. He's done nothing wrong, but I feel so fucking off-kilter.

Confused.

Nervous?

Why would I be nervous?

I'm trying so hard to maintain some fucking semblance of zen, but the acid is still eating a path through my insides. My chest is too tight.

"Four cars up, far right lane."

I keep roughly the same distance between us until we follow them into the parking lot of *The Rox City Diner*. It's a medium-sized, fifties-inspired diner, with all original furniture and fittings. It's popular for Rox students going off campus, and it fits her style perfectly. Like it was made for her.

I grimace. *It doesn't fucking matter if it's her style.*

I creep into a space several cars away from the Aventador, but still within eye-shot of the diner's front windows. As soon as I turn the engine off, I've got an arm across Lake's chest, pinning him to his seat.

"*Stay.* We're only here to observe," I remind him firmly.

Lake whines as he watches Sabine exit from the passenger side, slamming the door behind her. She's already changed out of the stained shirt and blazer, and into a cropped, zip-up hoodie over a tight, white babydoll tee—both with a low neckline.

Paired with her Rox Academy skirt and knee high socks, she looks like some fucking school-girl wet dream.

What the fuck.

His whine slips into a low, deadly hiss as the blond driver unfolds himself from the car.

I've never seen this dude before, and the motherfucker is big. Between my interest in health and bodies, and time spent in the ring, I'm pretty good at sizing up an opponent's stats at a glance. From here, I can safely say I don't think he's *as* big as me, but he's not far off. I have maybe a couple of inches or so on him, but dude is ripped. He's covered in ink as well, so pain's probably more a friend than foe.

There's something in his bearing too—in the way he's holding himself. There's a good chance this guy is

Ace muscle, and we just haven't come across him before.

Or worse. He's muscle for one of the *other* guys.

Goddamnit. I can honestly say I have no clue how a fight with him would land up.

"Fuck, he *is* pretty," Lake's still losing his shit beside me, worried about the guy as a sexual rival. I'm not. I'm worried about whether he's a *business* rival. If and how I'm gonna need to take this fucker out.

Objectively, I can agree the guy's good looking, but I still don't like the way he moves. Like a fucking snake in the grass. He's draped over Sabine, laughing and pawing at her, smirking down at her outfit like she's dressed up especially for him. In her heels, they're almost the same height.

Sabine's smiling right back at him. It looks uncomfortable on her face but it's probably the most genuine smile I've seen from her yet. She doesn't look quite as icy and closed off like she does at school, she looks almost relaxed. Like there's a real connection there.

The two of them disappear inside, taking a seat in one of the front window booths a moment later. They're sitting across from each other, and the flirty grins and easy banter between them doesn't seem to have slowed.

When I'm certain Lake isn't going to jump out of the window, I lower my arm and drop my head back against the headrest. That ugly feeling still slithers through my gut, twisting tighter the longer I watch her with this stranger.

What am I even thinking? She's a fucking stranger too.

She's not though, that treacherous little voice reminds me. *She's home.*

Just as the waitress finishes delivering their food, a giant with dark, shaggy hair and two full sleeves of dark ink approaches their table. He doesn't hesitate before squeezing his bulk into the seat next to Sabine. He then kisses her temple before bumping fists with the guy she arrived with.

My spine straightens at the same moment that Lake leans forward, even more ready to leap out of the car. "Now who's *this* motherfucker?"

Great. We could power the entire Twin Cities with the chaotic energy he's now putting off. He's practically vibrating through the leather of the seat.

I'm mystified. I thought she was meeting Blondie for a hook-up. So who the fuck is Shaggy? He's awfully familiar with our girl as well.

Our girl?

Christ, I'm losing my goddamn mind.

The three of them are obviously close though. Sabine's comfortable as she eats, gesturing wildly. The new guy watches her with nothing but affection.

The more I stare at the newcomer though, the more uneasy I feel. There's something about him that I can't quite put my finger on.

"Does the second guy look familiar to you?"

Lake doesn't answer me straight away, and I feel my sanity fray just a bit further. "Lake?"

"Yeah, hang on a sec, bro," he mutters. I turn to look at him, reluctantly taking my gaze off the trio. His fingers are flying furiously across his phone. No doubt looking for a lead.

"Yep. Here. Rafe Morales. He's got an older brother, Knox. Brother's twenty-two. Graduated from Rox Academy a few years ago." Rafe's one of Tristan's teammates. Cocky son of a bitch, but he's not as painful to hang out with as some of the other Rox jocks.

I narrow my eyes, considering. Now that Lake says it, the guy does look like he could be an older, buffer version of Rafe. I guess that's what I was seeing.

"Alright, so that might be Knox Morales, but who the fuck is the first guy? And how does she know either of them?" Frustration leaks into my voice.

"No idea, brother. *Oh shit*. On the move."

While I'd been busy trying to sort my head, the three of them have evidently finished their lunch and are saying their goodbyes. Knox pulls them both in for a tight group hug, dropping a kiss on both their heads before shoving them playfully towards the door.

The dynamic is more fucking confusing than ever.

"What do we know about the older Morales?" I throw at Lake, rolling my shoulders and cracking my neck as I get ready to start the 'Stang. Sabine and Blondie are still making their way back to his car.

"Not much, except that it looks like he left Rox City after he graduated. I got nothing after that." He tilts his head, his eyes gleaming. Despite his vibe bordering on frantic, however, he's still completely in tune with me. As always. "You think they're Aces, don't you?"

I grunt. "Not ruling it out. They look like muscle for hire and dude's driving a pricy as fuck car."

Does that mean Sabine's an Ace too?

My teeth ache with how hard my jaw clenches at that intrusive thought. I already figured she'd be hazardous for our sanity, but that would just be the goddamn icing on the cake. I won't know for sure though until we can dig up more dirt on those two muscle-bound pricks.

I continue to gnash my teeth as we shadow the two of them through the main streets and out towards the more industrialized sections of the city. The old Victorian style buildings of the business district slowly give way to strip malls and then to warehouses.

As the traffic thins, I'm forced to drop back further and further. I can feel my pulse thundering in my temple.

We're not far from the docks when I lose sight of them.

"Fuck!" I slam my hands on the wheel and speed up.

"Hey, *hey*, there. Bro, right there," Lake almost yelps, gesturing down the side street I was about to blast past. I yank the wheel and pull us over to the curb of the road we're on, a few car lengths down from the corner. I kill the ignition. The muscle in my jaw throbs along with the ticks and clicks of the engine cooling down.

Lake's already got a map of the area pulled up. "Looks like that's nothing but a dead end street. A few warehouses and an old metalworks." He clicks around a bit. "At least two of those buildings are out of commission." Glancing up, he looks around at the ones he can see. "Private, I guess."

He's looking at me now, waiting for my okay to pursue. Like he needs me to let him off leash. No matter how far his control slips, or how far inside his head he gets, he will still always seek out the structure and discipline that only we can provide him.

I grimace. I wish I could just turn around and go back to the Academy. "Alright, let's go. Just keep it on a simmer."

He's out of the car and across the street before I can even lock the car. My mouth pulls even tighter and my stomach roils with anxiety as I race after him, cursing the gravel and broken glass that crunches loudly beneath the leather shoes of my Academy uniform.

As we both move around the corner, we slip instinctively into the shadows of one of the building's many overhangs. Our carefully placed footfalls slow even further, both aiming to stay as close to silent as possible despite the detritus beneath our soles.

Up ahead, maybe fifty paces away, the Aventador is parked at an odd angle, right out front of the building we're crouching against. It's a nondescript warehouse, a few shot out windows and a rusting framework. The door is long gone; nothing but a yawning entrance to the complete darkness beyond.

Now I that have a clear view of them, I can see that Blondie's got Sabine pinned up against the car, caging her in with his large body. He's got a fistful of that long, pale blonde hair clenched tightly behind her neck while he talks quietly against her ear.

I'm frozen.

What the hell is this? Is he threatening her?

But no, she's not fighting him. Her eyes are closed and posture tense, small tremors running through her like she's connected to a live wire.

Without warning he flings her away, shoving her in the direction of the warehouse. Her whole body bursts into motion, and then she's disappearing into the pitch black doorway.

Lake and I move at the same time like ghosts, picking a path through the shadows towards the douchebag.

"Run, run, run, little girl!" he bellows at the darkness, following it with raucous laughter. The asshole peels off his aviators and throws them on top of his car, before turning and locking eyes with us.

Shit.

We're made.

Yeah, this prick has Underworld written all over him.

"Enjoy the show, boys!" he smirks, sweeping a shallow bow like the absolute dickhead that he is. And then he too disappears into the pitch black building.

"*What the fuck,*" Lake breathes, his eyes glazed over with excitement. I hesitate as we both reach the threshold, trying and failing to make out anything in the inky darkness beyond. My scalp prickles. Lake has no such misgivings, taking a step towards the open door before I manage to grab his shoulder and give him a hard shake. He jerks to a stop, but doesn't move his focus from the entrance.

I waggle my cell in front of his face. "Infrared. Need it to navigate and hopefully get a video of our little spook to take back to Tristan."

Lake nods absently, pulling his own out of his pocket and bringing up his IR camera app.

I exhale. It's a long harsh, ragged breath that does nothing to calm the growing storm inside.

Alright, Winters. Time to pull back the curtains.

CHAPTER XI
SABINE

THE AIR IS thick with our frenetic energy and the coppery smell of structural decay. Ten steps at this pace and I know there will be another doorway—this one leading down to a rotting catwalk. The entire blueprint of this warehouse has been seared into my brain from the moment we chose it. I can recall each sub-level in perfect detail and navigate them with my eyes closed.

Which I may as well be doing as the pitch black inside this building is *absolute*.

I burst through the opening in question, covering my mouth with a fist as I kick up a clouded bouquet of sawdust and red dirt. The stench of damp wood, rusting metal, and nesting rodents that surrounds me does nothing to deter the frenzied pumps of adrenaline singing through my veins. If anything, the blatant danger of running blind through a rotting building is only amplifying the rush of excited dread.

I know the lack of light in here is not the only reason my pupils are no doubt as big as saucers. My heart is thundering wildly and my lungs constrict, gripped by a renewed wave of icy-cold anticipation. It leaves my gut in a happy, jumbled mess of writhing carpet snakes.

I fucking love it.

It's *exactly* what I needed to reset my brain.

The metal catwalk rings out like a tuning fork with my first footfall. I pause and tilt my head, listening. I always try to vary my paths as much as possible, but Rhett is a fucking bloodhound. If I didn't know better, I would think he was using night vision goggles to cheat through these sordid little games of cat and mouse.

I hear a soft movement from below. Giddy, I retreat back through the doorway, my movements deliberately more measured this trip through. I don't want to give myself away just yet. I'm not nearly ready for this hunt to be over.

No matter the game, I never bother finding a home base. I just out-pace and out-maneuver, utilizing my agility and stamina. He'll expect me to keep moving, as always. Perhaps this time I can use that fact to my advantage.

The southern end of the hallway outside this particular room leads back towards a cluster of abandoned offices. Only five steps into the hallway, however, and a shiver of awareness skates down my spine.

I freeze, goosebumps rippling down each of my limbs in delicious, bone-tingling expectation. Straining, I desperately will my ears to pick up *any* hint of movement. Breathing, footsteps, *anything*.

There—the slightest rustle of clothing from the northern end of the corridor. Directly behind me.

I still can't see a fucking thing. There is absolutely no light for my eyesight to adjust to. I'm not even entirely sure that I *actually* heard anything over the erratic sound of my own pulse.

But I swear I can *feel* him. Feel him lurking in the inky blackness, just on the edge of my senses. Feel him in the way my heart pounds in my chest and between my legs.

"Little girl, why aren't you running?" comes the low, menacing taunt from the dark. He's close.

The warning edge to his voice should feel sharp like a slice, a stab; instead it feels like the stroke of a lover's hand. As always, it knocks me off-kilter in the best of ways. I can practically feel every hair on my body standing on end.

I whirl, all the air in my lungs leaving in an ecstatic rush as I dash down the hallway, heading in my original direction. Blood roars like a tide in my ears but my mind is now blissfully empty. None of the usual pandemonium.

Only one thought remains.

Run.

I can't hear his footsteps, not over my pulse, nor my hysterical pants, nor the dramatic clicks of my own heels. But I do hear his wicked laughter. It bounces off the metal siding, coming from everywhere and nowhere all at once.

Fourteen paces before the corridor ends with a sharp left hand turn into a receiving area that's surrounded by another warren of rooms.

Nine paces.

Four.

But I don't make it to that turn because a massive weight collides with my back and suddenly we're airborne. I only have one hitched breath to brace for impact, and then we're crashing through the aging, fiberboard composite wall that previously signaled the end of the hallway.

The wall practically disintegrates beneath us in a cloud of decaying MDF dust and shards.

I don't get the chance to clear my lungs or regain my bearings before a large hand is clamping down over my mouth. Its partner tangles roughly through my hair, yanking my head back with a sharp jerk.

"Not fast enough," Rhett hisses victoriously in my ear. Without sight, all my other senses are working overtime. His voice thunders, and his breath feels scorchingly hot against my cheek. What feels like hundreds of pieces of destroyed cladding stab cruelly into every surface of exposed skin that's pressed into the floor.

Arousal pools violently in my pelvis at the guttural, primal sound of his voice, and my wanton pussy opening the floodgates in response. I can't stop the low, strangled mewl that escapes my throat, vibrating pitifully against his palm.

Rhett gives my locks another rough tug. My neck strains, and my arms swing out and backwards, clawed fists connecting with his shins as he crouches over me.

"Listen to you moan, you wicked little slut," he growls, shaking me by the hair with a clenched fist. "You wanted the big bad wolf to catch you, didn't you?" Another jerk. "You didn't even *try* to get away."

This time it's not a moan I give, but a muffled curse. He chuckles darkly in response, before shoving me face-down with the hand that grips my hair. The large hand sealed firmly across my mouth protects most of my skin from the debris of our crash-landing, but I can still catch jagged pieces pressing into my forehead and the top of one cheek.

No pain follows though; my system is too busy overloading. Too much adrenaline and too much dopamine. I can feel the tenuous agreement between my mind and body on what should and should *not* be happening to us splintering like sugar glass.

The hand in my hair suddenly disappears. He's using it now to secure one of my flailing arms—twisting it behind my back and pinning it beneath a heavy knee. The other arm swiftly follows.

He shifts then so that his other knee is between my legs, forcing my thighs apart. My neck is again bent back at an awkward angle, this time by the hand still covering my mouth. I pull in short, quick breaths through the small part of my nostril that's blessedly exposed. My eyes are watering and a single tear runs unbidden down one cheek and drips onto the floor.

With a hand now free to explore, he finds the hem of my skirt. Rhett's confidence in the complete darkness is always slightly jarring. "This *fucking* skirt again," he rasps. "If I lift this tiny, godforsaken thing, what am I going to find?"

I give an experimental tug of my wrists. Instead of gaining any leverage, the bones simply grind beneath the weight of his kneecap. My groan vibrates against his palm. He's got me thoroughly and helplessly trapped.

And I'm loving every cursed second.

"Are you going to be wet and ready for me? Is that what I'll find?" He flips the material up and over my asscheeks, exposing my drenched panties to the air, and sending a renewed wave of goosebumps racing over the back of my thighs.

A swipe of two fingers confirms his suspicions. "*Yes.* Fucking *flooded.* Such a juicy little whore for me."

Before I can even think of protesting, he grabs a hold of the lace and tears them from my body with savage force.

For a moment, I think he's going to return his fingers to my undeniably slick pussy—instead I hear the jangle of his belt and the distinct sound of his zipper as he shoves his jeans down his thick thighs.

He doesn't stop for a condom. He always goes in raw. It only serves to make this more depraved and dangerous for me.

For both of us.

My heart rate ratchets even higher. My clit throbs and my abdomen clenches. I can already feel the deep-seated heat of my orgasm beginning to gather like storm clouds on the horizon.

With his cock now free, Rhett slides off me, hovering over me with his upper body. "Time to pay the piper," is all he grinds out before lining up and thrusting viciously inside. He buries himself straight to the hilt, fast and with unerring accuracy. No preparation—only the generous lubrication of my fear-induced arousal.

But just like the knowledge he's taking me with nothing between us, the pinch and burn only adds to the experience.

I'm too slow to register that my wrists were released the moment he repositioned himself, and he's already dropping his torso, swiftly pinning my arms between us with nothing but his large chest. Now I'm *completely* prone.

He slams that free hand down by my head, using it now for leverage. Each subsequent movement, like his initial intrusion, is hard and aggressive.

Dominating.

Almost like he has something to prove.

I've never been so turned on.

"*Fuck. Yes.* Tightest little snatch around," Rhett says with a strangled groan, before pulling back and plunging back in.

I feel that groan everywhere our bodies meet. The feverishly warm skin of the seal still in place across my mouth. The crushing weight of his chest against my back. The firm lines of his pelvis pressing into my ass. The cold steel of his Jacob's Ladder as it drags across my battered G-spot.

I can feel my climax still gathering steam. And not quietly. This one won't be gentle. No, this one's going to rearrange my fucking psyche.

The snaps of his hips become sharper and more

combative as he begins to rut with total abandon. The slap of flesh against flesh rings out in the pitch black and his pounding propels us deeper into the destroyed room.

"You're soaking my dick, filthy girl," he pants out against my neck.

My eyes roll back, and my walls contract sharply in response to his words.

Right there. Right there.

I moan desperately against his palm.

"Yes, right there, I felt that. *Right fucking there.* Feel's so fucking good. So *fucking good.* You're going to cream all over my cock and I'm going to drench your insides. Because you love this, don't you? *Dirty. Little. Cum slut.*" Rhett delivers each word against my neck through clenched teeth and between increasingly frenzied thrusts.

I'm done. I'm cooked. Fucking serve me up.

"Here it comes, all for you, baby," he grits out, before burying himself deeply one last time. Everything is so heightened, I swear I can feel his cock pulsing, his piercings rippling along my sensitive walls as he fills me.

Just as he promised.

My orgasm barrels into me with all the force and finesse of a fucking freight train. The darkness behind my eyelids—now squeezed firmly shut—crackles and whites out with its sheer intensity. For a long, blissful eternity, I don't hear or feel anything but the limb-shaking pulses of pure pleasure. I release the strained grip that I've been holding on to each of my remaining senses with, and just—

Let go.

Sinking. Floating. Heavy. Light. Warm. Safe.

Free.

Free from the crushing thoughts always crowding my skull. Free from the responsibilities of my role.

Just. *Free.*

After a minute, or maybe a month, or perhaps a year, I become vaguely aware of a gentle, baritone voice in my ear.

"Baby. Baby, I'm here," Rhett coos, smoothing lank, sweat-tangled hair back from my damp forehead. "I've got you, baby. You did so well."

I groan as I attempt to roll off my stomach, knowing full well I will feel every aching atom of my body once the bliss seeps away.

"Jesus, fuck," I croak. "Bringing your A-game, Orbison."

I hope he can hear the smile in my hoarse voice. My skin is covered in fiery abrasions, and no doubt I'll be walking suspiciously for the next few days, but the inside of my head is a fucking *nirvana* right now.

Rhett chuckles, all male smugness, as per his default setting. He's still stroking my head gently. "What the lady wants, the lady gets."

Suddenly, his strong hands are lifting me up and out of the ruins of our frenzied rutting as if I weigh nothing. I cling to his massive biceps, my mind slipping back offline as it luxuriates in its quiet, shimmery post-O haze.

From far, far away, I hear, "Come on, let's get you back to our place and clean you up."

WHEN I CRASH back to reality, it's with a sudden hiss of pain. Rhett looks up from where he's knelt beside me, dabbing antiseptic over one of my shredded knees. He chuckles softly and says with a panty-melting grin, "Welcome back, sweet thing."

I slow blink, then squint, finding the lighting so harsh after fighting against such absolute darkness. I have zero concept of any time passing—not since he picked me up to carry me from the warehouse.

I take a quick, internal stock of my body. I can already feel the deep aches and stings of the cuts and bruises forming across multiple parts of my body.

Christ, I am going to be sore tomorrow. The twinge between my legs only brings a smile to my face though.

So does the relative peace and quiet inside my skull.

It's a rare blessing for me to experience the euphoria of falling into subspace. It has taken Rhett and I *months* of moving the boundaries on our sexual experiments and some extreme forms of play to finally get me there. Now, if only I could recreate said feelings with a lot less of the threat of tetanus, and a little more Egyptian cotton instead.

I push up onto my elbows with a grunt and see that I'm laid out on Rhett's bed in the Rox City apartment that houses the rest of our Crew. A glance down confirms that I'm wearing nothing but one of his huge shirts. I can see that my thighs and one of my knees have been cleaned, treated and dressed.

I pat my hair, finding it wet. "Did you shower me already?"

Rhett bounces his eyebrows. "You were positively filthy, Ms. Winters. And you were under for a while."

He drops his gaze back to my battered legs, giving me a small lift of one shoulder. His smile is a little less cocksure. But he knows better than anyone how hard I struggle with intimacy and feelings. It's kind of difficult to properly invest yourself in functional relationships when you're nothing but a walking, talking Tin Man without a real heart.

I clear my throat. "Thanks." My voice still sounds a little husky. "Definitely in my top five abandoned warehouse railings. I think I can taste colors now."

Rhett's smirk is still there, but now it seems a little strained. "Anything for you, baby, you know that."

I swallow thickly and squeeze my eyes shut. There's a dull ache somewhere in my chest. If I knew any better, I'd say it might feel something like…*regret*.

But almost as soon as it's there, it's gone. Seeping back through the cracks and hollows of my empty ribcage.

"I know," I whisper.

He didn't question my need to careen over the edge this afternoon.

He just took one look at my soiled uniform and the frustration simmering around me like a living thing and simply asked what I needed.

He never asks for more, he just *does*.

But, I wish—more than anything—that someday he *would* ask.

And that I could somehow learn how to give it to him.

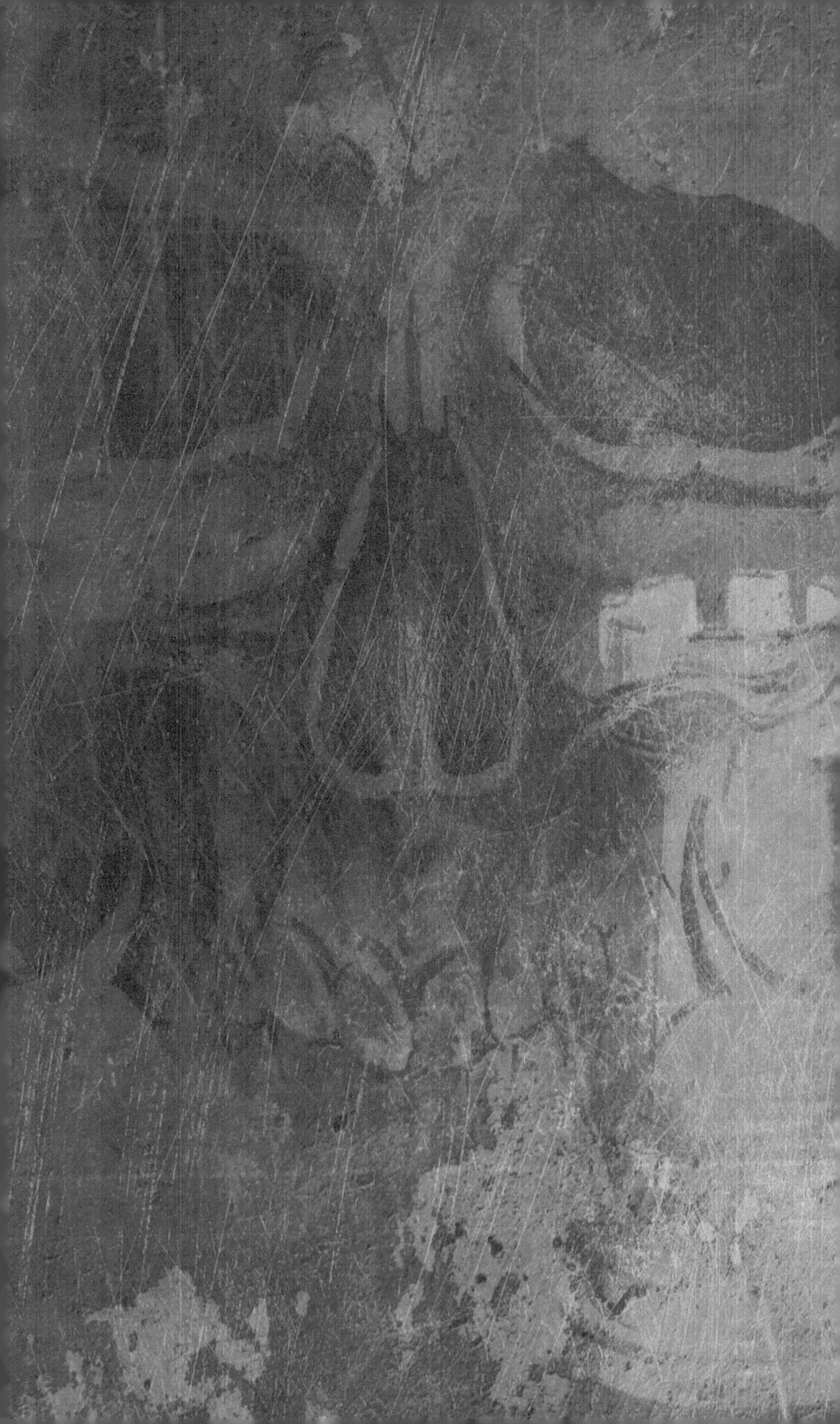

CHAPTER XII

I STARE DOWN MOROSELY at the small handful of Xanax in the palm of my hand. Two days. That's exactly how long I got before the peaceful afterglow of my playtime with Rhett began to wear off.

Three, before it was gone completely.

Parts of my body still bear the tell-tale signs of our elicit afternoon, but the only side effect I even remotely care about is how little chemical assistance I needed during the come-down.

Because now it's the end of the first week and I'm already *itching* for a fix of something—*anything*, really—that will give me back more of that blissful *nothingness* inside my head.

I consider my progress thus far. I think I've made a pretty decent start, at least for a rookie. After the dining hall Prefect Bullshit, I doubled down and I now have several new recruits and viable prospects in tow. Seven in total, including Jasper and the young receptionist, Janey. Two of Jasper's team mates with the stereotypical penchant for performance-enhancing drugs were my next logical targets, along with a few members from the janitorial staff.

If I maintain this pace, I should be able to keep on track with my target goals. I could take the night off, right? Go and snort or fuck some of this restlessness out from where it buzzes beneath my skin.

I throw the pills back dry and stare blankly ahead into my locker. Usually, the siren calls of addiction are too hard to ignore, but for once, a small voice of reason—*which oddly sounds just like Jax*—is doing its best to cut in.

I can just imagine him now.

Dark eyebrows pulling together, the small crease forming the only outward sign of his quiet vexation.

He'd remind me in that ever deep and sensual baritone of his, that although this latest Gray Man power play was a long time coming—and his father's betrayal inevitable—we mustn't lose sight of the forest for the trees. War *is* coming, and nobody knows just how the goal posts will shift when the battle lines are finally drawn.

"Stay on track. The senior back-to-school party is tomorrow night," he'd point out evenly.

"Yep. I haven't forgotten."

"The intel on your target was largely insufficient and you've yet to lay eyes on the location."

"Yep."

"*Sabine.*" His voice is now thick with warning, but laced with a hint of exasperation. Hypothetical Jax is secretly a daddy and *loves* Bratty Sabine.

Christ.

My horny hindbrain has derailed my pep talk and now my thoughts have devolved into a very vivid and recurring fantasy—one that involves a growling Jax, tie loose and shirt sleeves rolled up, wanting nothing more than to bend me over his knee and punish me for all my slack groundwork and sassy back talk.

Telling me how much of a bad girl I've been.

I really do need to just go out and get laid.

My conscience did make a good point while masquerading as Hypothetical Jax, though. The upcoming party *will* be an important opportunity to observe my classmates outside of school, and I really wasn't able to find out much about the host location.

The Guardhouse, despite only opening last year, has quickly become the favorite off-campus haunt of the older Academy students. Investigations into the building's records gave us nothing concrete—only a slew of shell corporations, the mysterious amendment of its heritage status, and a distinct lack of Council-approved blueprints for me to study.

A clandestine nightclub, owned and operated within Roxborough City limits? Employees who turn a blind eye to underage patrons on the regular?

Screams *Strange Aces hunting grounds* to me.

But there's no reason why I can't please both the devil *and* angel on my shoulders. I can be productive whilst also enjoying myself, can't I?

I'll go tonight, scope the layout, find someone to blow off steam with, and potentially snag me some working leads from among the dealers that should be there pushing the crowd. They'll all undoubtedly be some flavor of Ace, but I've only got about a week's worth of pills left. Booze would be much easier to get my hands on, however it only does so much for my sanity.

And nobody wants to deal with me when I'm *truly* sober. Honestly, I'd practically be performing a community service.

That's settled then.

Just as I'm closing my locker door, I feel the hairs on my nape flare and my shoulders tense. The hallway behind me has long since emptied out, but someone large and silent is hovering just in my peripheral vision.

My first instincts say Callum. I haven't spoken a word to him or his friends since I stormed out of that courtyard.

But I've seen each of them around, of course. Sometimes together and sometimes separately—and at least one of them always seems to have eyes on me. I know Callum followed me to the Diner. I saw his car in the lot.

It's obvious that I'm now under some kind of mutual surveillance. Maybe I should be flattered, but as I still don't know who they work for or why, the realization only serves to amp up my reservations about them.

I pull up a cold, tight smile, like a warrior raising a shield before battle, and turn, braced for the inevitable verbal sparring.

Sabine Winters is dead.

Who the fuck are you?

Why are you here?

However, instead of a brooding, tattooed slab of yummy Rox Boy, I find *Leon James Baker, 19, linebacker and co-Captain of the Roxborough Titans. Football scholarship student.*

Hmm. That was definitely unexpected. Why would a popular jock like Leo Baker risk being seen approaching me? It's no secret that I've pissed off the Rox Academy socialites. I'm toxic. Spoiled goods.

Admittedly, Leo hasn't been a priority person of interest for me since wading into the viper pit of Rox Academy. On paper, he's what I would call *a nice guy*. His parents are still married and heavily involved in their church. He helps coach a casual Pee Wee football team through the community rec center during the off-season. Tall, broad and athletic, with a defined jaw, sandy-blond hair, and warm brown eyes. He's traditionally handsome and looks ten shades of guileless.

By all accounts, he's your standard issue All-American Boy Next Door.

"Hi," he says with a sheepish grin, a blush staining the tops of his bladed cheekbones.

He's nervous. My frigid expression thaws a fraction, and my right eyebrow twitches in amusement. Christ, he's like a big, wide-eyed puppy. Total golden retriever vibes.

Then it occurs to me that the two main sports teams always make a point to avoid each other during breaks.

I wonder if this here is some form of basketball *vs* football rivalry? Since I've landed myself on the Kraken's shit-list, I'm now Titan catnip? I mentally file that away on my *To Investigate Further* list, before taking a second to run my eyes over him from head to toe. Really take stock of him now that he's more than just a polaroid in a file. He's well over six feet and built like a football player in his prime. He looks good in his academic uniform. Muscles on muscles.

Now, I wasn't exaggerating when I told Queen Bee I don't make a habit of hooking up with high school boys. I find that most of them tend to *way* over-sell themselves and their bedroom prowess.

And this one looks greener than a leprechaun's dick.

But I *am* looking for a quick ride, and the boy *does* have a championship coach…that means he's probably pretty decent at following instructions, right? And with shoulders and hands that size, there's a good chance he's big *everywhere*.

Worst case scenario, I could always use our time together as a teaching moment.

But promises of mediocre dickings aside, I have to remember that he might actually be useful as a source of information, and I still need to increase my numbers.

"So, uh, I was wondering if you'd want to go grab some food? There's this diner—"

"You want to take me to *Rox City?*" I interrupt his adorably fumbling proposition. Now there's the prospect of food involved? My libido says *done deal!*

He scratches the back of his neck. "Well, yeah, if you want to," he huffs out.

"Sure. I could eat," I give him a non-committal shrug, and adjust my bag over my shoulder. "You're buying though," I add with a raised brow, just to test the waters. I need to know if he's going to let me call the shots.

Leo only chuckles, flashing me that goofy grin again. He sweeps an arm out in a mock bow, like he's ushering along royalty. "Yes, of course. My treat. Let's go, princess."

I give him a sharp bark of laughter. I did *not* expect that level of back-sass from the poster boy for Wholesomeness himself. This shy, goofy puppy might surprise me after all.

As I begin walking with him towards the front doors, I catch a flash of untamed blond curls from the corner of my eye.

The flame of Lake's Zippo dances as he flicks it open and closed with sharp, ominous snaps. I follow the movement for a moment before glancing up at its owner. Normally brimming with mischief, his gaze today is instead dangerous and simmering with fury. His jaw is clenched tight.

He must still be pissed off about our last interaction.

But wait, it's not me he's glaring at—it's the footballer that's escorting me out of the school.

Fucking great. I guess I was right about the team rivalry.

What headache have I just stepped into there?

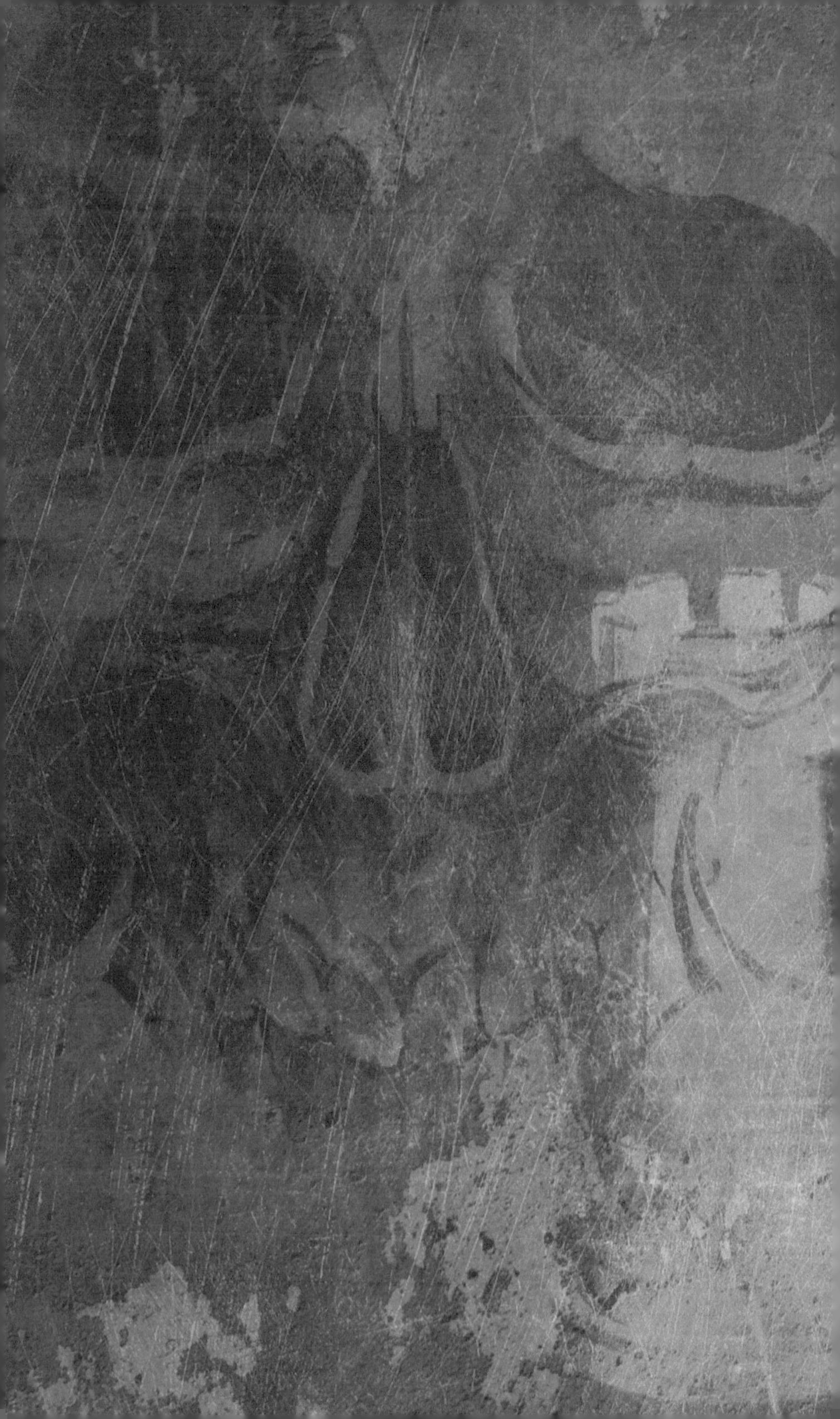

CHAPTER XIII

OF COURSE A GOLDEN boy like Leo drives a Ford pickup. In fact, if I was pressed to picture the guy *as* a truck, I would wager it would be this exact pristine, sky-blue older model F-150.

He sits tall and straight as he drives us to the diner, throwing me occasional, sidelong glances. I almost want to take my hands and run my fingers through his neatly styled hair, mess him up a little. He's just so *clean cut.*

I text both Rhett and Knox my plans for the evening, so someone knows where The Librarian is likely to be, and then we're pulling into the parking lot. I didn't think I'd find any sort of enjoyment in this city aside from its gothic architecture, but this diner is definitely growing on me.

Leo, the gentleman that he is, opens my passenger side door, and then holds the front glass door for me as well. I grant him a little mocking smile, but he only answers it with another one of his wide, *aw shucks* grins.

Lord have mercy, this boy. I am going to have so much fun mixing chocolate syrup into this bland, vanilla milkshake. I really want to be the one to darken up all that pure-white, All-American, civilian goodness.

He ushers me over to a rear corner booth that I am pleased to note gives me a decent view of the front door, the exits and the rest of the patrons. Without any of my Crew with me, I need to be able to have my own back.

We both drape our blazers over the table near the window. Leo rolls up the cuffs of his shirt, giving me a nice view of his tanned, chorded forearms. Yum.

"Alright, spill it," I say as we sit, pretending to browse one of the greasy, laminated menus. I have it memorized from my first visit here—the weekend we settled down in Rox City.

"Spill it?" He's desperately trying for nonchalance but the tops of his ears are a bright red.

"I'm practically radioactive, Lassie. So why are we here?" I close the menu and place it down, clasping my hands together on the tabletop.

The vinyl seat groans as he shifts uncomfortably. "What the Prefects did in the dining hall was pretty nasty. Thought you could use a more friendly welcome to the Academy," he offers.

"Mhm. And?"

His eyes dart to the side. Mine narrow at the painfully obvious, guilty tell. It was just a bit of cold soup. After blowing off the initial steam with Rhett, I'm not losing sleep over it.

"Aaaand?" I drawl. "I'm not stupid, Leon."

His brows pull together slightly at the use of his full

name. He looks down at his large hands, clenching them into fists.

Shit. I keep my face carefully blank. I guess nobody calls him that, ever. Or nobody calls him that in a way he appreciates.

"Uh, look. My boys and I—" His eyes curve briefly over my scar. He pauses awkwardly before fixating back on his hands. "My *team* and I don't really see eye-to-eye with any of the ballers. Especially the uh, Rox Boys." He clears his throat and flexes his fingers.

"They seem *real* interested in you, though."

It's not surprising that someone else aside from me has noticed. They're so confident in their place at the top of the food chain, and they really have no interest in subtlety. It *is* surprising that it's coming from this zipped-up footballer.

It's all just furthering my suspicions about an underlying Kraken-Titan sub-plot. How deep does *that* rabbit hole go?

"So you thought you'd try and get a shot in at stealing their shiny new toy?" I chuckle. It's not a nice sound, but I try to soften it with what I hope is a friendly smile.

I really do need more practice with…*people-ing.*

"You might have noticed that I'm not exactly eating lunch at their table. I'm not *theirs.*"

My stomach does a weird little clench. *The fuck?*

I don't actually *want* to be theirs, do I?

Leo's eyes widen slightly and now the flush from his ears starts to spread to his neck. Whose idea was it to send this guy into the trenches? He's a worse Front Man than I am.

"Uh, more like the enemy of my enemy, right?"

Before I can answer, we're interrupted by Darlene—a harried single mother of three teenagers who always looks like she's running on about eight cups of black coffee and two hours of sleep. She takes exactly no shit from any of the customers and she's by far my favorite waitress here.

"What can I get for you kids?" she prompts without looking up from her notepad.

"Triple cheeseburger with a side of loaded bacon fries and a double choc shake," Leo recites politely.

"Sounds good, I'll have the same," I add, aiming for my best impression of cheerful. Darlene grunts in an affirmative way before whisking off in a squeaking whirlwind of rubber soled shoes.

Leo's brows climb up his forehead but I hold up a hand before he can make some asinine comment about girls and food. "I've heard it all. Yes, I have a large appetite and stupid-fast metabolism. Yes, I *also* sometimes wish those carbs would make their way to my tits, but alas, here I am, living firmly in the Land of A Cups."

The poor guy just coughs into fist, his brown eyes watering as he tries to hold in his laughter. "I, uh, think your tits are just fine," he gasps out.

Such a gentleman. Be still my heart.

"Of course they're fine, Casanova. But I *would* like to be able to rock a few more strapless options in my wardrobe. Like…a nice busty corset, you know?" I punctuate my words with a lift of my tits, like I'm wearing said corset, watching with secret glee as the flush creeps further down his neck.

I don't usually give half a fuck about the size of my breasts, but sometimes—especially when I'm out drinking—I do find myself wishing I could channel my inner pirate wench with a tad more accuracy.

Deciding to give Leo a moment to salvage his dignity, I flick my eyes to the front door and back in a routine sweep. There are twelve other patrons and three staff that I can currently see from my vantage point. I recognize two fellow Seniors—Elijah Collins, a basketballer and Teagan Roberts, a Kraken cheerleader. They're sitting opposite one another in a booth near the front windows.

I do my best to keep my gaze from landing on them for too long, but I don't miss the harsh scowl that Elijah is directing at Leo.

Okay. Now I *have* to get the story there.

I prop my chin on a fist and waggle my eyebrows salaciously at the footballer in question. "Alright, big guy. I'm in. But! *Quid pro quo.* I want the behind the scenes at the Academy."

The look he gives me is part incredulous, part suspicious—with just a tiny dash of relief. Obviously he didn't expect me to be so amenable. I mean, he basically just admitted to wanting to use me against his closest rivals.

But two can play at that game and it's not my fault he's like a big ball of dopey putty.

I sit back and cross my arms. I may as well push this ship straight out of the harbor and set it sailing in the right direction. "So. You got a game tonight?"

Leo smiles broadly at that. Typical sports bro. Dangle just a little interest about their chosen ballgame in front of them and they eat that shit up. "Nah, first game's next week. Coach lets us have the Friday off before the season starts, since we've been training all break."

"Hmm," I muse. "Are you going out then? I was going to go check out this Guardhouse I keep hearing about." I lean back as Darlene appears next to our booth bearing a tray topped with our orders. She unloads our food and drinks without fanfare, and once she's assured that we don't need anything else, she's gone just as quickly.

Leo falls upon his loaded fries, but a thoughtful look creeps across his face. "You want to go to the Guardhouse tonight?" he asks between mouthfuls.

"Yeah, I thought it might something fun to finish my first week with." I pick at my own fries in a casual way, but make sure to shoot Leo a look from beneath my lashes. "I understand if it's not your scene though."

He swipes a finger across his upper lip, like he's trying to hide a smile. "Yeah, princess, we can go to the Guardhouse," he grins, dimples on full display.

I pause, my focus now completely on the footballer across from me. Why does his enthusiasm make me feel like I've just walked into a trap? Trying to cover up my discomfort, I take an exaggerated bite from my burger. Maybe this boy's not as naive as I first thought.

Just as I go to reach for my fry basket, my hand crashes into a decidedly larger, tattooed one. I give a very involuntary, very unladylike squawk, watching in horror as none other than *Callum motherfucking Jameson* dips in and steals one of my loaded fries.

Right in front of me.

There's a self-satisfied, shit-eating grin on his face as he licks his lips, but his eyes aren't mirthful. No, they twinkle with something else. Something darker, and more dangerously sexy.

Restraint.

He's on a knife's edge. *Why?*

And when the *hell* did these two arrive, anyway?

I curse my total slip in spatial awareness. It only takes but a second, but here's the glaring proof. It's why I never usually go places without at least one of my Enforcers. But I couldn't exactly drag Knox or Rhett along to an innocuous 'dinner date' with a senior classmate.

My narrowed gaze is pulled away from Callum's handsome fucking everything and over to his partner-in-crime, who is sliding gracefully into the seat next to Leo with an equally unhinged look on his face.

Lake throws an arm around the linebacker's shoulders and plants a kiss on his cheek. He reaches over and also helps himself to a fry, trailing gooey cheese across the tabletop as he does. Zero fucks given.

"Hello ladies," he sings, glancing between us with a smirk that is borderline lethal.

Leo curses under his breath, anger now tingeing his cheekbones a deeper, more mottled red.

Callum—having already molested my meal—shoves in next to me, much less gracefully than feline Lake. His arm and thigh collide with mine, forcing me to scoot along the worn seat with an angry squeak of leather.

Leo flings Lake's arm off with a snarl. "Get the fuck off me, Miller."

Lake's chuckle is relaxed, and all dark amusement. "Now, now. Don't be such a prude, Baker." He raises an eyebrow. "Just ask Winters. She knows all about the importance of *sharing*, doesn't she?"

His tone *sounds* jovial, but like his smile, there's a sharp edge. It's him in a nutshell, though. Flirtatious, but with an undercurrent of violence there that's only *just* being leashed. It's stupidly attractive to me, just like he is, but I can't let these fucking Roxborough wannabe-bangers derail my schemes, no matter how last-minute.

I pick up a fry dripping with cheese, examine it and then casually toss it at his head. He's too graceful though, dodging my bacon loaded missile with ease.

"If you're looking for someone to turn you into a pretty meat sandwich for the night, Miller, you're barking up the wrong tree. We've already got plans, and they *don't* involve spit-roasting little blond fuckboys."

Shit. Now I have images running through my head of me and someone else double-teaming Lake Miller and *fuuuck*.

DOWN, GIRL.

God, I hope Leo is going to let me climb him like a

tree later or I'm going to have to find someone else at the Guardhouse to take this growing edge off.

Or maybe Rhett can tag me into whatever sexy Friday night plans he's got going on.

I swallow roughly, trying to cover it up with a sarcastic *sorry to disappoint you* face.

Lake's hazel eyes only glimmer while he groans, "Baby, you've got *such* a filthy fucking mouth." He spreads his hands, slouching back like the insouciant devil that he is. "We just wanted to give you a proper welcome to the City of Sin, didn't we, Cal? You *are* the *new girl* after all."

There's something odd about the way he draws out the words *new girl.* Like there's a question or a challenge hidden beneath his teasing tone.

Callum still hasn't said a word, but I can feel the heat of his huge body radiating down my side. I watch as he plays with the metal napkin dispenser, pushing it back and forth across the scratched laminate table top between two calloused hands.

Their memories of the courtyard can't be *that* short. Just who am I to them? Am I the *new girl* or am I the *dead girl*?

I scoff. "Of course! The shining examples of school spirit and leadership that you both are." Taking a long, noisy sip from my shake, I look pointedly between the two of them. "But that's entirely unnecessary. Leo has already offered to show me the Roxborough ropes. So go terrorize someone else."

Leo is audibly grinding his teeth now. "Yeah, Sabine and I have plans, so *fuck off, Miller.*"

Lake's grin never wavers. In fact, it widens, and I automatically brace myself. "Some other time then, Winters. We do so enjoy a good chase."

My eyes snap up. There was no mistaking the innuendo that time.

What the fuck?

Looks like it wasn't just Callum in the car on Monday, and they didn't only follow me here to the Diner…But all the way to the warehouse.

Sooo not good.

Lake, of course, looks smug as all fuck, confident that he's sliding beneath my skin—making himself at home there, rent free. And he wouldn't be *entirely* wrong. *Cheeky fucking bastard.*

But it's not the Rox Boys' *voyeurism* that's got me off-balance. Nay, it's the knowledge that in less than a week I've already been compromised, and my targets have potentially gained dangerous insight into a very significant and private part of my life.

My scalp prickles under the pressure of that knowing glint in his eye and I blink, trying to re-orient myself. I'm confident that if I could feel more than an echo of embarrassment, my face would be a five-alarm fire right now.

Rookie shit, Winters.

Callum grunts deeply and shifts next to me, his gaze sliding away from our table and in the direction of the front door.

That noise though—it's almost like a confirmation that he was there— one that scrubs out the unease with the answering surge of arousal that blossoms in my pelvis.

Fuck.

I glance back at Leo, who's not even attempting to hide his annoyance. His molars must be dust by now, and those red cheeks are now a red face and red neck. I'm almost fascinated by the vein that's throbbing angrily along his already prominent jawline.

With one last panty-melting smirk, Lake unfurls from the booth and is gone—his seeds of discord sown and his giant inked shadow following directly behind him.

As soon as they disappear into the parking lot, I give my leftovers a glum look and shove out of the booth myself. I'm now too on edge to eat, and instead find myself really fucking eager to get to the fun part of the evening.

"C'mon, Baker," I sigh. "I need to go hard tonight. Hard enough that I can pretend to forget."

"Forget what?"

"Everything."

CHAPTER XIV

I UNDERSTAND NOW why this place is so popular. Formerly a heritage-listed, decommissioned garrison, its footprint is huge—sprawling across three floors and a basement level. It's dark and gritty and smoky and loud. Very appealing for bored, rebellious students needing to cut loose from their stuffy Academy rules.

I let a rare smile ghost over my lips. Seems like a place to find ten kinds of trouble. *It's perfect.*

Reaching back, I grab Leo's large hand, tugging him behind me as I push my way towards the bar. I'm forced to take short, careful steps, having since changed into a killer black wiggle dress with red trim and matching studded Valentino pumps.

But I don't mind. My heels and bony elbows are always a perk in a crowded club, and with a few well placed jabs, I manage to quickly clear a place right in front of one of the hottie bartenders. "A Southside, for me," I shout, feeling Leo's heat move in behind me. His hard chest presses against my back as he leans over and yells his own designer beer order over the industrial bass.

As soon as our drinks are in hand, I turn and make a beeline towards one of the many shadowy nooks that line the main dance floor. They look perfect for more private conversations, clandestine hookups, or general people-watching. I dare say I will be making regular use of them for all of the above.

Silhouettes move within the neighboring alcoves, each spaced evenly around the three walls not already dedicated to the lengthy bar.

The bar itself spans most of the eastern side behind me, ending near the entrance. A wide set of stairs in the north-western corner lead up to the next level. The shadowed hallway I spy tucked away in the opposite corner of this first floor, looks promising. If I had to guess, that'll be my ticket to The Guardhouse's basement level.

The dance floor is at capacity; undulating waves of sexual tension and booze and an endless rotation of sweaty bodies. I've counted twenty-seven Academy students already, and that's just the dancers whose faces I can see. I expect that count will be much higher by the time I'm done here.

Nobody catches my interest, so I hustle my burly date inside the first empty nook I find, which is only a few paces wide but ringed by black suede bench seats. There is a heavy curtain that hangs at the entrance, but I don't bother pulling it shut. I'm sure it would help to dampen the jaw-rattling house music, but I'd prefer to keep one eye on the crowd if I can.

Charades and lip-reading it is.

I snatch the bottle away from Leo's grip and shove him rather unceremoniously towards the cushions along the back wall, enjoying the surprised grunt that reverberates against my palm as I do. The air is thick with smoke and body heat. He's got a lop-sided grin and a thin sheen across his brow that shines in the flickering strobe of the club's lights. I know he has his own ulterior motives for approaching me, but right now, the look on his face says things are going much better than expected and he's eager to please.

I take a big gulp of my gin cocktail before abandoning both drinks on the low, glossy table sitting in the middle of the space.

Then, grabbing the sides of my form-fitting dress, I shimmy the material upwards, allowing just enough room for me to spread my legs and climb aboard Leo Baker's lap. His thighs are huge and by the time I'm able to straddle him properly, I can feel that the hem is well past the bottom of my ass cheeks. This dress doesn't exactly co-operate when it comes to panty lines, so I usually just go without.

It's extremely dark and private in these side rooms, but I'm positive that if the dancers nearest to us took the time to really look in here, they'd be getting one hell of a show. I hope this hapless footballer isn't put off by the idea of an audience.

"Hi," I grin down at him, throwing my arms around his neck and secretly loving the wary, boyish excitement that lights up his face. I wonder how far Leo will let me take this, considering it's our first time together, and he seems like a gentleman. Testing the waters, I drop and grind against the crotch of the pair of jeans he changed into during our quick stop by the dorms.

He lets out another pained grunt that I feel rather than hear. *Yes.* I can also feel the tell-tale beginnings of that boyish excitement coming to life beneath me. His chest heaves as my fingers slither through the back of his hair.

Then I begin to move with a slow, seductive rhythm against that bulge now pressing behind his zipper.

"Hi," he mouths back to me, a little dazed. His huge, sports-calloused hands begin to creep tentatively up the back of my thighs. When I don't stop him, he continues to drag them cautiously up under my dress until finally, he takes two handfuls of my ass. He gives both cheeks an experimental squeeze.

"I'm not made of glass, Baker," I huff out with an annoyed laugh. There's every chance he didn't catch that over the music, so I further relay the message by gyrating my hips and pressing down harder against his growing erection. His throat bobs and he licks his bottom lip.

Bless him.

I assume he's used to being with a different kind of girl. Maybe one who prefers a few perfectly nice, perfectly wholesome dates first. Who's not exactly into a good ol' fashioned man-handling. I can certainly appreciate that—it's not for everyone.

Then his eyes flick down to my mouth and I see the resolve in his eyes as he starts to lean up.

Shit.

I quickly turn and push my face into an arm that's currently covered by my cropped leather jacket—a jacket I needed to cover my upper back tattoos. Can't risk someone with the right connections seeing them and understanding their significance. The ink on my thighs is visible but they don't hold the same meaning.

Feeling him pause, I cringe, and silently hope I wasn't too obvious with my rejection. Poor guy. It's not a move that anyone wants a hook-up to pull, especially when things are heating up.

I just...don't kiss.

Anyone.

Ever.

Sex? Sex for me is transactional, and I know that makes me a selfish lover. I can't help that it's never just about getting each other off for me. The real goal has always been those precious moments when I am no longer trapped by the nonsense in my head.

Kissing though? Some leftover part of my younger self still believes in the sanctity of that special brand of theater—the way our mouths intimate everything that we're feeling without the need for actual words. The problem, of course, is that *I'm* in possession of a heart that's nothing but a barren, emotional wasteland, and I just can't bring myself to let my lips lie. To anyone.

So I hold on firmly to the fairytale.

Leo drops his forehead against my collarbone in defeat, giving my ass another solemn squeeze. He's resigning himself to us not taking this any further. But he's wrong. So wrong. I'm just not letting him past *these* lips.

Dropping my hands down between us, I get to work on his belt and jeans, hoping to distract him from looking too closely at my kissing hang-up. With his neck now free and clear, I give it a nice long slow, lick followed by a bite to his earlobe.

I'm rewarded with a hoarse groan and another, more forceful, squeeze.

Thatta boy.

Rocking back to give myself more space to play, I attempt to lock eyes with him. I want to see what his face does as I skip the rest of the preamble and go straight to pulling his dick out. It's quite comical really—and I watch in amusement as his heavy-lidded expression tap dances between proud, athletic stoicism and horny, teenaged delight.

I'm sure my palm is still cold from the condensation of my cocktail glass, but it doesn't seem to matter any. His cock is plenty hot and beautifully hard, jerking once as I grip it in my hand.

My pussy and I are pleased to find we were not wrong in our forecast of his proportions.

"Sabine," he croaks, brown eyes rolling back as I squeeze tightly, giving him a few firm pumps with my fist. When my thumb brushes over the head, finding the beginning drops of pre-cum, I gather what I can, spreading the moisture down the large vein on his shaft during my next few passes.

More often than not, I prefer the freedom of

submission. Surrender is the fastest route to the peace and quiet I crave, after all. But when the mood strikes, I can and do enjoy being the one in the driver's seat. Leaning over, I squeeze again and snarl against his ear, "Eyes up here, Baker."

With obvious effort, he slides his gaze back to mine.

Better.

Flashing him my canines in a wide smile, I rise up to my knees. With one hand, I line his cock up with my entrance, teasing it through the slickness already there and waiting. The hussy never takes much sweet talking. She's always good to go.

Leo's eyes flash as he finds a brief moment of clarity before he's lost beneath the waves of lust. "Condom," he forces out, trying his hardest to maintain eye contact with me and *not* look down at where my soaking wet pussy is pressing against his swollen, leaking glans.

I'm a terrible fucking person. The thrill of going bareback with a stranger is just too fucking good to pass up. It's pretty much an addiction at this point. "I'm clean," I mouth back over the music.

Jax knows I have no sense of self preservation and makes me get tested bi-weekly. Sebastian also made sure a long time ago that his precious asset could never be compromised by something so *pedestrian* as pregnancy.

But I'm not too far gone to remember it's never just a question of *my* consent. So I hover, waiting, but still sending up desperate, slutty prayers to Eros and Aphrodite and Cupid and Freyr that he won't insist on stopping right now just so that he can wrap it up.

He tips his chin down, never breaking eye contact, giving me the green light to proceed.

Thank all the gods and goddesses.

I drop down hard and fast, taking him all the way to the root. The sharp initial pinch takes my breath. The stretch and burn that follows is *magnificent* and I mentally pat myself on the back for taking a chance on this well-kept, well-endowed footballer.

"*Fuck,*" he barks. "Winters, *fuck.*" A single bead of sweat skates down his temple as I start to move. His hands never venture any further north, but his thumbs begin to press into my lower waist; his equally large fingers dig into my ass.

After a heavy exhale, he cants his hips up, pulling me down hard and grinding our pelvises together. His eyes have not once left my face, and so I force myself to relax and let him take over the rhythm. My hands find the back of his hair again.

Alright, Lassie…Let's see what you've got.

The angle means his large cock is now doing a bang-up job of working my clit and G-spot in tandem. A simple Chair Cowgirl is way too mellow to ever earn a place on the mantle of my personal *Best Sex Ever* annals, but I'm horny and Leo's pace is strong and steady.

When I stop overthinking the mechanics of my choice of partner, his efforts are enough to gently coax a climax to the surface. The heat of it begins to slink in, languidly curling around and around in my lower abdomen like a lazy house cat, and my head drops back. My upper body feels loose, even as my lower muscles begin to tighten.

The powerful industrial bass continues to thrum across my heated, sensitive skin. Beneath the cloying scent of smoke, I catch the lingering hints of Leo's sweet, malty beer on his staccato breaths.

Somewhere on the edge of my periphery, I sense the intrusive press of someone's dark gaze between my shoulder blades—but then Leo's measured push and pull of our hips begins to take on a new urgency, and I try to shove thoughts of an audience back down beneath the rising wave of pleasure.

I feel the muscles in his thighs tense, and I watch with satisfaction as the veins on his neck begin to strain. *"Fuck,"* he pants out again, before slamming up hard, holding me still as he empties himself.

Leo's release—*and the possibility of someone watching us*—has my own orgasm cresting hard and fast, almost in spite of its slow build up. I ride it all the way into shore with deliberate, greedy circles of my hips. The footballer's already lost to post-orgasmic bliss, eyes shut, chest heaving. Before my body can fully relax however, I'm off his lap and pulling my dress down to cover my ass.

I glance up and catch Leo watching my movements with a cautious look on his face. His forehead glistens and I've made a downright sex-mess of his hair. I know he's rightfully wondering if I'm about to bail. It's not that I'm exactly opposed to hanging out with him right now, but I do still have other things I need to do tonight—like scouting The Guardhouse for a dealer.

And possibly uncovering the identity of our mysterious voyeur.

His cum is hot and tacky between my inner thighs, emphasizing the fact that I'm not wearing any panties. As much as I love the debauched feeling, I should probably start the rest of my night by going and tending to this mess.

I snatch up my drink, down the rest of it in one go, and point in the direction of the restrooms. Leo nods once.

I step out of the booth and skirt my way around the edge of the dance floor; the whole time vigilantly searching for possible leads on a seller. Knowing this is an Ace-owned club, chances are good that *someone* around here will have some decent shit on them.

Maybe, if I'm back in Fortune's good graces, I could even find some uncut *Asphodel*. It's such a gamble getting a hold of pure *Ash* these days—now that the Suits are getting mixed up in the Ace's local import and circulation.

But it would go a long fucking way in smoothing the edges of this constant, growing agitation that fucking Leo barely touched. My mouth waters at the possibility.

Mmm. Come to Momma.

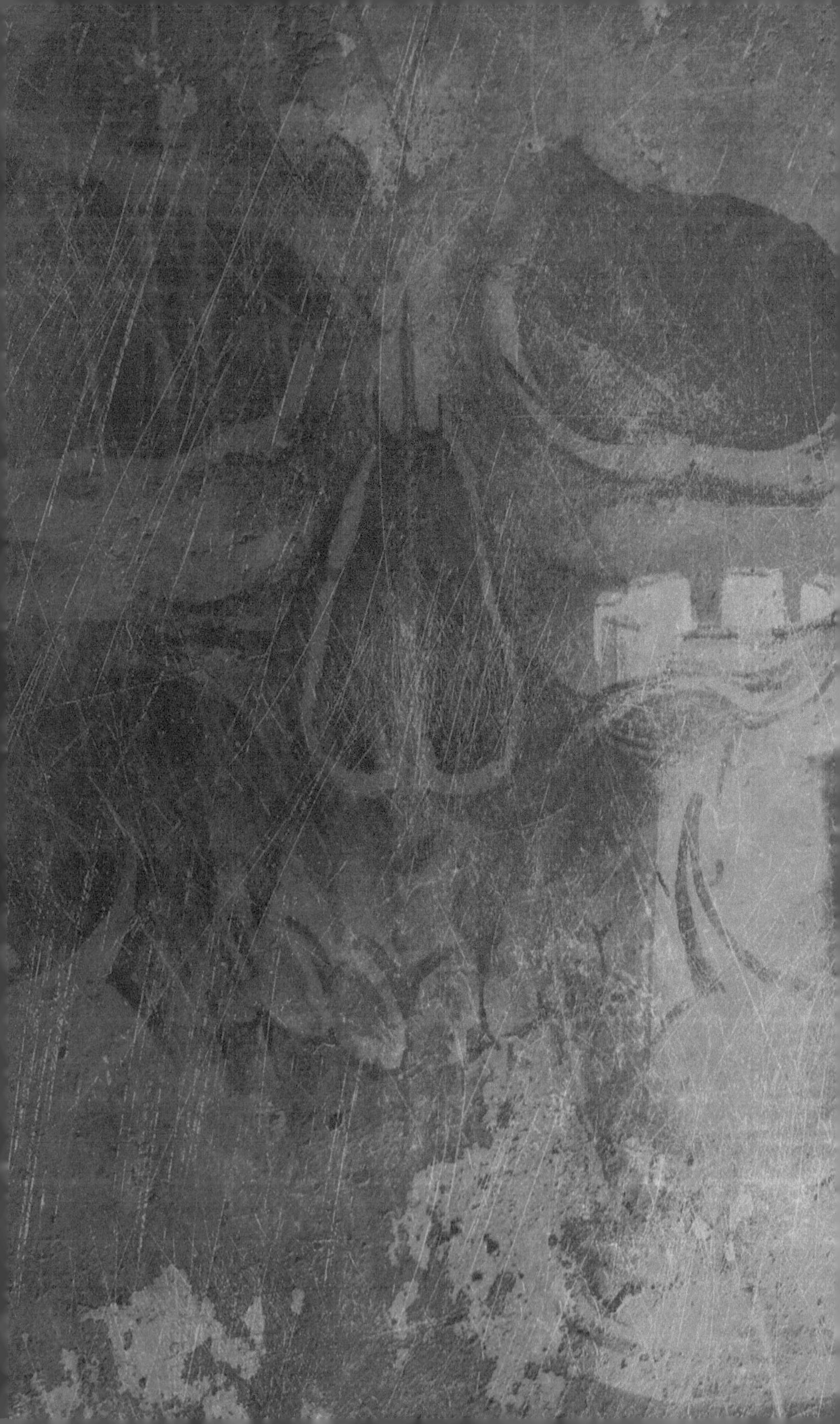

CHAPTER XV

TRISTAN

LEO *FUCKING* BAKER.

Of all the bullshit moves on the board that I expected from her, I never could have anticipated the *sheer fucking audacity* of this one.

I can't even begin to describe how paper-thin the grip on my sanity is right now. A cold, paralyzing rage is creeping across the edges of my vision like a black fog—its hateful fingers threatening to strip back the composure I'm usually so diligent in maintaining. After all, it wouldn't '*reflect well*' on Martin Sinclair should his '*perfect son*' ever give in to the incessant urge to hold down and choke the life from someone.

Though I may be about to make a very public exception.

There's an aggravation that's starting to coil through the bloodlust like a serpent, nipping and squeezing at my throat. My chest. My guts. It's crushing, and each breath feels more labored than the last.

But I refuse to consider that this sick, choking displeasure might be anything else.

Because I'm not…*jealous.*

I'm angry.

Livid in fact, because just as all our cautious scheming had *finally* begun to produce real, tangible results—someone's gone and moved this unknown piece into play.

I don't—*can't*—do unknown.

I also don't have a single fuck to spare for any living person that's not one of my three brothers. Not even my mother.

Certainly not because I left the remaining pieces of my heart in the hands of a blonde-haired girl on an asphalt-covered playground six fucking years ago.

Why would I still care?

Before I can even think to second guess myself, I'm pushing away from the private recess I've been occupying since I first spotted my gray-eyed ghost. I'd watched Sabine saunter in—with Leo *fucking* Baker on her heels—wasting exactly zero time in finding a darkened corner to pull him into.

And despite knowing from the moment she climbed aboard his lap *exactly* how it would end, I couldn't bring myself to look away. Couldn't stop the painful fucking hard on that followed.

How the fuck did they even meet? When Callum and Lake told me they'd followed the two of them to the diner, I thought that would be the extent of it. I didn't imagine she'd actually take it further.

Actually…fuck him.

But what I just witnessed proves that she *absolutely would*, and *did*. Without hesitation.

That harsh revelation leaves an acidic taste on my tongue, and without my consent, the fragile illusion of outrage starts to splinter, giving way to the insidious, suffocating miasma of betrayal instead.

Knowing she was fucking someone else.

Someone that wasn't me.

Someone that wasn't...*us*.

The denials I've been loudly shouting in my head all week are starting to sound like a high pitched whine, and those grasping, clawing fingers dig in harder, working to expose my soft underbelly.

I dog her steps, still seething, but for an entirely different reason now. My pulse is thrumming in my ears, vibrating with the need to confront her and teach her a fucking lesson. Demand that she tell me just what the fuck kind of game she's playing at; who sent her here and gave her permission to upend my careful plans and twist my whole fucking body into knots?

Answers. Yes. *Answers.* That's the only way I'm going to be able to wrestle back some kind of control.

Just as she's nearing the restrooms, we both clock the pair of casually dressed guys standing nearby and lazily surveying the crowd. Just above the place where their necks meet their right shoulder is a tattoo of an Ace of Clubs. The tattoos mark them as low level members of the Strange Aces, barely higher than Prospects.

She thinks she's been so slick in keeping her eye on everyone at the Academy, watching us all like a fucking hawk. But she's not the only one who's been observing, taking measure of the threat right in front of us. When she thinks no one is looking at her, Sabine's face is oddly devoid of expression. Almost as if she's not fully present, too busy in her own head. Even now, despite having just fucked some guy's brains out in a *very* public place—she appears strangely detached.

But as soon as she spots those two thugs, it's like a switch flicks and she's online for human interaction. She immediately affects a *white-girl wasted* persona, complete with pasted on smile and wobbly gait.

I stop within hearing range as she makes her way over, pressing myself behind a nearby pylon. There's only one reason to approach guys like them. My jaw clenches.

"Hi boys," she chirps loudly, swaying on her *fuck me* heels. They're several inches tall and she's almost at eye level with them. Absently, I find myself tracing the lines of her dress that's doing a poor impersonation of something that might actually cover a grown woman's ass—and then I'm drawn down, *down* the considerable length of her legs.

Fuck.

Those legs.

I tear my eyes away angrily, and back to the two bikers. From where I stand, I can only see one weapon holstered on each of their hips. They look incredibly bored with their post.

"Can we help you, sweetheart?" one of them asks her with a smirk. His hair is thinning in the front, and his dark eyes are mean. They glitter under the lights as he tracks them over her body. He's probably in his late twenties but already has the thoroughly strung out, middle-aged look of unchecked addiction.

"I'm hoping that you can," she replies with a flirty look and conspiring smile, and they both straighten.

Jesus Christ. How do they not notice how *forced* that smile is? It looks so…*empty.*

She's fool's gold. Shiny and beautiful to look at, but I see the truth whenever the light shifts and her mask falls away. There's something broken and rotting right beneath the surface.

"I'm new to town, and I really need to fill my prescriptions. Do you think you can maybe give me directions to the nearest pharmacy?"

As if her fucking Baker wasn't the extent of her sins, she confirms my suspicion that she's hitting up these bottom-feeders hoping to score. Not only that—that streetwise mouth of hers tells me it's obviously not her first time.

My teeth grind so hard I expect to hear a crack.

The second Ace laughs, hooking his thumbs in his belt loops and tugging while he shares a smug look with his Club brother. "Yeah, I think we might be able to do that. You got bus money?"

This one's not bad looking, with his hint of surfer vibe, but his hair is cut in a douche-bro style, and he's got that overly inflated sense of self-entitlement that so many low-ranked bangers seem to have.

Sabine flashes him a stack of notes that must come from a hidden pocket somewhere on that sorry excuse for a dress.

The other guy tilts his chin back towards the hallway that leads to the Underground. "Slash's Compounding's still open downstairs. First landing, can't miss it. Tell 'em Beetle and Malibu sent you."

Beetle and Malibu. No guesses there who's who.

She gives them a finger wave and spins on her heels, ostensibly to continue on her way to the bathroom. But really, it's a piss-poor attempt to hide her obvious interest in the mention of their boss. I saw the way she perked up at his name.

Slash is well known to us. He's one of the few guys in charge of their distribution that's earned the MC's highest rank of Spade. We know enough about him from their numerous attempts to recruit us since this place opened. He's rarely here in the flesh.

But how the fuck does *she* know Slash? Sabine Winters hasn't been in the city since…No, we would have found her by now. Heard *something*.

All of these fucking unknowns are going to send me to an early grave.

She reaches the restroom door and pushes through. Again my body seems to make my decision for me, and I'm stalking forward, following her through the swinging door. I kick it shut behind me, the music instantly cutting off, and pause for a moment to watch her.

Without so much as a glance back, Sabine strides confidently towards a plastic dispenser on the far side of the room, most likely looking for something to clean Baker's cum off with—and fuck, does *that* have crimson red bleeding violently into the black fog's edge. Of course she doesn't make it to her destination, because I'm flicking the lock and then I'm across the room, grabbing her nape and slamming her up against the wall.

She hisses out her surprise, and I track that familiar, reflexive need to go on the defensive in the way she tenses and readies her muscles. One spiked heel swings backwards looking for a target, at the same time an elbow shoots out, seeking the middle of my chest. I manage to twist my upper body so that her thrust only grazes my ribcage, but her foot connects sharply with my shin. I grunt at the short burst of pain but I don't let her go.

Her cheek is pressed against the cold tile but she's facing the cracked length of the mirror. When she sees who is responsible for the weight at her back, she huffs out loudly in frustration, and then drops her shoulders.

Our ragged breaths mingle and echo around the room. She smells like sandalwood beneath the acrid smells of the club.

"Sinclair! Nice of you to drop in. Can I offer you something to drink? Beer? Coffee?"

I grab her shoulder and spin her roughly, my right hand deftly sliding from the back of her neck to nestle against the front of her throat. The blue lights in here are designed to make finding a vein hard, but it also makes it difficult to determine the true color of her eyes.

I know they're gray—but are they *her* gray eyes?

Sabine doesn't bring her own hands up in an attempt to remove my hold. If anything, she presses into it. I squeeze my fingers in warning, expecting to see fear blossom across that guarded gaze. Instead, the suspicion

I see there is overtaken by something that looks a lot more heated.

My thumb sweeps over her pulse point and I feel it when it jumps, the elevated beat mirroring my own. Was her heart racing because she's on edge, or because she's... *turned on?*

My cock gives an answering twitch.

For the first time since I committed to delivering this lesson, I realize that I might be the one who's in over my head here. My eyes dart to the prominent scar on her temple. A stark reminder that I have no idea who she is any more.

What she's capable of.

The thought leaves a sour weight in my stomach, and indecision crowds in. I can't decide if I want to continue meting out this punishment...or somehow get her to open up to me.

As if she can see the war raging in me, a sultry smile tips Sabine's darkly stained lips. Something about it feels a lot more genuine than the one she gave the two Aces outside. Or perhaps I'm just hallucinating, what with all of the blood that's now very much occupied elsewhere.

"I'm not usually big on jewelry, Sinclair, but I do *love* a good hand necklace."

Oh, this fucking girl.

And just like that, I'm back on this encounter remaining firmly educational.

"Christ, you have a *fucking mouth on you,*" I growl out. The grip on my composure is tenuous now, but I do my best to keep from letting the equal parts turmoil and desire reflect in my expression. With the last threads of my control, I sew a cool, unflinching mask back into place. "Why don't I give you a better use for it?"

My tone is definitely colder now. Good. I *need* to keep my wits here. I take a small step back and with the hand still around her throat, I shove her down.

Sabine doesn't flinch as her knees hit the floor with a dull smack. She simply looks up at me, eyes shining with unconcealed arousal.

Fuck. Weak.

With my other hand I free my pulsing cock from the tight confines of my zipper. It's long and hard as fucking stone, already dripping at the head with the agony of watching her with Baker. I squeeze Sabine's neck again and her dark red mouth pops open, tongue out, showing me the hint of the piercing on her frenulum. Everything zeroes in on the sight of her kneeling before me, waiting and ready.

Still not giving myself a chance to second guess my actions, I punch forward with my hips, and surge past her lips. I don't give her time to adjust her jaw—I just surrender to the brutal pace needed to whip this smart little ass of hers back into line.

Yes. Fucking, yes.

The fingers guiding my cock move up to spear roughly into her hair. I press down with my nails into her scalp in a way that matches the possessive hold of the other hand gripping her throat. With my palm where it is, and the folds of her jacket, I can't really see much of her body. But it doesn't matter—the physical sensations are already too much. Her mouth is hot and warm and so fucking *right*.

Every fibre in my being is struggling to hold back from fucking her face right through the goddamn wall.

Despite the unrelenting thrusts, however, she doesn't appear distressed at all. I can see tears forming in the corners of her eyes from the force of my assault, but her calm focus never wavers. Never leaves my face. Even now it's like she's still watching every micro-expression. Cataloging.

No—evidently, she's *just* as into this.

Her tongue determinedly lashes a path up and down my cock as I move in and out. Her fingers dig into the backs of my thighs, pulling me forward. Urging me on.

Everything about this feels otherworldly.

"A good start, but I know we can do better," I grit out, each word laced with a beast that's *this* close to fully slipping the leash.

Obediently, her chin tilts, opening her throat. The submission sparks something on a primal level. Without thought, I shove deeper until my cock slips snugly into the tight embrace. A wanton moan escapes through the seal of her lips. It sends a desperate vibration, one filled with urgency, all the way through my balls.

But I don't know whose urgency it is—mine or Sabine's.

"I'm not done with you yet, so don't get too comfortable." I say through clenched teeth as I pull out and ram in again. And again. I should have found her limit by now, but still she doesn't choke or gag. The tears have gathered and spilled over, but her fingers continue to press into my thighs, goading me.

I don't stop until I feel her nose and lips pressed against my pelvis.

My hand flexes, right where I can feel the tight swell of my shaft in her throat.

God Al-fucking-mighty.

She's taken everything. Every single inch.

Sabine swallows hard against my palm, the movement only further strangling the head of my cock. My eyes roll back in my head and lights flash behind the lids. An involuntary groan escapes.

I move the hand away and tilt my head so that I have an unobstructed view around her jaw. Mesmerized, I gently stroke two fingers over the bulge there. It's the hottest fucking thing I've ever seen. "You took it all, Jelly Bean. Look how well you took it," I rasp out. The old, long-forgotten nickname slips out between us like a treacherous thing.

When she doesn't seem to respond to it, a pang of disappointment spikes in my chest. But it's then that I notice her wet cheeks are starting to flush, and I pull back, reluctant, but knowing that she needs oxygen. I'm not exactly small.

Sabine, of course, seizes my kindness as an opportunity to unleash her smart mouth again. She pulls off with a gasping breath, my dick slipping out with a trail of spit connecting it to her puffy lips. "I might not have a gag reflex, Sinclair, but I also don't have fucking gills," she sasses up at me.

Fuck, if every word of hers doesn't just serve to stoke the flames higher.

"I've had enough of your wicked tongue. Now breathe through your nose." I shove her back down on my cock—though I'm much more chivalrous this time, and I *don't* pin her face directly into my core. She gives an indignant, garbled sound of protest, but then she yanks my thighs in towards her, like she's trying to feed the length of it all the way down and into her guts, so I ignore it.

Both hands are in her hair now, and I'm starting to really lose myself. As I pound into that godforsaken mouth, I feel a sudden kinship with Lake's growing obsession towards her.

Twisting and binding.

An addiction.

She moans again, heralding the familiar pleasurable tingle that shoots along my spine. The muscles in my legs tighten and my balls draw up. I look down, seeing the fire in her eyes, and despite the mascara making tracks and the saliva smeared across her cheek, she's breathtaking.

Sabine.

The girl who left me standing, waiting, bleeding out next to a jungle gym when we were twelve.

My Jelly Bean.

The startlingly hopeful thought that it's actually *her* threatens to steal what little air I had left in my lungs. The thought of having her here, all grown up and *mine*

mine mine calls up that beast again and sends me hurtling over the finish line.

With one last deep, broken groan, I unleash a torrent straight down her throat. Her name is a tortured whisper.

I pull away, half-delirious, the strings of saliva leading to her lips now laced with my cum. Fingers flex and slip out of her hair and I fall forward against the tile, leaning on my fists. My chest heaves with erratic breaths, and my vision dances with white spots and the weird blue lighting of the bathroom.

After a long moment—silent, but for our panting—I take two unsteady steps back, and look down to tuck myself away. That's when I notice there's a perfect lipstick imprint on my pelvis, circling the base of my cock.

Jesus fucking Christ.

I'm not even a religious man, but the way she has me blaspheming is something of a divine thing.

Sabine hasn't moved. Just kneels there, staring back at me with her half-hooded eyes. It's the most life I've seen on her face since she arrived at Roxborough. Then she pushes up to her feet and theatrically brushes her knees off. "Well, thanks f—" she starts, but I press forward again, my focus on her swollen mouth. The aggressive movement has the desired effect and cuts off whatever sarcastic quip she was about to throw at me.

Suddenly all I can see are those abused lips. I'm just about to crash my own against them, when there's a sharp intake of a breath and her face jerks away. My spine goes rigid. There's something like trepidation in her eyes when she looks back and is finally able to meet my scowl.

What the fuck was that?

Why wouldn't she want to kiss me? Does she think I care that she just had my dick in her mouth?

Determined not to let her wrestle back the upper hand by rejecting me further, I reluctantly forgo the kiss. For now.

Instead, I drop my face towards hers and say in a tense, heated whisper, "You seem to have forgotten that you belong to *us*, Winters, so consider this to have been a *gentle reminder*." I angle away, searching her expression. Trying to get some kind of a read on her. *Nothing*.

I feel a muscle jump in my jaw as I grit my teeth. "Just try and forget us twice, *I fucking dare you*."

And with that, I shove away from her and flee the scene of my crime—unlocking and striding through the door before she can ask me what the fuck those words meant. I'm too raw, too caught up in the memory of her mouth and the knowledge that I might finally have her back.

My gaze locks with Baker's as I step outside. He's talking to the two Ace lookouts and my gut sours at the sight of the prick.

But then I feel Sabine spilling out of the bathroom behind me and I watch as he sees the state of her hair and makeup and puts two and two together. The way the shock on his face morphs into an expression that's midnight black is fucking glorious. I answer with the smuggest smile I can muster.

I glance back at his date, just as she's realizing she's been caught stumbling out of the bathroom with another guy. I'm surprised not to see any guilt on her face, only a hard expression that says the last thing she wants right now is guy drama.

Good. It means she doesn't hold feelings for him. So long as it stays that way.

And maybe seeing Baker with the two bikers means she won't want to get involved with the Aces either.

I lean in once more. *"Ours. Don't forget it."*

Then I'm cutting through the crowd towards the entrance, desperate for a moment to rebuild the walls she's managed to fracture in the short time it took for her to swallow my dick.

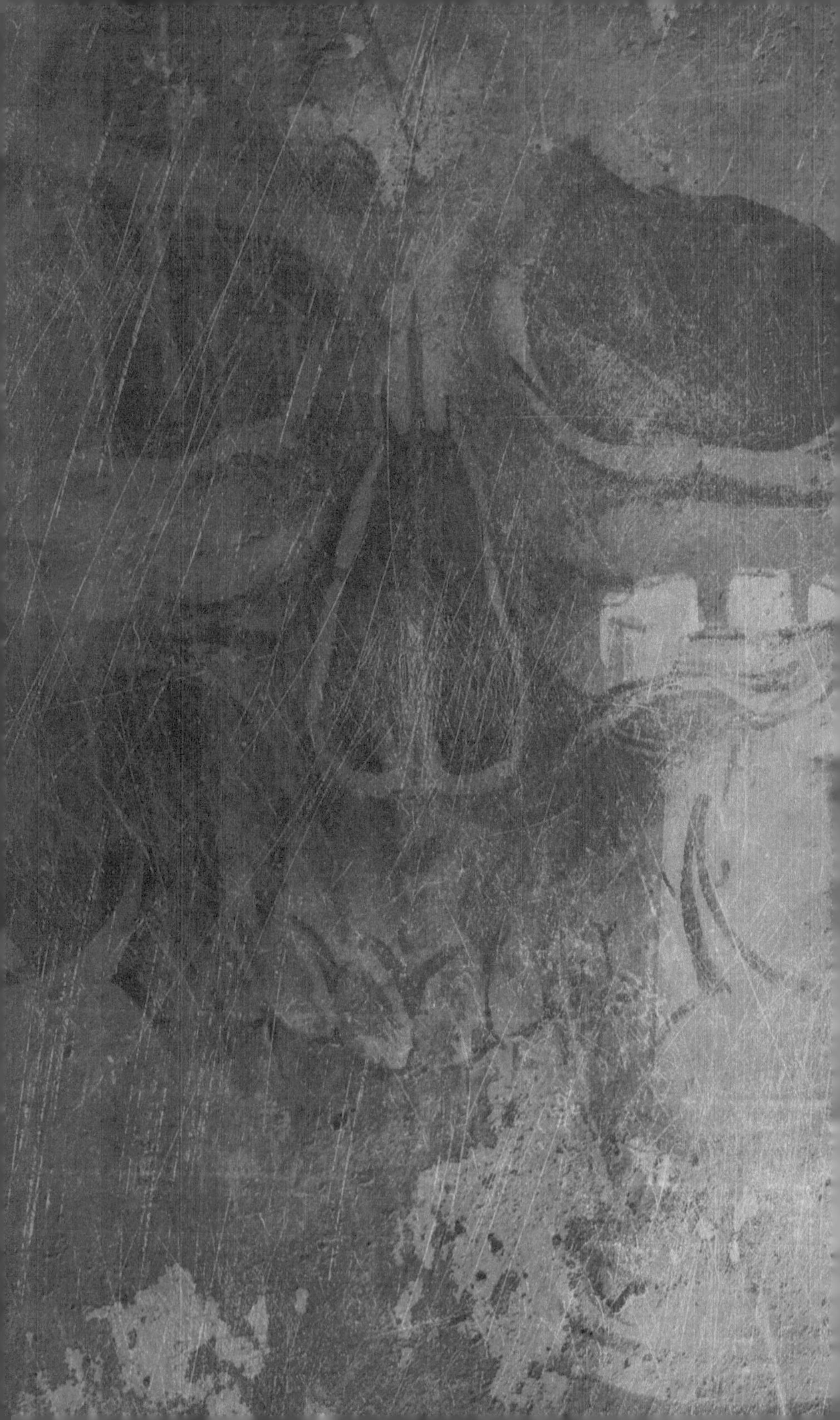

CHAPTER XVI

SABINE

THE ATMOSPHERE when I return to the Guardhouse on Saturday feels significantly more charged after my encounter with the Head Prefect.

After Hotty McFuckface left me standing outside that bathroom—directly in the line of sight of a livid linebacker and rocking my freshly face-fucked hair and raccoon eyes—I had decided to just call it a night and took an Uber back to the Academy.

Ours.

He said it like he had any right to tell me who I could and couldn't be with. Like he already had some claim to me.

No, not just any claim. A *prior* claim.

I don't enjoy the way that makes my chest feel. Like something is trying to move in and fill the empty space there. So I shove that reflex down and file the whole incident away to live amongst the rest of the Rox Boy mysteries I've yet to unravel.

Mercifully, I've yet to cross paths with Baker tonight. If he's even here. Last night was like getting busted by a one-night stand, shoes in hand, trying to sneak out because you thought they'd be occupied in the bathroom. Only *I* was the one occupied in the bathroom. With his most hated social rival. *Oops.*

Now who really wants to be forced to sit through *that* kind of awkwardness?

Scattered throughout the first level's dance floor is a mixture of Clubs and Diamonds on necks—and even a couple of Hearts. I watch them all closely as I slowly circle the room. Their faces are hard, eyes moving constantly over the crowd. I assume their idea of a good time doesn't usually include chaperoning for a bunch of spoiled seniors during their back-to-school rager.

On my third lap, and after documenting all the faces I can make out against the pulsing lights and smoke, I start to notice two things. A significant portion of the upper echelon of students are missing from the enthusiastic throng before me—including the Rox Boys—and whenever a member of the football team passes by, the MC guards all give a small dip of their chins in acknowledgement. The bro nods are a tad disconcerting, because I don't see them affording the same respect to the ballers, and that tells me it's probably not a star player thing. I file it away.

Catching a flash of Sloane's red hair reminds me that although I have yet to find an Achilles heel for my main groups of targets, I do still have a clear and exploitable weakness for at least *one* significant Family gunning for the Crown.

I groan and absently rub at the scar on my temple. My

head is starting to ache just thinking about the tangled politics of the Underworld, and I already took the last of my stash earlier. After I got back to the dorms I realized rather belatedly that my little rendezvous with Sinclair meant that I didn't end up visiting Slash. So I *really* hope I can find someone to buy from as I do my work, otherwise I'm going to be forced to become best friends with the hot bartender over there.

Deciding to follow the cheerleader's lead, I weave my way to the stairs and head up to the second floor. I'm assuming this is where some of my missing classmates will be.

As soon as my feet hit the landing, I do a perfunctory sweep of what I can see of the layout from here. There's another dance floor but it's much smaller. The majority of the space is taken up by a haphazard cluster of mismatched couches and low tables. Another long bar takes up most of the back wall. To my left I spot someone that has my lips turning up. Maybe I can check *Replenishing My Supplies* off the to-do list after all.

Standing with two of his buddies near the railing that overlooks the first floor, is *Axel Nathaniel King, 18.* Despite being the son of one of Rox Academy's tenured teaching staff members, it is a poorly kept secret that Axel is *always* holding. It was one of the first big Rox truths I learnt during my first week.

I'm trying not to get ahead of myself, but since it's the first big party of the year, I'm cautiously optimistic that he's brought some decent stuff with him.

Sauntering over, I plaster what I hope is a friendly

smile on my face. I'm wearing my cropped leather jacket again, but this time it's over a plunging blood-red skater dress with half sleeves. My Louboutins are still pushing six inches but I wanted to keep a bit more movement in my clothing tonight, just in case I need to go into stealth mode.

Axel's eyes track down my chest as I approach and he flashes me his best salesman's smile. "New girl, enjoying the party?"

The music isn't as deafening as it is downstairs, but it's still a struggle to be heard. I lift my shoulder and shout in return, "I guess it depends. Did any of your girls make it? I was hoping to dance with some of them tonight."

He leans back against the railing and cuts a look towards his friends, before giving me another considering once-over. "Maybe. Who are you looking for, baby?"

I sidle closer and lean against the barrier beside him so he can better hear me over the bass. "Have you seen Charlie, Molly or Crystal around? Roxy? I'm so fucking bored, I'd even hang out with Mary Jane at this point."

Axel squints his eyes at me, pretending like he's trying to decide whether I'm worth taking a risk on.

He's another stupidly good-looking Rox senior. He doesn't play sports for any of the Academy's teams, although he's fairly tall, with the lithely toned body and style of a skater. He's got two snake-bite piercings and a dark swathe of hair that almost covers a pair of green eyes always flashing with attitude.

I almost wonder why he and Lake aren't friends. They've both got the same devil-may-care air.

But I recognize the song and dance. I also know he's going to sell to me, regardless. I know I'm right when he blows out a dramatic breath and asks with a lop-sided grin, "Yeah, I got you, baby. How about you come and party with Elyse and I?"

Elysium. Not the uncaring bliss I'd get from a bump of *Asphodel*, but it'll be good for a few hours of fun, uncomplicated rolling. It would mean I'll even be able to continue working. That is unless he's actually got something a bit stronger with him and he's simply keeping his cards close to his chest. "Sure, after you."

Axel pushes off the railing and swaggers towards a private hallway that leads directly off from the second level's main area. The walls of the passageway are covered in all kinds of graffiti, painted in a fluorescent paint that glows brightly beneath the black lights overhead. We pass a few closed doors before he leads me to one right near the end. Inside is an empty, unassuming room—all that's inside is one of his buddies sitting on an old couch and casually holding his stash for him.

I guess I'm about to find out whether I'm just wasting my time or if I need to go find tonight's Beetle or Malibu downstairs instead.

Tyrone stands without a word, throws the duffel to Axel and heads out the door. Seems a bit lax after all the cloak and dagger, but I'm in no position to complain. I just want a fix at this point.

Axel kicks the door shut after his friend and

immediately unzips his bag. I spin to follow him as he walks towards the couch. "Are you just looking for a quick hit? I've got some bars and shit in here as well."

My ears perk up. "Yeah? I'll grab whatever downers you've got on you to take home, and I'll get a few drops of Elyse for now."

He holds up a clear zip-locked bag with what looks like a hodgepodge mix of benzos. "I've got—" he starts before I cut him off with a wave.

"Don't care, I'll take them." I toss him the wad of cash I had put aside from last night.

"Alright, baby. Rock'n'roll," he says, pocketing the money and holding out the bag with a smirk. I take a step towards him, arm reaching for the baggie. Just as I go to grasp it though, Axel nods at someone behind me.

A pair of hands snatches my outstretched arm, before a second set grips my opposite biceps just as roughly.

"What the fuck, Axel?" I cry, giving an annoyed shake of my arm. "There's more than enough to cover it there, why're you getting frisky with me?"

"Because you make it so easy for us, you fucking junkie." Unease pours down my back at the taunting sound of the redhead whose swaying hips I had followed up here in the first place.

Sloane. I didn't even hear the door open.

Just like when Tristan grabbed me in the bathroom, I'm at the whim of my the strength of my captors. Being light and fast on your feet does nothing when I've already lost the advantage and I'm outmatched by sheer size. I twist my head from side to side, finding that I'm being restrained by two of the remaining Krakens I hadn't managed to recruit yet. *Brett Donoghue* and *Liam Byrne*. They're both big strapping lads with Irish family names. I guess it's possible they're already spoken for by the O'Sullivans.

Looks like they're also going on my *Disposal List* for lost causes.

I attempt to track Sloane as she stalks around me, coming to a stop next to Axel. She looks like a total bombshell tonight, with those fiery locks and an emerald mesh dress that clings to her like a dream. It shows off a lot of skin with that illegally low back.

"What's next, Walker? Pig's blood?" I ask her with a flat laugh.

Her answering laughter is a little more animated than mine. "No, I think what a crackhead like you needs is something a little stronger." She trails a finger down my sleeve and taps in the crook of one arm.

I frown. "Crackhead?"

She tips her head to the side, hair sliding off her shoulder as she does. "Tweaker? It doesn't really matter. We all know you slam back pills at your locker or in the girl's bathroom at all hours of the day."

I scoff in an attempt to cover my surprise. Well, fuck. I suppose I wasn't exactly tip-toeing around, but I hadn't expected anyone to actually fucking *notice*. I suppose the cold hard truth is everyone with an addiction *always* thinks they're being more subtle than they actually are. Why would I be the exception to the rule? I'm such a fucking idiot.

I look at Axel. "Sensing some hypocrisy here, King. Shouldn't an enterprising guy such as yourself be securing a regular customer, not joining in on…whatever this is?"

Axel shrugs, spreading his hands. "Nothing personal, new girl. Just trying to make it to graduation."

Asshole. What that does give me though, is some unexpected insight into Sloane's influence at school. Sounds like she's not above bribery tactics herself.

To Sloane, he says curtly, "It's in the front pocket."

Movement from my periphery announces the arrival of Reid. She saunters over to Axel's bag, rummaging around in the front compartment until she pulls out a pre-loaded syringe. She holds it up triumphantly before walking over to place it gingerly in Sloane's hand.

I eye the needle. I might have no real sense of self-preservation, but I still like to be armed with the knowledge of exactly *what* I'm putting in my body. Call it a little island of sanity in my usual stream of madness. "What's in it?"

I know what it *looks* like, but I've already underestimated these fuckers once tonight, and something tells me that whatever is in that syringe, it has *not* been prepared for my health.

"*Ash.*" Sloane confirms, and her smirk is pure villainy. "Mostly."

Mostly?

"It's an *Asphodel* hotshot?" I ask in a hard voice, watching her wave the syringe around and testing the tight grips still holding my biceps hostage. "What else is in it?"

She lifts her shoulders and drops them in a dramatic shrug. "Do you really care?"

I go to respond with my usual snark—maybe something about how I don't like track marks and prefer to take my drugs up my nose like any respectable closet junkie—but I don't get a chance to answer because Brett clamps a meaty hand over my mouth. At the same time, Liam grabs the collar of my jacket, yanking it back over my shoulders and peeling down the leather sleeves, effectively trapping my hands.

The two of them wrestle me forward, with both forearms now stretched awkwardly out at each side. Glancing down, I can see the prominent veins in the creases of my elbows, even in the dim lighting.

The hairs on the back of my neck are starting to stand up, adrenaline trickling in at the thought of the imminent drug high. *Aw, hell.* I wish I had the good sense to feel scared, but the reward system of my brain only cares about the promise of sweet, sweet dopamine.

Sloane gazes at me from beneath her lashes. I expect her to start monologuing me to death, but she doesn't give me anything more than another cruel, victorious smirk.

I bet it probably looks a lot like the ones I gave her in our last two encounters.

But I'm not fucking smirking now.

CHAPTER XVII

SABINE

INSTEAD, I'm watching as she angles the syringe over the exposed stretch of skin in the crook of my arm. She lines it up right where the veins are most visible, before driving it roughly in and depressing the plunger.

The hypodermic needle breaks through the flesh with a sharp pinch, followed by an awful burning as the concoction dumps directly into my bloodstream.

My breath sucks in with a pained hiss. I try my best to bite into the meaty palm of Brett's hand, but the grip he has on my face only serves to press my lips back against my teeth instead.

Fuck. *Fuck,* that really fucking hurt.

Fire is spreading swiftly up my arm, sending an ache all the way through the limb and into my chest. It seems like several maddening minutes pass before I can feel anything past the initial scorch of the injection.

But then, feel it I do.

At first there's just a few sparks, like the puff of embers from a bonfire into the night sky. Then the drugs take root and those flames roar to life—surging outwards in hot, rolling waves to overwhelm my nervous system like a hit of epinephrine.

At first, it had almost started out with the feverish, cleansing rush of *Ash*, but this? This is more like *Ash*'s huge, angry cousin—out on bail after spending years behind bars getting ripped, then coming home with an axe to grind.

The heat builds and builds, searing my insides until they surely must be blackened and stripped of flesh. I gasp, desperately needing the oxygen, and feeling like every blood vessel in my body is dilating to capacity.

I bet my pupils are blown to hell.

Speaking of—my vision goes out in a brilliant flash of white, followed by a dancing mural of reds and purples. Everything jumps and writhes before me like a living Van Gogh painting.

I can't even appreciate the weird beauty of it, because the drug is still meting out a steady, painful path through my system like a wildfire raging out of control.

There's a harsh, grating sound in my ears, one that's fighting my climbing heartbeat for dominance. When there's a flare of pain in my jaw, it vaguely occurs to me that the sound must be my teeth grinding together.

Then that brief moment of lucidity is gone, along with all feeling in my fingers.

My breathing was already very labored, but now it's like the entire weight of the universe has decided to rush in to wrap around my rib cage, crushing it like a vise.

I'm now convinced every bone must be broken.

Surely my heart can't take this kind of pressure? It must be about to combust right there in my chest.

Abruptly the twin grips on my arms fall away, and without the added support, my knees give out, and I slump to the floor. My arms are still pinned to my sides by my sleeves.

I hear a moan.

It might be mine but I can't be sure. I think I'm dying.

I must be dying.

"I knew it—you do look *right* at home on your knees, Winters." Sloane's voice reverberates, coming from everywhere and nowhere at once.

I'm not able to formulate any kind of answer, except for a shameful kind of gurgling noise that originates from somewhere in the back of my throat.

Lights continue to dance in front of my face and giggles echo around me.

Sloane says something else that I don't quite catch, but then hands are adjusting my jacket, before picking me up under the armpits and dragging me.

Where are we going?

I can't feel my hands or my tongue. My feet are five hundred pounds of lead, trapped on the ends of legs that also feel as though they have thousands of fire ants crawling up them. I wish someone would remove my skin for me. I think I'd prefer to live without it right now.

We only make it a few feet before I'm unceremoniously dumped on the floor again. I can hear movement and voices but they sound distorted, like I'm underwater.

A thud, which could be the door. Or my sanity.

And then nothing but the muted sound of whatever music's playing outside the room and the deafening *swoosh* of my pulse.

Belatedly, I realize my view is blocked by something dark and solid. I attempt to focus on the unmoving obstacle, hoping to use it to orient my rioting senses and at the very least, persuade my optic nerves to *settle the fuck down.*

When it seems like I can blink without my eyesight doing a backflip, I try to make sense of what it is I'm looking at. It takes several moments longer, attempting to corral my thoughts into some kind of sensible order, but I finally realize that I'm looking directly at the back side of the couch.

Now that I have some idea of where I am, I decide I need to take stock of my current physical state. I attempt to turn my head, but as I do, pain rips through my neck and ricochets down my spine.

Christ on a fucking cracker. Death, take me now.

My vision swirls again, and I do my best to breathe through my nose, but that only seems to force my jaw to clench more tightly. I let it out in little pants instead.

Slowly, after what could be minutes, an hour—or decades, for all I know—the muscles along my vertebrae begin to relax enough that I am able to roll gingerly onto my back.

I lay there, chest heaving—wondering how I could possibly have let myself get to the point where the need to secure my next fix was more important than securing my blindspots.

I know I made it too easy for them to get this ammunition in the first place. Sloane is a princess in our Underworld after all. I'd just assumed Daddy had shipped her off to keep her out of the muck, or perhaps hidden her here for her protection.

I try to concentrate on just breathing, even as a million questions continue to cascade through my brain.

Did her father also give her an official recruitment directive, or is *she* the one using her peers as she sees fit?

Had she actually *intended* for this attack to be lethal?

Have I grossly underestimated Sloane O'Sullivan?

Christ, I'm lucky none of my Crew were here to witness this. Not that I think any of them would narc on me to Sebastian, necessarily, but...I fucked up. Royally. I've broken the two key rules of mission engagement— *Don't lose your head* and *never show weakness.* There are Suits that have definitely been 'retired' for less.

Before I can slip into a spiral of further overthinking and self-dissection, something cuts through the quiet.

My still-addled brain needs a moment to interpret the noise, belatedly translating it as the sound of the door snicking shut, and feet shuffling across the threadbare carpet.

"Sabine?" A throaty voice calls out in hushed tones.

"Over here," I croak.

I'm relieved to find that my faculties are beginning to recover and my tongue is working again. I suspect that my tolerance to narcotics after two years of drug abuse has unintentionally worked in my favor. Instead of being a lethal dose—or at least a highly incapacitating one—the injection only knocked me soundly on my ass.

Regardless, I think the worst of it has begun to pass.

There's a beat of silence and then a shock of white hair is hovering over me. He has two faces that look kind of ghostly and transposed right now, but I'd recognize them anywhere.

"Wren. Hey." *Lord*, it feels like I've been gargling glass shards, and my voice sounds all kinds of wrong.

Wren's eyes roam over my face in that casually detached way that he has. "I saw you come in here with Axel and Sloane. But you never came out after they all left."

He runs a hand absently up his arm. He's wearing a plain black t-shirt tonight, and I can sort of make out that his tattoo sleeves are made up of dozens of tightly packed flowers. Briar roses, maybe? My vision is still doing gymnastics.

"What the fuck actually happened?"

I swallow a few times, trying to dislodge that harsh, sandpaper-like texture from my mouth and throat. "Dirty drugs. How long have I been in here?"

He glances at the door briefly, before dropping his gaze back to mine. "I don't know, a couple of hours maybe? I was kind of preoccupied."

I close my eyes, a quiet flush of relief in my chest. I'm almost positive now that their original plan included me not walking out of this room *at all*, so a couple of hours? I'll fucking take it.

My eyes open as I hear him let out a long, unsteady breath. "Do you…need me to call someone?"

I consider his offer as I do another sluggish inventory of my physical and mental state. Maybe I *should* just suck it up and get Rhett or Knox down here to take me somewhere safe.

No. No.

I got myself into this mess. I'm on my own.

"Nah. I'll be fine. It'll take a lot more than whatever weak shit they just shot me up with." That's a lie. It wasn't weak at all—I'm just so broken that the poison only managed to fill in the cracks already formed by my habit instead of making more.

Wren's pale eyebrows shoot up. Oops. I guess he must have assumed I was in here willingly, and doing this to myself.

Does everyone *know about my habit?* Fuck.

"How then?" he asks incredulously. There's a deep scowl on his face. It's probably the most emotion I've seen or heard from him thus far.

I cough, wincing at the throbs of pain that reverberate through my ribs. "Donoghue and Byrne took me by surprise. King supplied, and Sloane forced it into my arm. Shit fucking *hurt.*"

I moan. I haven't felt that kind of pain or loss of control since my days with…Let's just say—it's been a while.

He's quiet. His face is still a little out of focus, but his wavering expressions says he knows what I'm not saying. That I initially followed King into the room of my own volition, hoping to score *something*.

"Wait here," he says, finally, before turning and disappearing from my view.

"Sure thing," I wheeze out into the empty room.

I still have no way to gauge how much time passes as I lay there waiting for his return, but I do notice sensation beginning to creep back into my limbs, and that my thoughts aren't nearly as scattered.

Finally I hear Wren slip back into the room, his footsteps more urgent as he returns to my spot behind the couch. He crouches down, holding out a plastic bottle of water that's dripping with condensation.

I want to weep with joy. My tongue feels like a giant wad of cotton and I've never needed fluids more in my life.

"Legendary," I croak, reaching out a shaky hand.

He pauses, suddenly considering my prone position. "Do you…need help sitting up?"

"Probably," I huff, trying to slide my elbows underneath me in an awkward attempt to prop myself on my forearms.

Wren places the water down before slipping his hands under my armpits and hauling me up. Between the two of us, we manage to get my mostly dead weight up and leaning against the couch.

He cracks the lid on the bottle and hands it to me. Then the only sounds are my desperate gulps as I guzzle down the water like I've stumbled across a desert oasis and I'm dying of thirst.

As I finish, I let out a loud, satiated sigh, before dropping the empty bottle into my lap. My throat will be raw for a while, but I no longer feel like I should be spitting up mouthfuls of blood.

I catch Wren's eyes darting towards the door again. "What is it? Do you need to go?"

He looks back at me, hesitance clear in his expression. "I should…"

I was kind of preoccupied.

"Just help me to my feet, then you can go," I say, trying to contort my own face into something I hope resembles a wink and a knowing look. It's hard to tell. Parts of my face still feel numb.

He grunts, then scoops me under the armpits once more, only this time he hauls me all the way to my feet. I hiss like an angry cat at the sudden vertical movement, swaying like a drunken sailor as I fight the rush of vertigo. "Jesus Christ, Wren, a little warning," I grit out.

He lets out a small huff. "Thought you were tougher than a little dizzy spell."

A giggle—that sounds more like a gurgle in my ruined throat—bubbles up at his uncharacteristic cheekiness. I shoot him a wobbly grin. "Jacobs, don't find yourself on my steadily growing shit-list. Just don't."

He responds with a small grin of his own, and it feels like a victory. I need this boy as an asset for our organization, but there's just something about him. He feels more…*organic* than most of the students I've encountered so far.

What you see is the already stripped down, authentic

version of Wren Jacobs. I can guess that not everyone will necessarily make it past the barriers he has in place, but you sure as hell won't be served up anything less than the truth when he does eventually let you in. It's refreshing, and that's why I'm almost certain that I wouldn't mind having him on my Crew. In fact, I kind of…really want to be his…friend. That's not something I find myself wanting often. I'm too selfish to form lasting, healthy friendships. I always end up taking more than I can give back.

Without realizing it, Wren has already hooked one hand under my elbow and is steering me towards the door. Tremors run up and down my legs, and my knees feel like they're made of Jell-O, but my steps get steadier the closer we get. By the time we make it to the end of the dark hallway, I'm no longer leaning on him for support.

We both come to a stop in the shadows, each of us taking in the crowd still occupying this level's dance floor and lounge area. I see Wren's gaze jump to a small group of Rox Academy students currently sprawled across a settee on the other side of the room.

It's a mixed group, and I can't tell who has him so transfixed, but it's obvious to me that I'm not going to be able to compete against their attention tonight. Knowing I also have a lot of lost ground to cover, I elbow him weakly in the ribs. When he gives me an annoyed look, I tilt my head in their direction and mouth over the music, "Go."

His brows pinch slightly as he subtly checks over my

face and posture. His annoyance softens and then he mouths back, *"You good?"*

I nod once and then shove my reluctant rescuer lightly in the small of his back. He stiffens at the touch, but doesn't say anything else, doesn't even glance back. He just angles around the living mass of writhing dancers and couples, presumably heading back towards his friends.

That sharp twinge in my guts that follows is just the lingering effects of the *Ash*.

It's definitely *not* envy.

CHAPTER XVIII

WITH THE SUPPORT of Wren's arm now gone, I slump wearily against the wall beside me. I feel like I could sleep for a whole fucking month, but I'm still just lucid enough to make use of the poor lighting of the hallway as cover while I catch my breath.

My arms feel weak and heavy, and my fingers don't want to cooperate, but after some fumbling, I manage to pull my phone out of my dress's skirt pocket.

Tipping the screen towards me, I blink at the sudden brightness and scowl when I see that the display reads **11:37pm**. That means I lost just over three hours. As I shove it back into my pocket with a curse, I try to remind myself that I might not have even had those hours to lose, if the drugs had done their job properly.

It doesn't help at all. I need to try and salvage this night.

I bite down on my lip, the sharp pain only marginally helping to focus my untethered thoughts.

Okay. Concentrate. Where are your targets?

When I checked on the dance floor with Wren, I had

to consciously ignore the undulating surfaces and ghostly after-images thanks to the drugs, but I do know I didn't see Sloane anywhere.

In fact, there doesn't seem to be *any* Prefects, *or* either of the sports teams up here. Have they gone back down…or up? I've yet to see what's on the third floor.

But as my eyes go to seek out the stairs to the next level, my attention is snagged by another similarly narrow and darkened hallway—this one on the exact opposite side of the open space.

Just inside, a tall and darkly dressed figure leans against the wall, arms crossed, their face and shoulders completely shrouded in darkness. The pulsing lights don't reach that opening either, and there's something menacing about the way the shadows there almost seem to drape around their lurking occupant.

I can't make out who it is, but now that I know they're there, I'm almost positive that their eyes are also on me.

The longer we stare at each other across the room, the greater my curiosity becomes. I'm not entirely sure whether it's a symptom of the drugs still lingering in my bloodstream, or if it's just my usual troublemaking urges, but I'm suddenly overcome with an insatiable need to seek this person out.

With a groan, I launch myself away from the safety of the hallway, staggering a little as I do. Luckily, I manage to catch myself with a steadying hand on the wall beside me, right before I can faceplant.

Shit.

It'll be hard enough navigating this club while high off my fucking face—let alone in six inch heels.

Blood rushes to my head and my vision is swimming as I bend down. Keeping that hand on the wall for support, I grit my teeth and focus on removing my shoes, one at a time. Once they're finally off, I straighten, breathing heavily and gripping the pair of Louboutins in my other fist.

No way am I leaving these babies behind.

I'm determined to inch my way around the room until I can reach that other hallway, so I concentrate on putting one foot in front of the other. I find that using the walls as a guide helps me skirt the edges of the crowd quite effectively; the cold, flat surface passing beneath my palm helping the floor feel more stable beneath my bare feet.

As I draw closer, the shadow straightens, dropping their arms to their sides with fists tightly clenched. A single step forward is just far enough that the lights from the dance floor now cut a slant across their face. My labored steps come to a halt.

Emerging like a paralysis demon from a waking nightmare, is Atlas Rhodes.

Fittingly, he's dressed all in black, with a dark button up shirt and ripped jeans. His long tresses are pulled back at the base of his neck into a messy bun. Whenever the smoky beams bounce off his face, his eyes seem to flash aggressively.

The music continues to pulse between us; the smell of liquor, cigarette smoke and the arousal of dozens of grinding couples hanging thick in the air. One moment seems to stretch into eternity, and the weight of his attention becomes almost painful to bear.

Christ, he's beautiful to look at.

The thought slips in unbidden, just as he's the one to break our stare-off, spinning to stalk back into the darkness behind him. A twinge of panic sparks, needing to keep him in my sights before he can slip away like Hades back down into the Underworld.

Just where are you going, Hades?

With a jolt of renewed determined, I rush after his retreating form—all thoughts and plans for the rest of my night at The Guardhouse pushed firmly to the back of my mind.

I've got a Rox Boy to hunt.

THE BONE-DEEP THROB of the Guardhouse's industrial bass ebbs away as we reach the end of the passageway.

After a sharp corner, we're met with a dim set of stairs and without pausing, Atlas leads our descent. Like the rest of the club, the stairwells are lit by black lights, decorated by loud neon murals, half-smoked roaches and cigarette butts.

Several rotations later and the stairwell empties out onto an old metal platform that stretches into the distance. My brain is still foggy but I feel like we've ventured down far enough that this must be the basement level.

He obviously knows that I'm following him, but Atlas never once looks back at me. His fists are shoved deep in his pockets, his shoulders set and stride determined. He's keeping pace half a dozen steps ahead of me, outlined by the low glow of the pendant lights that form a long strip above us.

Soon enough, the only sounds are my short, expectant breaths, and the echo of our footsteps on the aging catwalks.

The building's not that far from the Tethys, and it's obvious from the damp down here that the platforms were added solely to raise the floor against flooding.

Before long, the catwalk splits around us at a four-way junction. From the left, I hear the sudden and distinct swell of a cheering crowd—dulled as if coming from much further underground. It sounds hungry though, and now I'm wondering what kind of blood sports must go on down here in the dark.

Atlas strides ahead without slowing.

Just before we reach the second junction, he veers off to the right, disappearing soundlessly through a large fire door that's sitting slightly propped open.

Cursing under my breath, I quicken my own pace until I too reach the gap. I pause, trying to listen for movement beyond, but all my senses are still so overstimulated and unreliable that I can't exactly trust my own hearing.

I decide to just hope for the best, stepping as quietly as I can into the cool night air of what appears to be an adjoining side street. Almost immediately, however, the distinct sound of masculine voices from somewhere down the alley has me melting into the shadows cast by a nearby dumpster.

Under *normal* circumstances, I'd say this is me in my element, sneaking around and conducting covert surveillance from the shadows. I'm sure-footed and lithe enough that I'm able to render myself almost invisible if needed.

I also normally do so with a lot more planning, and a lot less double vision.

And shoes.

Soooo…this should be fun then.

I do my best to creep along behind the container with cautious, wobbly footsteps. The space between its massive body and the wall of the Guardhouse is just large enough for me to fit through without scraping up my shoulders.

The smell is fucking atrocious however, and I can feel my body temperature dropping further each time a bare foot connects with the frigid pavement. I remind myself that at the end of the rainbow is the possibility of some juicy Rox Boy intel.

When I reach the edge of the dumpster I peer out, squinting in the direction of the voices, and trying my hardest to stay mindful of both the lighting and my breathing. My gamble pays off, and the new vantage point rewards me with an unobstructed view of five men, meeting roughly thirty feet away, at the dead end of the alley.

Despite my rioting vision and only a solitary security

flood light to see by, there is no mistaking the identity of one half of the huddled group—not after a solid week of obsessing over their every move.

Lake stands relaxed and supremely confident, talking casually to two unknown men. He's flanked first by a hovering Callum, and then a brooding Atlas, tension obvious as he joins them.

There's no sign of the final Rox Boy, but I don't even care right now. This could be the exact fucking break I need in order to uncover the real power behind this mysterious quad.

Anticipation buzzes across my shoulders and down my spine. I press a fist to my mouth as my stomach unexpectedly lurches with nausea.

"He's impressed so far," one of the men is saying. He looks to be in his early thirties, with a clean shaven face and casual but expensive clothes. His hair is slicked back from his forehead in a neat hairstyle. I can't see if he has any gang marks from where I'm hiding, but that accent is *definitely* not from around here.

He sounds like a New York native. But there are no chapters of the Strange Aces up that way. They all fall within the Southern sovereignty. Northern Transplant perhaps?

"We've given him no reason not to be," Lake shrugs, replying with all the bravado of a seasoned crew member.

Hmm. Who is *him*?

The guy flicks his cigarette away, the glowing butt skittering away into the darkness. "We were figuring youse'd be getting more pushback from the Suits or Mahoney's guys by now."

Mahoney's guys. Nobody would refer to their own crew that way.

So *not* Aces then.

Plot twist.

His bald companion hasn't said a word, keeping his eyes trained on Callum like one would watch a dangerous guard dog pacing behind a chain link fence. Callum returns the attention with his own glare, the muscles along his jaw popping with tension.

Lake shrugs again, smug as fuck. "We're always careful." His posture and tone is even and unruffled. He doesn't elaborate. "And we've delivered the update, in person, like he wanted. So I think we're done here."

Atlas stares off down the length of the alley, but is careful not to look directly at where he *must* know I'm hiding. There's an odd sort of flutter in my abdomen when I consider the fact he hasn't ratted me out yet.

Unless he's just biding his time.

The *Ash* is making me feel a confusing mix of both giddy and paranoid. *Ugh.*

I miss how the New Yorker responds, distracted by a scuffing noise coming from behind the exit that I left angled open by its rusty closer. A second conversation drifts out. As I strain my ears, I can just hear what must be two Strange meatheads talking animatedly about the *sure pussy* he's just scored for the night.

I mentally groan as their footsteps come to a stop, and I concentrate on slowing my breathing even further.

Keep moving, I chant silently.

One of the bikers laughs then, kicking at a pipe near the door with a heavy boot. The two of them stumble out into the alley, pulling out their packs of cigarettes. Instantly I recognize them as Beetle and Malibu—Slash's spotters from last night.

Oh boy.

Beetle straightens, his obnoxious guffaw cutting off as they round the dumpster and finally notice that their little smoke spot is already occupied. His beady eyes dart back and forth over the gathered men. "You gentlemen lost?" he sneers. Malibu steps up next to him, a hand hovering behind his back, right near his waistband.

Fuck. If I know anything about Clubs, it's that they all tend to be really *really* fucking trigger-happy. It's like they think it's easier to prove themselves to their president if they make sure to always shoot first. Questions be damned.

New York turns with his palms out in a placating gesture, a charming smile in place. No doubt whoever this guy works for, he's one of their Front Men. "Just visiting with my nephew here, thought we'd step outside for a minute and enjoy the fresh Roxborough night air."

Anyone worth their salt could smell the bullshit a mile away, no matter how smooth a talker this guy is. Beetle's eyes narrow, but he doesn't go for his weapon. Malibu's hand returns to his side.

It looks like Beetle's actually going to buy it. I sink my teeth into the fist still pressed against my lips, trying to stifle the hysterical giggle that wants to escape at their gullibility.

Then he gets a good look at Lake and his friends and a line forms between his brow.

I can almost hear the grind of the gears turning in his dense-as-fuck-but-loyal Club head. I've no doubt the Boys are regulars at The Guardhouse, not with how easily Atlas navigated the basement area. I'd also wager they've been approached by the Aces a few times. It's no secret they love snapping up young Rox City thugs.

Now Beetle's got to be wondering who is trespassing in their chapter's territory, since the boys *don't* work for Trick.

That much I'm sure of.

New York's silent cohort obviously reads the same thoughts on Beetle's face that I do, because he pulls out his own gun—and still without a word—drops them both with two shots each to the chest.

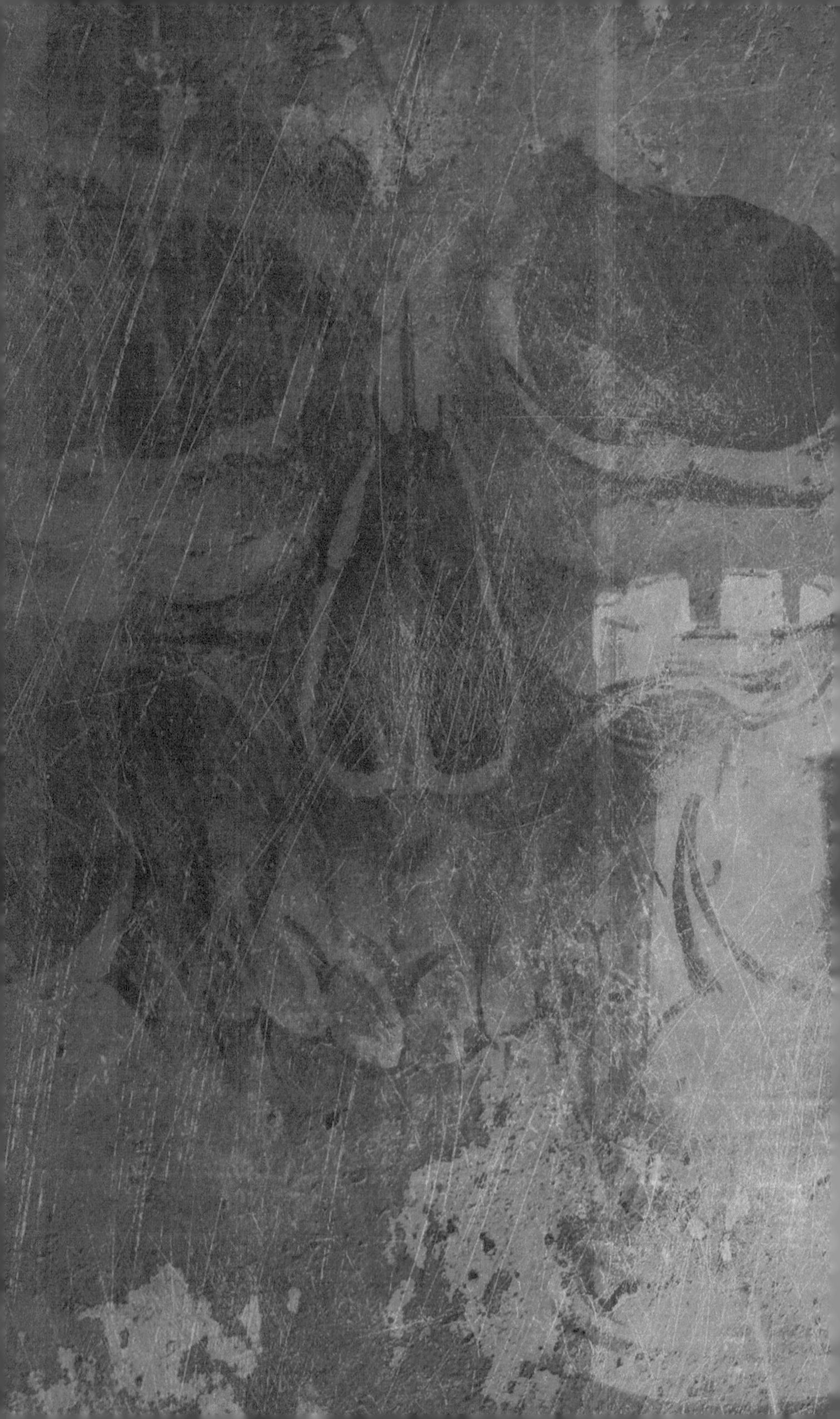

CHAPTER XIX

ALRIGHT, *that's* my cue.

I take a small step backwards, needing to put some space between this alleyway and I before the sound of gunfire brings more Aces.

But of course, because the lingering effects of the *Ash* have my spatial awareness taking a fucking vacation, the arm still holding my shoes connects with the side of the dumpster with a loud *clang*.

In the silent aftermath of the shooting, it sounds like a death knell.

The Rox Boys all go on high alert and both New York and Silent Bob dart their gazes over to where I'm hidden.

Fuck!

My scalp prickles and I feel a rush of bile race up my throat, burning the back of my tongue.

Why did I think I could pull off spying while off my fucking face, again?

Without waiting to be discovered, I start moving back along the wall. My best chance will be trying to slip back through the open exit before they can lay eyes on me.

The moment I step out from behind the dumpster, however, I'm met with both the cold kiss of a muzzle against my temple, and a smug northern accent. "What do we have here, boys?"

New York gives a light tap with the gun, signaling me to turn around. I am in no state to consider running, so I lift my hands up, spinning slowly to face the group. I have to fight an aggressive rush of vertigo, but manage to school my expression as I do.

Not my first rodeo.

I clock the fact that both strangers have their guns trained on me, followed by the varying range of emotions on the Rox Boys' handsome faces.

Callum seethes with anger, the muscle in his jaw jumping. Lake looks excited, but whether that's excitement at seeing me or just straight up pure bloodlust is anyone's guess. Atlas looks coldly indifferent. That fire in his eyes I saw earlier is banked, but not quite gone. He's impossible to read accurately right now.

Not that he ever gives me much to work with.

My eyes slide back to the out-of-towners. Dealing with mid to low-ranking syndicate reps *should* be as easy as breathing for me, but my brain is still too sluggish to properly calculate all the best possible angles and outcomes right now.

What I can assume is that they have prior orders from their boss to go strictly unseen, because Silent Bob here had no qualms about stepping in to clean up two potential Ace witnesses. All I can hope for now is that my knowledge of the thorny dance of Underworld etiquette will be enough to avoid a bullet in my own chest.

"When did the North stop respecting the Treaty and *Hospitium*?" I level in a flat, unaffected voice.

It's probably a stretch as to whether The Law of Hospitality actually does apply here, but one could broadly argue that we *are* in Ace territory and are therefore their guests.

It's the best I have right now, so I press on.

"Two dead Aces, in Ace territory. Two dead Aces who in this instance, did *not* instigate conflict." Again, one could argue that the two Clubs were the ones who started shit with their posturing, but Bob *had* shot first. That's going to be the important distinction here.

"I know things are a little...messy in the South right now, but I'm sure even the Arbiter wouldn't pass up the chance to oversee a Treaty violation."

New York immediately jerks his barrel up. Silent Bob's hand only drops slightly, but a frown forms on his face. The overhead light glints off his bald scalp.

I let a frosty smile slide across my face at their reticence. No Underworld citizen—Northern *or* Southern —wants to find themselves facing the Arbiter. I might be unsure which Family, club or syndicate they're from, but chances are still good they're from the North, which means they'd *also* be incurring Midas's wrath.

I think I'd rather face the Arbiter.

"*Ah, fuck,*" New York mutters. There's a light sheen of sweat on his forehead. His gaze sweeps over the Rox Boys, looking at each of their faces, searching for something. Whatever he sees there, must help him make up his mind.

My chest tightens when I see him roll his shoulders back. My gamble hasn't played off.

Unfortunately, there's only one decent card left in my hand, but it's the one I refuse to play just yet. *The Codex.*

No. If I balk and show my entire hand this early, there'll be no taking it back. Not without needing to kill everyone here. I've already given so much away with just this one cryptic conversation.

There's no chance for me to fold, one way or another, because Callum makes the decision for me.

He moves faster than his size gives him credit for, everything happening in the space of a few scant heartbeats. New York's head snaps back as he takes a shot in the forehead. Bob's a true professional and doesn't so much as flinch as his comrade goes down. He makes a valiant effort to bring his gun back up, but ends up taking one in the neck.

The silence that follows is absolute, the three Rox Boys alternating between staring me down, and looking at the multiple corpses now littering the ground before us.

Atlas's glare is the color of deep space, but he doesn't necessarily look surprised at the clusterfuck turn of events—or my newly exposed Underworld leanings.

Lake and Callum however, don't even try to hide their shock now that the danger has passed.

"The actual *fuck*, Winters?" Callum bellows. He just about grows three sizes, the visible tattoos on his neck and arms rippling as clenches his fists. He looks and sounds positively livid.

Instead of answering him straight away, I do a quick scan of the surrounding eaves, and satisfied there are no cameras, I move towards Silent Bob. I crouch over his body, discreetly checking his pulse. He's gone, and New York's headshot ensured he was toast before he even hit the ground. I highly doubt the Rox City police are going to do forensics on such an obvious gang shooting. Not when I'm sure Trick has them all on his payroll.

Straightening, I nod towards Atlas. "I was following the White Rabbit here, and seems I fell down the hole, straight through to Wonderland."

Lake lets out a throaty laugh, and Callum's scowl deepens even further. Atlas doesn't say anything. He doesn't need to when his look already promises severe consequences.

I'm still a little confused as to why he clearly led me here in the first place.

Does he suspect that I've been watching them all with just a little too much interest?

Was this a trap?

"What? *Christ*. Rabbit hole?" Callum tries again, frustrated. He seems more prone to bouts of explosive anger than Tristan or even Atlas. It's why I suspect he's the brawn and not the brains.

A nearby car door slams, reminding me that we are still standing in the middle of the aftermath of a bloody shootout. In enemy territory.

Callum shoves a huge hand through his auburn hair,

tugging at the longer strands on top. *"Fuck.* We've got to move. Winters, you're coming with us."

Lake whoops and snags my free hand. "Let's go, Wifey." He tugs me violently in the direction of the street. I clutch my heels to my chest, trying to keep to the balls of my feet as we run. I can hear Callum and Atlas's thundering footsteps behind me.

When we reach the end of the building, Lake's shoving me towards the back door of a gorgeous black Mustang GT. I clamber in only to find the missing fourth member.

Tristan spins in the driver's seat, an incredulous look flashing across his handsome face, before it's quickly hidden by that signature mask of icy, bridled control.

A vivid memory of watching that mask come undone as he skull-fucked me last night floods my already overwrought brain.

And my underwear.

"You have exactly two seconds," he seethes as Callum falls into the passenger seat. Atlas slides in behind me and Lake darts around to the rear driver's side door before folding himself in on my other side.

I'm now firmly nestled in a delightfully muscled Rox Boy sandwich. It doesn't even matter that one of the slices of bread is sending me death glares. *Yum.*

"Drive," Callum grunts and Tristan flares his nostrils but peels out with protest.

"UPDATE," he barks once we're a block away from The Guardhouse.

Lake leans up behind Tristan to rest his chin against the shoulder of the front seat. No one's bothered to put on a seatbelt.

"A couple of dipshit Aces stumbled on the meet, but Monelli took them both out. Then our girl here showed up. Reynolds was all set to try and take care of her as well, but of course *Callum* got in first." He slumps back, pouting and blowing at curl on his forehead like a petulant child. He sounds genuinely disappointed that Callum was the one that got to do all the killing tonight.

"Both?" Tristan asks evenly.

"Both," Callum confirms for him.

"And why the fuck was she there in the first place?"

"Why are you talking about me like I'm not even here?" I grumble. *Rude.*

"She followed me," Atlas cuts in with his dark, gravelly voice and *Good. Lord.* My thong, as flimsy as it already was, is now *definitely* a lost cause.

These boys are a goddamn hazard to panties everywhere.

Turning my head, I raise my eyebrows and snark, "So you *do* speak, *Hades.*"

He doubles down on the eye daggers.

"Hades?" Tristan and Callum both scoff loudly at the same time, evenly matched in their annoyance at this whole night.

I let out a chuckle that sounds slightly unhinged, even

for me. I'm still high as a kite and I have *negative* filter right now.

But the truth is, I've been tossing these ideas around for a while. Top tier assets need company-issued aliases, and this group certainly contains a *Pantheon* of god-like bodies with temperaments to match.

Mhm. Something about the mythos just seems to *speak* to me.

Or perhaps that's just the drugs.

"Yes, *Ares*, I think it rather suits him, don't you? The way he skulks around, unseen. I just *bet* he's one who likes to watch."

Those eye daggers are now longswords. Disemboweling.

I almost want to point out to them that Hades is also known as the God of Wealth. We weren't able to find who they were working for in our deep dive into their personal lives, but it wasn't hard to find Atlas's portfolios, and to see the stock market magic he's been working for their group.

But *they* don't know that *I* know that.

Yet.

"Oh Callum's Ares now, is he?" Lake slips his arm behind my neck and leans into me. I can feel his hot breath on my jaw. My pelvic floor does an involuntary stomach crunch.

"The God of War? No brainer. Just look at him," I nod towards the huge, tattooed thug simmering angrily in the front seat. He's hunched over, fists clenched on top of his thighs. I can see all his muscles in High Definition as they pull tight beneath his Henley.

Lake chuckles appreciatively. "I *definitely* see it. So, who am I then, my love?" I turn my head towards him, finding his hazel eyes bright, glittering with their usual mirth. He's so completely unfazed by the events of tonight.

No one would suspect that he and his friends just watched four men die in a seedy alley.

Anyone with two eyes could see they've each got a little damage; each very dark *and* very delicious. There's no denying we'd be an unholy match made in hell.

That thought sends a frisson of lust and danger up my spine.

Ours. Don't forget it.

I hum and pretend not to have heard the words *my love,* and instead deliberately run my eyes over his face. He's cheeky to be sure, and I'm well aware of his penchant for hacking. He's very skilled at retrieving information. Tonight's meeting showed me that he's probably also their endearing messenger boy. "*Hermes,* of course. The Trickster."

The grin I'm rewarded with is perfectly wolfish.

Fuck. Fuck. These boys are too fucking hot for their own good.

I can't slip up and get in over my head here. I still have a mission and they still have an unknown benefactor. There's entirely too much Underworld political fuckery at play here.

"And Mister Sinclair?" Lake/Hermes urges me with a purr.

Tall, broody and golden-skinned? With his blinding good looks, love of music and interest in studying medicine next year? *Easy.*

"Apollo." My voice is unintentionally husky. Raw.

Like you'd expect if one had recently had their throat summarily assaulted by said Sun God.

Tristan/Apollo's eyes snap up to meet mine in the rear view mirror. He could go head to head with Atlas/Hades with the weight of that dark glare. I hold my breath. His gaze feels like a crushing judgment around my chest and lungs.

But then he looks back at the road and the spell is broken.

Does he regret last night?

It didn't *feel* like he thought it was a mistake. It *felt* like a claiming.

No, I'm pretty sure that *was* a claiming.

"Why were you in that alley, Sabine?" he asks in a carefully even voice after a taut moment of silence.

God, if only it wasn't so hard to stay on your verbal toes when you're shit-faced.

"I'm a nosy bitch. I saw Hades inside the club, and was interested in seeing what one of the infamous Rox Boys might get up to during one of their parties. Is that why you chose to have it there and not at your place?"

Apollo's control cracks just a little and I see his fingers tighten where they hold the wheel. It's possible he's remembering what he saw *me* get up to the night before. I hope he is. I need him as off-kilter as I am. But more likely it's simple frustration that he doesn't have the full picture and *boy*, do I know how that feels. It feels like an ice pick to the temple.

We definitely both share the dire compulsion to keep count of each and every one of the cards on the table.

"Speaking of being a nosy bitch. I definitely had you four pegged as baby Aces before tonight. So who do you *actually* answer to?"

I swear you could hear a pin drop.

Almost immediately, Apollo's shoring up his defenses, arctic features shutting down either further, white-knuckled grip forcibly relaxing. The tension flees his shoulders so completely as to leave no evidence that he was ever on edge. It's a complete transformation.

I glance around between the four of them. Even Hermes is now studiously avoiding my gaze.

"Nothing? Not even a hint? Man, you guys are no fun. I'll guess I'll just have to keep digging 'til I hit treasure." When they still don't reply to my quip, I sit up, spine straight. But then I get my first real look out the windows. I hadn't even noticed that we'd already made it back to the Academy. Too busy flirting with Hermes and enjoying watching the control seep out of Apollo.

Shit.

Hermes shoves against his door and then jumps out to hold it open, sweeping his arm in an exaggerated bow. As I slide across the leather seat to follow him out, Apollo's hard voice has me pausing.

"Everybody's got secrets, Sabine. So dig all you want, because so will we. You'd just better hope you fall on the right side of things when we all finally get to the truth."

entered that room for, and now I'm on day three of depending solely on my flask for moral support.

To say I'm a *hot mess* would be putting it mildly.

After Apollo dropped me off outside the dorms, I spent the rest of the weekend both recovering from the effects of the tainted *Asphodel*, and seething all over again about handing the Prefects their edge in the first place. Practically gift-wrapped.

Twenty-four plus hours of withdrawals hasn't stopped me from penning the mental shit-list of students that I needed to craft revenge plans for, however. I'm still able to be creative, even with a raging headache and wicked cottonmouth.

The harsh clang of a metal locker right next to my ear yanks me out of my melancholy, reminding me that I'm standing in the middle of the girl's locker room, and I'm still covered in sweat from my late-morning Gym class.

Groaning, I bend down stiffly and retrieve a change of clothes and my toiletries, before shuffling my way towards the showers. As I round the corner to where the shower stalls are, I'm relieved to see that I seem to be the last girl left. A damp mist hangs in the air, but I can't hear any running water, or see any silhouettes still getting dressed.

Choosing the shower at the end of the line, I drop my things on the bench seat and hurry to crank the tap on for the hot water. The tiled stalls are all open door, with only a shoulder high partition separating them. It means I have to be especially careful while getting undressed. The steam makes a good cover.

I begin to strip, suddenly keen to wash away both the perspiration from my grueling athletics session and the flop sweat of my ongoing detox. Just as the last of my sports gear comes off, and I'm about to turn my back to the scalding water, I hear a low whistle of appreciation.

"Nice ink," a feminine voice that I don't immediately recognize says from behind me. I freeze.

Fuck. *Fuck.* This is *exactly* why I'm supposed to be on my guard. Even though there hadn't been nearly enough steam in here yet to hide me completely, I'd thought I'd been alone.

I didn't physically check all the stalls though did I? The other locker bays before I left to shower?

No. I didn't.

Because I've been slowly losing more and more of my edge since I got here.

Christ. Who am I fucking kidding? This started *well* before I got to Roxborough. I've just always had my Crew to step in and stop me before I could manage to royally fuck things up.

Now that I've been forced to fend for myself, the cracks in my discipline and training are simply becoming more pronounced. It was only a matter of time before I lost my grip on those last vestiges of self-control and someone else paid the price for one of my failures.

Grudgingly, I turn and find *Zoe Elizabeth Nguyen, 17. State volleyball team. Scholarship student. Two older siblings, both graduated from Rox Academy and employed by the City.*

She's standing in front of my stall, fully clothed, phone in one hand. Her dark hair is wet and combed back from her own shower. She must have been bent over, getting dressed out of sight, which is why I didn't see her on my piss-poor survey of the room.

I have no idea what's possessed her to walk all the way down the line to my shower, but at a glance, her round face appears open and guileless. Most likely she simply heard the gossip about Saturday night and came over to gawk at Sloane's latest victim.

On the off chance that she's *not* here with an ulterior motive, then it's just extremely poor timing for both of us that has given her an unobstructed view of the sprawling tattoo that covers most of my back, shoulders and upper arms.

Zoe's eyebrows lift as I simply continue to stand here, naked and internally raging at myself. She's probably waiting for me to stop staring her down like a psychopath and respond to her compliment like a regular human being.

Sorry, babe. She has no idea the steaming pile of shit she just stepped us both in.

A pile of shit of my own making.

"Can I help you?" I ask instead, my head tilting to one side. Expression carefully blank.

Her eyes dart to my bare arms, confirming my suspicions. She did come over here to ogle the New Girl in all her junkie glory.

"Ah, yeah, I was actually coming over to speak to you at your locker when you disappeared into the showers. I wanted to see if you were...alright?" Her voice rises slightly, making the question sound not nearly as genuine in its concern. More cautious. Most likely because she was expecting to find me hunkered down in here licking my wounds, and now she doesn't know how to proceed.

"Alright? How do you mean?"

I need to know exactly what the rumor mill is churning with now so that I can try and get *some* kind of damage control under way. I just have no idea what that would even look like at this point.

Zoe shifts on her feet, looking down at her phone. She swipes it open before lifting it up, determination on her face as she holds it out to show me what she's pulled up from her texts. "Have you seen Reid's video?" she asks, studiously avoiding the serial killer-esque staredown that I have no intention of curbing.

The video. *Of course.*

I know I should have already been two steps ahead of this mess, but I've been too exhausted and pissed off to check on social media.

Did one of the Prefects purposefully send her in here to make sure I'd seen it? She's not part of Sloane's usual group of minions, but she's certainly popular enough to hang around in their close orbit. Perhaps this little visit is Zoe's personal attempt at moving up a rung on the Rox Academy social ladder?

At this point, I'm not sure it matters. She's seen my ink. After everything else I've fucked up this past week, I can't risk her running her mouth about it. The last thing I need is it getting back to Sebastian. Or to The Pantheon. They might not be working for the Aces, but they are definitely tangled up in the Underworld, somehow.

There's every chance they'd recognize the significance of the rooks on my back. Then it's *game over*.

Taking a step through the steam that's begun to belatedly gather in my stall, I drop my gaze to her screen. On it is a shaky vertical video of a familiar blonde's slumped form. Zoe presses play and the soundtrack of Reid's vicious giggles and Sloane's snarky commentary begins to echo loudly off the tiles.

I watch in a detached sort of way as a few seconds into the video, I collapse forward—legs folded beneath me at a painful-looking angle, and arms clamped to my side by the sleeves of my leather jacket. It looks like someone tried to peel it off me to gain access to my arm. An arm that clearly still has a depressed syringe embedded near the elbow. My moans join their laughter, low and agonized.

So much of this part of the night was lost to the first initial burn of the injection. But one thing I *do* remember?

The pain.

All the latent feelings of wrath that had been left on simmer after the weekend now bubble back violently to the surface. The edges of my vision spark.

After the video loops a third time, I finally force myself to look up at Zoe. She's not fast enough to hide the amused smile that's slipped into place as she watches me replay my own humiliation. That expression that had at first seemed so free of artifice, is nowhere to be found.

I'm not sure who I am more annoyed at right now—Zoe, or myself for how fucking shot to hell my instincts have become. There's no getting around the fact that she'd made her bed the moment she laid eyes on my tattoo, but the added deception just further sweeps away any reluctance.

This is the last *time I give* anyone *at this* godsforsaken *fucking school the benefit of the fucking doubt.*

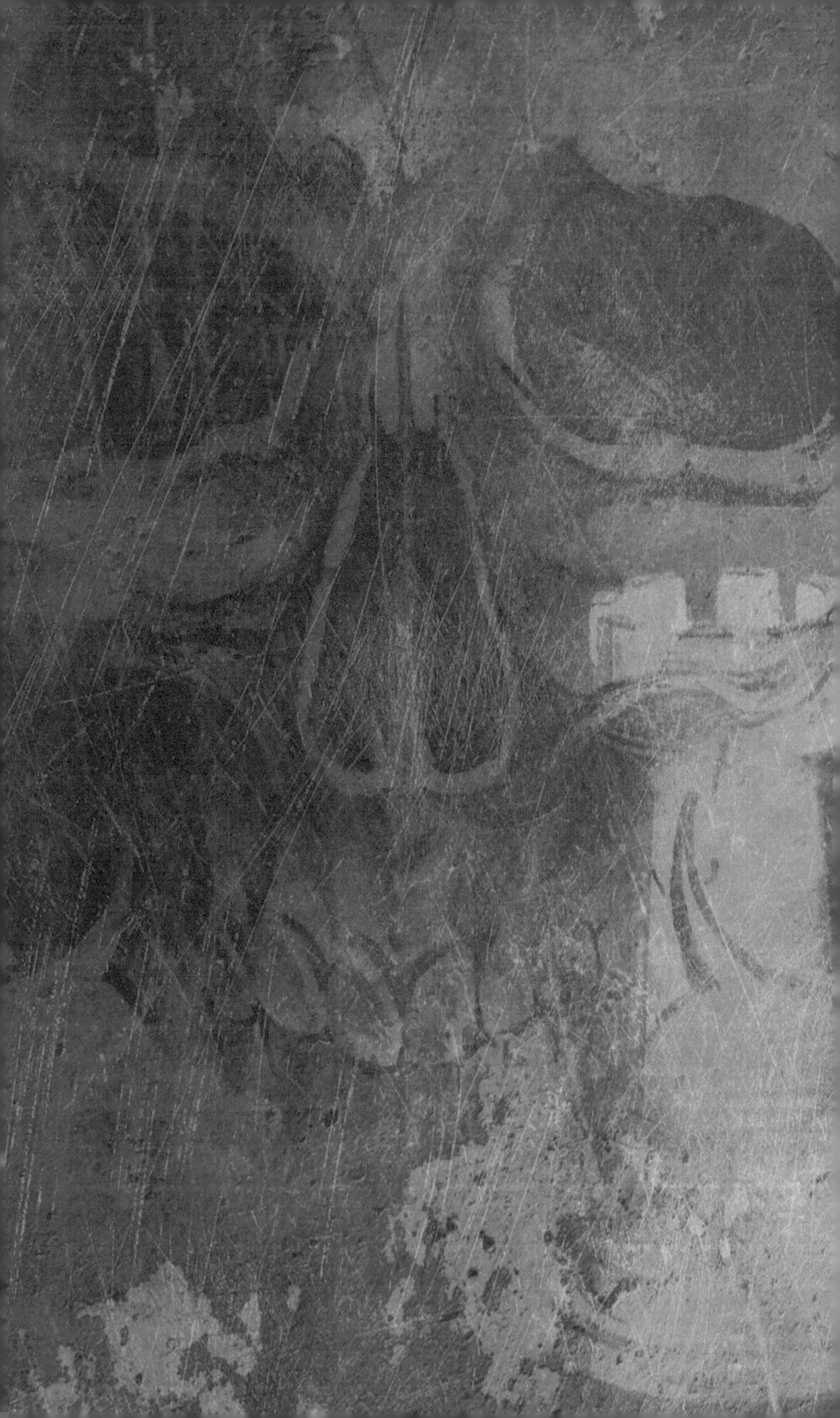

CHAPTER XXI
SABINE

A SLOW EXHALE.

Then I'm shoving all that frothing anger down and I'm inviting in the killing calm to settle comfortably across my shoulders. And like the drugs I lean on daily, I'm *addicted* to it.

My hand shoots out and I jab my thumb into the vagus nerve on her neck. "Sorry about it," I say, not sorry at all. There's no remorse, only the anticipatory rise of my heart rate.

I squeeze harder on the pressure point and Zoe's eyes roll back, her breathing starting to slow. I let go and watch as she slumps to the floor like a ragdoll. Almost in a perfect parody of my own recorded humiliation. That trouble-making thought doesn't get the chance to take hold, my brain already occupied with recycling this scrumptious morsel of adrenaline.

I stare down at Zoe's limp figure, reviewing everything I know about her. Her family, her sporting achievements, her academic record. There are no especially heinous skeletons looming in her closet. The truth is, she probably would have made a poor recruit anyway.

Accident it is.

I don't have any tools or weapons on me, and after assessing my options, a quick dry-boarding seems like my best chance to make this as clean as possible. I have to trust that the steam that has slowly been filling the room will be enough to provide some semblance of cover, but I do need to at least move us out of the thoroughfare between stalls.

I'm still naked but I don't bother getting dressed first. My clothes would get wet with what I need to do next. Reaching down, I grab Zoe under the armpits and drag her up and over the short upstand at the threshold of the shower. I then place her down on the floor at the base of the shower, careful not to lay her over the drain. The water spray begins to bead on her hair and brow.

Grabbing her discarded towel next, I twist one corner of it until it takes on the form of a snake. With one hand, I hold her mouth open and proceed to force-feed her the length of it. When it won't progress any further, and I'm confident her throat is fully blocked, I push her jaw closed against the towel and pinch her nose shut.

Zoe's eyes begin to flutter and a low, retching sound reverberates from the bottom of her throat. Still holding her nostrils closed, I lean that wrist down against the towel to prevent her from expelling it by reflex, and then use my free hand to apply more pressure to her vagus nerve.

It has the desired effect of calming the rising flight-or-flight response of her body's struggle for oxygen, and soon enough Zoe's shoulders drop back to the floor. She's fully unconscious.

My heart thrums like a hummingbird. It's lunch time, so the chances of any one coming into the locker room now are slim. But they aren't zero. I strain my hearing, desperate to catch any new movements. I won't be taken by surprise a second time.

Miraculously, we remain alone.

The wait is grueling, but after I count out a generous ten minutes—more than enough to ensure brain death—I ease back, checking Zoe's pulse as I retract the towel. She's gone.

Standing up, I groan, stretching and rolling the aching muscles in my back and shoulders. Pins and needles prick along my extremities. I must have been tensed up like a coiled spring the entire time I was crouched. Ready to pounce on the next intruder.

When I've got all the feeling back in my fingers, I kneel back down, scooping one hand behind Zoe's head and placing the other beneath her jaw. Then I take a deep breath in and hold. On the exhale, I yank up and to the side quickly. There's a quiet crunch as I adjust her neck to sit at an unnatural angle. After I leave her slumped against the back corner of the stall and under the water with a wayward sandal next to her—the final effect looks like an unfortunate slip-and-fall.

Satisfied, I gather up everything I brought with me into the shower and start rushing through getting dressed. My hair and makeup is going to be the bare fucking minimum I can manage so that I don't look like a drowned rat that's scurrying away from the scene of a homicide.

As I'm running some mascara along my lashes, I prop my phone against one shoulder and press the fourth person on my speed dial.

"Hello?" Foster's sullen tone filters into my ear. Over the line I can hear the frantic clicks of his keyboard and the gentle hum of a room full of electronics. There's no way of telling what I've interrupted. He could have been eating, gaming, jacking off or staring at the wall for all I know. He always sounds like a dollar store Eeyore no matter what he's been up to.

"Hey man, I'll need you to do a wipe of hallway cameras 26, 27 and 28 for the thirty minutes either side of this timestamp." I don't need to elaborate; I'm his only surveillance job right now and he knows by watching my phone's tracker that I'm still at Rox Academy. I also can't risk being overheard so I promptly hang up.

Just as I finish packing up the rest of my makeup, my cell buzzes in my hand. I frown when I see **Dionysus** flashing on the screen.

Dionysus…?

Oh.

I remember now.

Sometime during our early Sunday morning sexting —while I was undoubtedly still off my face—I had spilled the beans to Rhett about my Pantheon concept for the Rox Boys. Rhett being Rhett was *greatly* amused that my *"budding harem had matching nicknames"*, and then proceeded to pout at length until I agreed to assign him a likewise alias.

Dubbing him the God of Pleasure and Madness was only natural. In fact, now that I think about it—I can't believe it's taken me this long.

As a result of that conversation, he's now also taken to calling Jax *Daddy Zeus*.

Not gonna lie, I'm totally fucking here for it.

"Dioooo, what's good?" If he's calling me in the middle of the day, he's no doubt on brand for sowing some discord. I should probably be worried.

"What should I be calling *you* now? Aphrodite?"

I scrunch up my nose. "Fuck if I know. What's going on?"

Dionysus blows out a breath directly into the receiver and I brace myself. It's never good if he's the one hesitating. "Dominic's on campus. We just clocked him on the cameras outside your dorm building while we were getting ready for the wipe. Which, by the way—the fuck kind of mess have you gotten yourself into now, Ms Winters?"

I let out a long tortured groan, only just catching myself before I manage to wipe a hand down my face and mess up my freshly applied makeup.

Perfect. Gray Man bullshit, in the flesh, right after I've just thrown a chum bucket into the Roxborough Academy waters.

The skin across my temples seems to pull ever tighter as my live-in headache throbs savagely. There are no cameras inside the locker rooms for obvious privacy reasons, but it won't be long before Zoe's found and they'll put two and two together. Doesn't mean I need to make it easier for him and *openly* admit to my massive fuck up.

"You'll laugh," I hedge, hoping in vain he'll drop it.

"Oh *yes*, try me please. I want to be able to skip my core workout later," he says in the cheekiest fucking voice possible.

"There's a dead senior in the girl's locker room…on account of her having seen my tattoos," I mutter sullenly under my breath.

I have to hold the phone away from my ear then, because Dio positively *howls*. "How the *fuck* did she manage that? Who got the drop on you?"

This bullshit is *exactly* what I was trying to avoid. "I don't want to fucking talk about it," I snark back.

"Oh my sides, shit. *Ow*," he wheezes. "We can't let you out of our sight for one fucking minute, can we, baby?"

I can practically *hear* the tears in his eyes. *Smug prick.*

Time to deflect. I'm running on borrowed seconds as it is.

"Where's Dominic now? I need to head him off. Can't have him lurking around." After witnessing the Pantheon meet up with an Underworld contact, I realize there's no telling how far they've ventured into our world. It's entirely possible they're already well aware of who Sebastian Grayson and his Second are.

It's the same reason I couldn't risk Zoe casually mentioning my back tattoo to the Prefects over lunch and having the Boys immediately clock me as a Gray Man.

See? Messy. Colossally fucking messy.

"Still outside the Briarthorn block. Doesn't look like he's being discreet about it either. Be careful, babe."

I nod to myself as I give into my ingrained habit of running through possible scenarios. Sending his Second to check up on me. Fucking power plays.

"Might want to add the Briarthorn cameras to your wipe as well then," I add before hanging up.

BY THE TIME I reach my dorm building, I've short-listed the most likely reasons for the impromptu visit.

Both Sebastian and his Second loathe setting foot anywhere this side of the Bridge, so I'm thoroughly convinced that they must have seen Reid's video. Zoe's copy of the video had come through in a massive group text, but I had to assume it was also on social media somewhere, and Dominic's here to read me the riot act.

Or they've simply decided its finally time for me to retire with an all-expenses-paid trip to the bottom of the Tethys. I'm not sure exactly how many second chances I was allocated for this mission, but it didn't seem like our boss was overflowing with good will all those weeks ago when he was gleefully assigning me to this hellhole.

Dominic's waiting for me beneath the shadowed portico of my dorm block. His face is like stone; hard angles and even harder to read. His brow is pulled down low, but that's kind of his default look. He's not on my list of people who really unnerve me, but he's got a direct line to Sebastian. And Sebastian *is* on that list.

"Librarian. Nice of you to join me," he says with that pack-a-day smoker's growl of his. His expression is still not giving anything away.

I tip my chin at him. There's no point in trying to small talk my way out of the inevitable. There's also no way this man in particular will let me. He makes it a habit to spend as little time in my vicinity as possible.

I'm also keenly aware of prying eyes.

"The Symposium is this weekend," he continues, and my guts do a massive backflip of relief. I carefully keep my features as neutral as possible. No relief, no disappointment, no sass. Dominic is *not* one to pass up on an opportunity to ream me out for giving attitude—*and he didn't mention the video first.*

He also didn't bring up the four dead bangers in the alley off the Guardhouse or the fact I just left behind a dead co-ed in the bathroom during lunch.

Those were also solid contenders on the *List Of Most Likely Reasons Sabine Meets Her End Today.*

I'm trying *really* hard not to count my fucking chickens. Did he really come all this way just to chit chat about…the *Symposium*?

This weekend marks the 63rd annual Underworld Symposium—a gala night always held on neutral ground and attended by Families and clubs and syndicates from both Sovereignties. The location is always a random pocket of No Man's Land, neutral ground that's overseen by the Gatekeeper.

It's the most highly anticipated event on the calendar, knowing it's a guaranteed way for everyone to safely get wasted and shit talk their sworn enemies without fear of bloodshed or reprisal. Although it's not officially hosted by one single party, *Hospitium* will still very much be in effect.

"Yes, the second Sunday of every September. I'm aware." I'm trying my best to keep the brattiness out of my voice, I swear, but it's a trial.

Dominic grunts but doesn't call me out on it. "Are the Sinclair kid and his friends going?"

Unexpectedly, my neck prickles and an uneasy...*protectiveness* trickles down my spine.

I mean, I'm here to recruit them *for* him. They'll have to meet him eventually. But for some cursed reason, the idea of Sebastian being in the same room as the Pantheon is making me really, really uneasy. The sensation is extremely foreign to me and entirely unpleasant.

I'm so fucking confused.

"Um," I swallow roughly, my throat raw and my guts churning like I just took that *Ash* shot in the arm all over again. "I haven't been able to confirm that yet," I rasp out. Does my voice sound weirdly high to his ears as well?

Dominic's forehead creases, and he looks like he's about to further burden me with his extreme disappointment, so I'm quick to add, "But I *was* able to confirm they're definitely working with a faction, but it's *not* the Strange Aces. I wasn't able to initially identify their contact's alliance."

"Initially?"

"I'm still working on it."

Dominic swipes a large hand along his jaw, pinning me with a *look*. "I expect a full report once you do. He's still not happy with you."

I don't bother arguing with that, and instead offer a small jerky nod and shrug combo that says *how could I forget?*

He stares me down for a moment longer before giving me a return jerk of the chin. "Make sure they're all there on Sunday night. The boss had a dress delivered to your room." Then he's melting into the surrounding shrubbery, looking to find his exit around the backside of the building.

All the adrenaline from the last half hour or so whooshes out of me, leaving my head spinning like a carousel, and my muscles feeling like they've been filled with lead.

I'm not entirely convinced that message warranted the in-person drop-in; but I'm sure Dominic just wanted to both physically set eyes on me, and ensure I still have a healthy fear of Sebastian after leaving Lexington.

I guess this means I get to see at least one more week of sunrises.

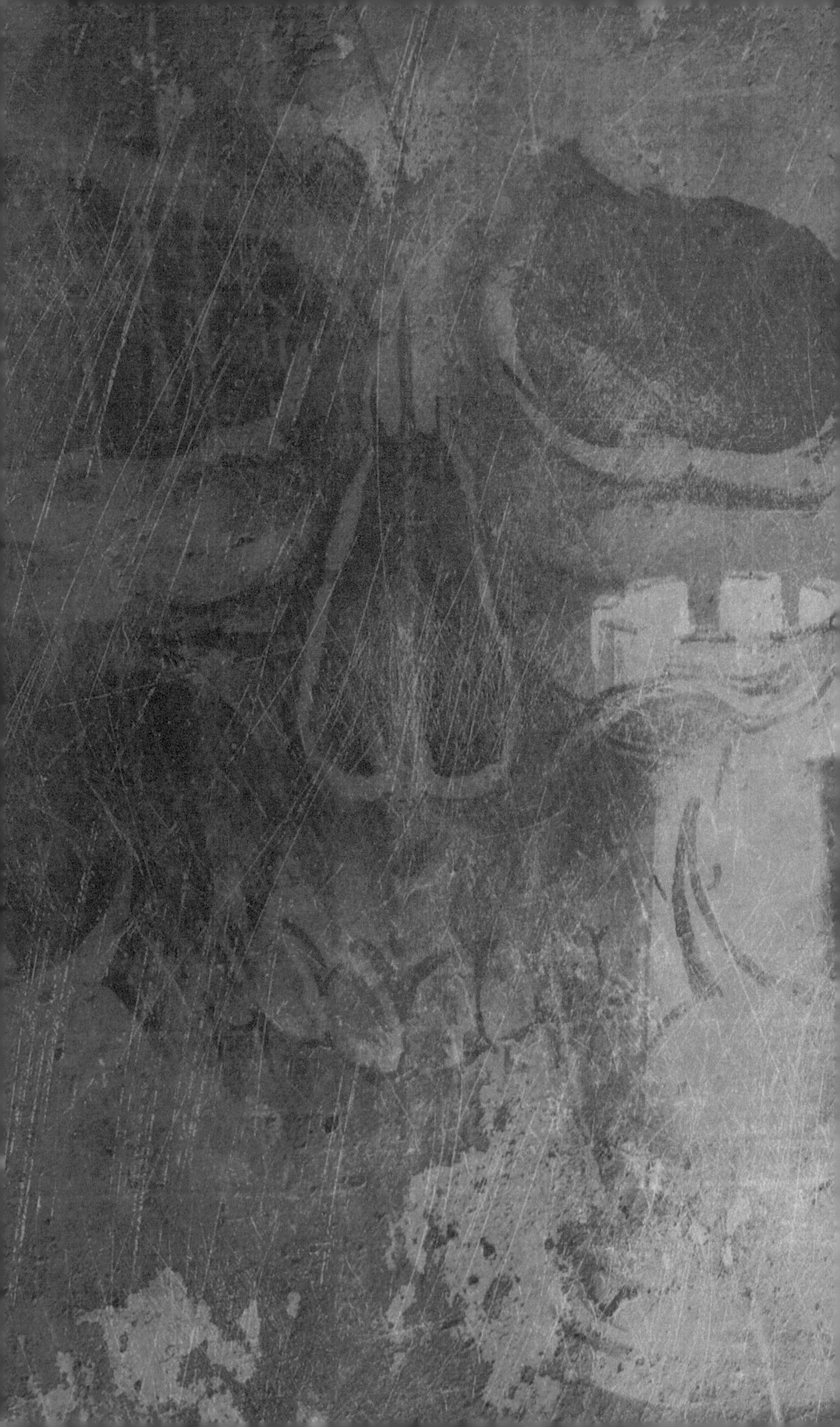

CHAPTER XXII

LAKE

HOW THE ACTUAL fuck I'm expected to keep my head in this stupid fucking ball game is anyone's goddamn guess.

I mean—it's hard on my so-called best days, right? The days where my heart *doesn't* feel like it's about to beat straight through my fucking ribcage and my head *doesn't* feel like a pile of snakes.

Days which—as any one of my brothers will tell you —are pretty fucking rare.

Even now, in the middle of a rostered season game, my skin feels tight and impatient, like it wants to just up and crawl straight off my body. It's like the unease is curdling deep down in my very marrow, somewhere just out of reach.

When it gets this bad, I'd do just about *anything* to gouge these feelings out. Well, most of those *anythings* are really more like *anyones*. It's not like it's hard to find warm, willing holes around here—especially if you're a fucking *Rox Boy*.

Jesus, who even came up with that shit? Probably that

newly endangered bitch Walker and her obsessed little Tristan Sinclair PR team.

No, I much prefer *Hermes. That*'s one name that brings back the smile to my face. I can feel the satisfaction of our little lost Wifey's claim slowly creeping back in and I welcome it.

I still can't believe she's actually here.

In the flesh.

Not dead, like we've believed for the past six fucking years.

Now my brothers just need to pull their heads out of their goddamn asses so we can make her ours again. *For real this time.*

The shrill, piercing sound of a whistle slices through my thoughts like a Razorhead arrow. The ref's calling the end of the quarter, and signaling the end of the game.

Fucking *finally.* Not that I've been paying much attention. Greenwich High is always a guaranteed win for us. God knows I could've spent the entire time on the court with my eyes closed and my hands on my dick, and I still would've had no trouble heading off any of their basic as shit defensive zone plays.

And I don't even like this game.

Truth be told, I'm only on this fucking team because of Apollo. Ares had thought it would be a *"good outlet"* for me. Something about too much excess energy spilling over into our 'extra curricular' work, and how I needed to *"pull my head in"* before I *"got us all killed".*

Apollo had agreed. *The beautiful traitor.*

Bunch of fucking mother hen bullshit if you ask me.

My grin slips and I scowl again. Now that I've stopped moving, my brain has started crowding back in and my limbs ache with my latest irritation.

From the moment that video hit the inboxes of the entire graduating class, I've been operating on an even sharper knife's edge than normal. I'm sure just about anybody could read the murderous intent that's been written all over my face since Monday.

Posturing little bitches. Just thinking about them has angry tingles prickling up and down my neck like TV static.

It wasn't a difficult thing to access Reid Adam's accounts and wipe the original's footprints from all her socials. Especially with everyone busy losing their minds after someone found Zoe Nguyen with a broken neck in the showers of the girl's locker room. It gave me the distraction I needed to work my magic on all the devices using the Academy's network settings.

I couldn't unring the bell on the mass text, however. Too many people had already seen it. Which I don't fucking like, at all. I also don't like that they were smart enough not to talk about it online where I could hack their message history, so I have no hard proof of what actually went down.

All I've got to go on is a video of our girl shooting up and totally fucking out of it. I don't care that there was a needle in her arm. I care that it doesn't look like she's in control. That she was in pain.

I could tell she'd been struggling to focus in the alley that night; the edges of her words had been a little slurred. I'd thought maybe she'd just been a little drunk, but after seeing that video, it makes so much more sense.

I wouldn't think she'd have bothered following Hades through the Underground if she'd only been drinking. But high? I can see it. A lot of the shit on the streets will turn you paranoid.

All I know is nothing about that video feels right, and I should know—control and I aren't on the best of terms.

I do my best to drown out the sound of the stadium's cheers and my teammates' bullshit, and jog over to our bench to cool down instead. As I run a towel over my neck and shoulders, I let my gaze roam over the crowd.

Holy shit.

She's actually here—sitting half a dozen rows away, and next to Wren Jacobs and Lincoln Reynolds of all people. Her face is carefully blank, and after scanning the other students around her it quickly becomes painfully obvious why.

Everyone within earshot of her seat is still whispering and giving her the *teen gossip* side-eye. It's been days now.

My blood pressure is rising and not in a way I normally enjoy.

As if she can hear every dark thought now churning in my skull, Sabine flicks her attention courtside, finding me straight away like we're two fucking magnets. Her eyes look dark and glimmering from where I stand.

A ghost of a smile appears, and then she tilts her head, taking me in as if she's busy weighing and measuring my soul from on high like some bored demigoddess. It sends a shiver rippling through tense muscles that I feel all the way down to my cock.

God, she's fucking gorgeous.

I know Apollo's had that mouth. Those lips look like they're made for sucking dick. But me? I can't wait to get *my* tongue on *her*.

I'm willing to bet she tastes so fucking sweet between those thighs that she gives me a goddamn toothache.

As she continues to stare me down, I let those thoughts play out across my face, hoping she can decipher my intentions. Then I jerk my chin towards the locker room. Apollo's busy doing Team Captain shit. It'll be easy to slip away.

She's thinking about it; I can tell. After a beat, she leans over and whispers something to Wren, who just shrugs once, and then she sends me a wicked smirk.

I've got my answer.

Fuck yes.

This will be the record for the fastest fucking shower of my life.

I HADN'T REALIZED JUST how completely wound up I was—totally convinced that Sabine was going to bail on me—until I burst out into the hallway and the relief splashes over me like sea spray.

My lighter snaps shut with a loud click and I shove it into my pocket of my gym shorts, taking a moment to drink in the sight of the woman in front of me. I feel my pulse spike again, but this time it's not with the same gut-wrenching anxiety that was churning in my guts during my entire post-game routine.

She's leaning against the wall, thumbs flying over her phone screen. Without looking up, she says, "What kind of mischief do you have planned for us today then, Hermes?"

I've got everything we need in the backpack slung over one of my shoulders. "Follow me," I instruct happily, grabbing her hand and making damn sure she is, in fact, following me.

"Yeah, sure. Why the fuck not?"

Yes! It is on like motherfucking Donkey Kong.

I drag her all the way through the back halls and via the shortcut to the parking lot. We need to blow this joint before a certain someone notices the keys to his Mustang are missing.

The big guy should really put a lot more thought into choosing his hiding places.

When we reach Ares's GT, my chest heaves with anticipation, laced with just a little trepidation, but I hold up the set of keys with a grin. "Can you drive stick, Wifey?"

For a moment, I think she hasn't heard me, then I realize Sabine's busy giving the car a *very* appreciative once-over.

I really want her to look at *me* like that.

Need it, in fact. Preferably while I'm busy licking her cunt from the inside out. Like, fucking *yesterday*.

"Stop calling me that," she answers in a distracted

tone, but then she proceeds to swipe the keys dangling off my finger. I guess that answers my question.

I clap my hands and round the hood for the passenger's seat. "No can do, babycakes. I know you and my brother didn't do much *talking* on Friday night, but I know that he told you that you're ours. So, best to quit fighting it and just *save your breath*."

Her eyebrows shoot up at my innuendo. Hell yeah, I love catching her off guard like that. After a lot of begging, I managed to squeeze every last play-by-play out of a smug Apollo.

Or should I say breath-play-by-breath-play?

Hmm. I wonder if her willingness to deep-throat would expand to other types of erotic asphyxiation? That'd be hot as fuck.

I volunteer as tribute.

I jump in and slam the door before she can quip back with something snarky and ruin this for us. We don't need those kinda mood killers here. There's only a moment's hesitation before there's a mirroring slam from the driver's side.

"Alright, where to?" Her voice is molten, like she's already horny as fuck and I chuckle, watching her. She's totally riveted, caressing her palms over the stained wood of the tri-bar steering wheel.

"The 'Stang's just the foreplay. You know the Southside Pier?" I ask, drumming my fingers on the dash while subtly checking our mirrors for signs of a pissed off tattooed man-hulk. So far, so good.

Sabine nods, firing the engine up—and then peeling

out of the lot like the Hounds of Hell are on her ass. I crank the window down and let out a long, loud howl of approval. First part of the mission is complete.

She whoops with me, smoothly changing gears and sliding us in and out of traffic like it's her fucking job. This is definitely not her first time behind the wheel of a muscle car.

This girl. Christ, I can't take my eyes off her and now I'm hard as diamonds.

I want to know everything about her. I want to strip her down to the bones and learn every notch and every ligament with my tongue. I want to bury my fingers and my cock so far inside she'll need an exorcism to get rid of me.

Who are you these days, baby girl?

For the moment, at least, she's trapped here with me. She can't dodge me—or the more important question that's been burning me up inside since the day we followed her. I'm diving in headfirst and grilling her before I can stop to think better of it.

"Who's the guy from the warehouse?"

The question being out there sends a pulse of something bitter roiling through my chest and stomach. *Are they together? Is he special to her?* My right leg is so jittery I can feel my thigh quaking.

She tosses me an assessing side glance, then focuses back on the road. There's a secret sort of smile on her face. I don't like that she's smiling at the same time that she's thinking about him.

It makes me feel a little homicidal.

Okay, maybe a lot.

"You can call him Dionysus. I wasn't kidding when I said he'd ruin you. He lives for that shit." There's a pause. "But now I've gotten a better vibe check, I'm thinking you'd probably both give as good as you'd get," she muses with a low laugh.

Well, *fuck*!

When I had first joked about sharing her with him, my chest had filled up with all kinds of acidic, jealous feelings. And they'd only gotten worse the longer the week went on. Not to mention, hearing that she had hooked up with Leo *fucking* Baker? She's honestly lucky there wasn't a higher body count this past weekend.

But with those few choice words, the murderous thoughts are quickly being replaced by a slew of boxer-tightening *hot-blond-guy-plus-dream-girl* ménage fantasies instead.

Goddamn. Now all I can think about is Sabine at the Diner talking about spit-roasting, and I'm wondering what it's going to take to get the two of them to make a meal out of *me*.

I groan quietly at thoughts of making an Eiffel Tower with this Dionysus and Sabine.

I've always wanted to go to Paris.

I reach down to squeeze my hard-on. The flimsy material does nothing to hide it either. "Drive faster, Wifey. I'm begging you."

Sabine snorts, but it sounds light. Nothing like the cool, mocking disdain we've gotten from her since she got here. "Don't start the party without me, Hermes," she snarks, and presses harder on the gas.

My cock pulses against my palm in response.

As soon as she pulls us into the curb near the Pier, I'm up and out of the car, backpack in hand. Her amused laughter follows as she locks up the car, but I'm too busy tipping my head to the sky and pulling in a lungful of the sea air.

It helps to ease the tightness under my ribs, but my heart rate is still ratcheted right up.

Luckily I have the solution for that problem.

As she sidles up behind me, I catch a soft whiff of sandalwood, picked up and carried by the soft breeze that gusts over us. I suck it in, letting it settle me. Then, as I did back in the hallway, I grab her hand and tug her along.

Christ, I seriously think I could get high off just this small amount of skin-to-skin contact with her. Actually fucking her is going to kill me.

I'm not heading for the boardwalk though, instead pulling her impatiently towards the sandy stretch of beach before us. When she sees where I'm headed, she yanks sharply against my firm grip. "Wait, Hermes, pump the brakes," she says, like I'm actually going to slow down. I'm dying of starvation and I'm this close to a Sabine-flavored all-you-can-eat buffet.

Wait. *Wait?* Is this where she starts to second guess coming with me?

Within seconds, my enthusiasm is draining away. My

vision tunnels and I can hear the taunting rush of blood pounding in my ears.

Why would she want to stay? Of course she's going to leave you here.

I spin, trying to bully my features into something resembling neutral, but I know my expression must be all kinds of fucked up. The way her eyes roam over my face, and then soften ever so slightly tells me she saw it, too.

She tugs on my hand again, and I reluctantly drop it.

This is it.

But she doesn't turn to head back to the car. She simply bends down—using that free hand on my shoulder for balance—before slipping off her Academy-issued shoes and knee-high socks. The school insists on everyone wearing their full academic uniforms to home games, even on the weekends. "Not walking on the beach in heels," she mutters, and I can feel my ears getting hot.

A quiet breath whooshes out of me.

Once she's ready, I'm off again, determined and powering towards my destination—a run-down husk of a lifeguard tower that's a ways down the beach. Her toes squeak in the cool sand as she hurries to catch up.

The wind shifts, and the seaspray hits my face. I feel like I might be able to finally take a breath again.

This. This is my domain.

Fucking and fighting are easy for blowing off steam, but *nothing* calms me like losing a few hours out on my board, surrounded by nothing but the wind and the swell.

By the time we reach the isolated hut, my veins no

longer feel like they're full of spiders and I'm as close to settled as I can get these days.

"What is this place?" Sabine asks, curious, eyes roaming over the weather-beaten shack like she can force it to give up all my secrets.

"Old lifeguard clubhouse and tower. They left it up after they built new ones closer to the Pier." I toss my backpack up and over the metal railing and hoist myself up. Most of the steps have rotted out in the salty air, and the rest are swollen with moisture. I turn around and offer my hand.

She grips my fingers and hoists herself up. But rather than climb over as I did, she slips between two of the handrails in a sexy as fuck feat of gymnastics. My face breaks out in a grin. "That kind of flexibility will come in handy."

Her answering grin is just as knowing. "You have no idea," she purrs.

"Lord have mercy on my cock," I murmur, palming it roughly again through my shorts. I feel like I've been hard for hours at this point.

Sabine follows the gesture and her smile turns feral. "C'mon then, pretty boy."

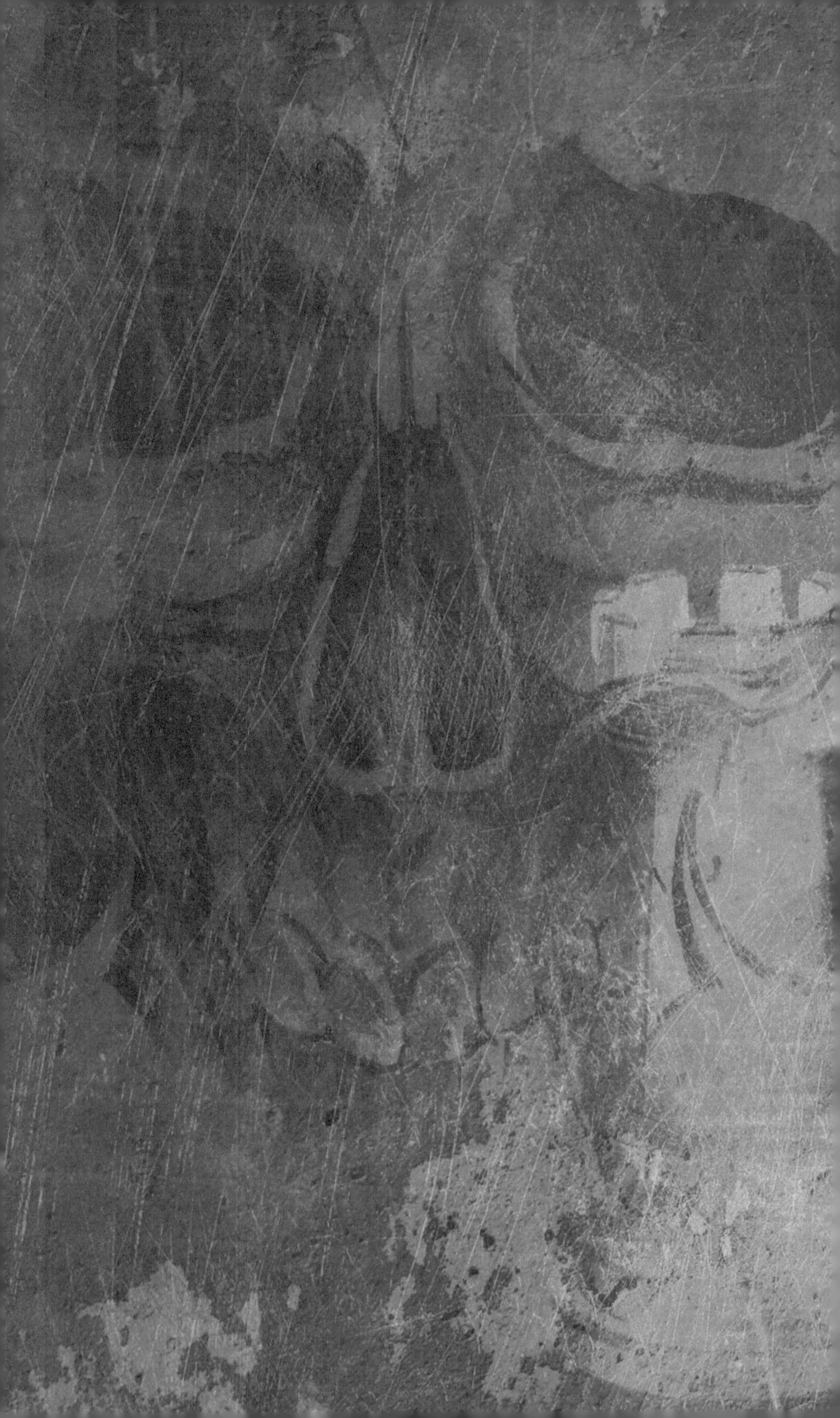

CHAPTER XXIII

LAKE

FUCK, *yes.*

I practically spring forward, shoving open a door that's been warped by the constant salt-infused damp, all the protective coatings long since worn away.

The inside of the shack is only in marginally better shape than the outside. The interior's been gutted, and the walls are stripped and pitted, but the huge fixed storm windows and roof are still intact, so it stays relatively dry.

I always assumed the original furniture must have been cleared out when they shut the place down. Over time I've added some ancient faded floor pillows and an old quilt of my mom's. There's also a fuck ton of mason jars with an assortment of candles scattered around the space. They're useful if I'm ever out here past sundown.

She wanders in behind me, surveying the place with a look of appreciation close to the one she gave the restored Mustang. "You put this all together?"

"Yeah. No one ever really comes this far down the

beach, not after they added all the tourist shit and moved the patrol area closer to the Pier."

I move forward, and fling myself into the cushions. I pat the one next to me in an open invitation. As I wait for her to join me, I pull my backpack between my knees and start emptying the contents.

"Hungry?" Arranged between us now are an assortment of Reubens and BLTs that Ares had lovingly created this morning. I idly wonder if he's noticed they're missing as well as his keys. At least I was kind enough to leave Apollo's gluten-free monstrosities behind.

No doubt he'd also be livid if he knew I'd brought along a bunch of energy drinks. Claims they fuck with my sleep, and are a bad trigger for my episodes.

I push thoughts of my overprotective brother away.

He's not here right now. It's just me and our girl.

Finally.

I go to pick up one of the sandwiches for her, but she beats me to it, tearing into a BLT like she's on the clock. "Make sure you chew first," I snicker at her, before I start in on one of the Reubens.

It doesn't take long for us to finish off the food, and then we're both flopping back down against the pillows and letting out matching sighs of satiation.

"Damn, girl, you've got a voracious appetite, don't you," I say in an appreciative tone.

"It's about to get bigger," she chuckles, magicking up two neatly rolled joints from thin air. She holds one out to me. "Courtesy of that traitorous fuck, King. I paid his dorm a visit this morning before the game."

"Oh, shit, now it's a fucking party," I crow, accepting the stolen joint. I light them for us, before returning the lighter to my pocket with a flourish.

"What's with the Zippo? I see you fidgeting with it all the time. Is it a stimming thing?" Sabine asks on a languid exhale, smoke leaking into the space between us like a slow-rolling morning fog.

"It was my grandpa's," I offer. "And yeah, gives me something to do with my hands when everything gets too…loud."

She shifts, and even with the smell of the weed filling my nostrils, I still catch undercurrents of her own unique musky scent. When I look at her face, I'm surprised to see something there that looks like understanding.

I raise an eyebrow. "Why do I get the feeling you know what I'm talking about?" There's a weird tug in my guts. Almost like if someone had sewn a thread through my navel and started yanking on it.

Sabine takes another hit before tilting her head so that the sun slanting in through from the observation deck highlights the angry-looking scar along her left temple. "There's a reason sobriety and me are not the best of friends. My head's a bit loud some days, as well."

There's no makeup covering it and her hair is styled away from her face. She hasn't even tried to hide it.

It's fierce. Just like her.

I must be feeling the effects of the weed starting to kick in, because before I can think, I'm leaning up and running my tongue along the length of it. Again.

Her lids—already at half-mast—fall shut with an

almost inaudible moan. Just like that first time at her locker, her skin feels warm and tastes so sweet. "Saturday night?" I ask her quietly.

She opens her eyes again, silently taking in my open expression. Despite the haze hanging in the air, her gaze is bright. Finally, with a resigned sigh, she mutters, "I was there to buy from Axel. I got caught with my pants down and Walker took the opportunity to stick me with a hotshot of *Ash*."

I rear back, coughing. Disbelief claws at my throat, along with the smoke from my last pull. My subtle high starts to slip away. "What the fuck? What was it cut with?"

"I actually have no idea. Luckily, I have, uh, a pretty high tolerance, so I was only laid out for a couple of hours. Took me the rest of the weekend to ride the whole thing out though."

Then something else about her words cuts through the fog and I'm feeling murderous all over again. "Wait? With your pants down? *Were you fucking King?*" I'm hissing like a cat whose tail just got stepped on, but I don't even fucking care right now.

The last thing I expect to hear from her is laughter. Or to feel her delicate hand sliding over the front of my shorts.

"*Down* boy, it was a figure of speech. She had a couple of her guard dogs with her and they got the jump on me," Sabine soothes in that sultry voice. "I should have been more careful," she adds darkly, like she's chastising herself.

Fuck everything about this. Fuck those cunts for touching her, and fuck her blaming herself.

Between one breath and the next, I'm hovering over her, pushing her shoulders back against the cushion she's propped against. I snatch the mostly smoked joint from between her two fingers, dropping both into the closest jar to burn out.

I'm diving down, ready to take her mouth with mine, when Sabine makes a weird noise in the back of her throat. I stop, pulling back, confusion and apprehension clouding in once again.

Is now *the moment she rejects me?*

She must see the agony playing out on my face, because she's talking to me again in those reassuring tones.

"Hermes, hey, look at me."

It takes everything I have not to just jump up and walk straight into the ocean. I drag my gaze back to hers.

"I'm sorry, okay?" Her voice sounds almost strained, like she's the one who's embarrassed here. "It's not you. I just…don't…kiss."

"What?" Her confession only serves to deepen my confusion. I feel like my brain is short circuiting.

"Uh, it's kind of stupid."

"Try me."

Sabine shifts her hips beneath me, reminding me that I'm still really fucking hard and my heart rate is *still* through the fucking roof, and that I really, really just need to be inside her.

She blows out a breath that's still tinged with smoke.

When I focus in on her face, I expect there to be a pretty blush across her cheeks, but she doesn't look flustered… just…uncertain?

"Kissing means feelings." She starts, all her usual confidence bleeding out of her.

"Yeah, I guess?" I mean, I get not wanting to make out with random hookups. They're usually quick in and outs.

But it's me. It's *us*.

I'm certainly feeling all *kinds* of things.

Dark, possessive, monstrous things.

I blink. She's gesturing to her head again. "I don't really experience emotions like most other people." Her arm flops back down to her side, almost dejectedly. "So the idea of kissing just feels…I don't know…*wrong* to me."

There's something in the way she says that, though. *The idea of kissing*.

"Wait. Are you tell me you've never kissed anyone?" A brand new emotion surges in, shoving aside the apprehension.

Sabine nods once, jaw clenched tight.

I can't help it. I roll off her and onto one elbow with a howl of laughter. If only she fucking knew.

Wait 'til they hear this.

This is fucking *priceless*.

Of course, her face goes carefully blank again, all vulnerability wiped away. There's only a slight crease left between her brow. "Why are you laughing at me?" she demands firmly.

I can only shake my head. Wiping the corner of my

eye, I say, "Alright. We'll circle back around to that another time. But let me put my mouth on you now. *Please.*"

Her blue-gray eyes are locked on mine, pupils blown wide with a heady combo of the weed and her arousal. She watches hungrily as I start to slither down her body, not moving to stop me at all.

Before I can finish settling myself between her legs, however, she seems to change her mind. I hesitate, lingering, as she begins to sit up, forcing me back onto my haunches.

That fucking insecurity starts crowding back in again, looking to find a new stranglehold in my chest.

But Sabine doesn't make me wait long. Fingers are suddenly spearing into my curls and she's switching our positions, yanking my head at an angle and guiding me roughly onto the flat of my back. All the air in my lungs squeezes out as I hit the pillows.

Before I can even register the motion, she's following me down and straddling me with a knee on either side of my head, giving me a breath-taking, unobstructed view of a lacy black thong.

Holy Christ.

For a moment, she just stares down at my face, features carefully schooled but eyes shining with unconcealed lust. If it wasn't for her chest rising and falling, she could almost be a Greek statue of one of those wild forest Nymphs.

She still has a tight grip on my hair, and she jerks it viciously, tilting my chin back and making my scalp burn with the most luscious spike of pain. I hiss out, before the sound tapers off into a moan.

Although in theory, I could easily flip her, I feel like my entire body is paralyzed. Somehow, the very idea that I'm here with her—under her, letting her take control, and completely at her mercy—it sends an intoxicating wash of calm over me.

Surrender.

"Hope you're still hungry," she purrs.

"Yes," I breathe, my entire being laser-focused into one pinpoint—the sight of her pussy floating above me.

"Good boy, that's what I want to hear. Now get to work."

Almost like my body no longer belongs to me, I watch with fascination as my hands slide up the outsides of her legs, lifting her skirt as I go. The rising hem starts to reveal a set of large, intricate tattoos on both her thighs and I hum in admiration.

One looks like the skull of a raven, or maybe a crow, and it's surrounded by a bunch of wilting wildflowers.

The other has more rotting flowers flanking a set of chess pieces.

The Queen standing over a fallen King?

They're both fucking gorgeous, if a little eerie. Kind of like the woman currently holding me hostage with said thighs.

My fingers trail over small bumps and raises in the skin as I run a finger over the ink. I suck in a breath as I realize what the sprawling line work is hiding. Dozens of tiny scars.

Sabine makes that disgruntled little noise in the back of her throat, like she did when I tried to kiss her. She grabs my hands, sliding them up higher. "You're not here to sightsee."

Yes, ma'am.

I still have the skirt rucked up beneath my palms, so I start shoving the hem into the waistband with untidy folds on either side. Now the only thing standing between me and my meal is this fucking thong.

Hooking two fingers behind the material, I allow myself exactly two seconds to relish the feel of how fucking wet she is, and then I yank down on it viciously. The flimsy thing tears away easily, and I'm greeted by a neatly trimmed triangle of blonde hair.

Sabine clears her throat, raising an eyebrow.

Flinging the scrap of lace to the side, I quickly return my hands to her thighs, running my palms all the way up the backs of her legs before grabbing her by the ass cheeks. Despite how tall and slim she is, my girl is working with a nice solid handful. I give them an experimental squeeze before I tug down.

"Okay, grant me a glorious death in battle, *mamacita*."

She snorts. "Let's see you earn it first, Hermes."

And then she's widening her stance, lowering over my face and finally, *finally* she's right where I need her.

Her pussy is already swollen and glistening; prominent lips open and waiting. In this moment, I don't think I've ever seen anything more beautiful.

I groan loudly when she drops even further and aligns herself directly over my waiting mouth. My nose buries immediately against her clit, like her cunt was custom molded for my face and my face alone.

Something tells me that she's not looking for a gentle ride today, and so I make the most of it and begin to eat her out with all the enthusiasm of a starving man. The fingers tightening in my hair tells me I've made the right choice.

"*Yes*, that's it."

Pretty soon she's taking over the pace, riding me from the bridge of my nose to my chin, and soaking my entire lower face with her juices. I slurp and lash and flick; laving her clit and both openings, and making sure to delve inside with my tongue when her movements allow me.

I go to pull back and beg her to cover my tongue with her cum, when she once again yanks on my hair. "Don't talk with your mouth full."

A new kink has been unlocked.

My cock is leaking like a fucking sieve, and I double down. Can't be coming in my pants before I've been inside her.

I feel Sabine's thighs already starting to shake above me, and so I latch my lips firmly onto her clit and suck. I didn't even get a chance to use my fingers yet. *Fucking hell.*

Her orgasm is swift and hard, sending her release pouring down my chin to join the mess already there. We both groan together, and I keep lapping.

She's delicious, a little salty, and I swear I could get

drunk off the taste. Finally, when I'm satisfied I've gotten every last drop, I pull back.

I know there must be a stupid grin on my lips and cum running down my neck, but I'm in fucking heaven right now.

Sabine straightens up but doesn't move away immediately. "Such a good boy, Hermes, licking up all your mess," she coos.

I swallow roughly. So fucking aroused by this magnificent femdom version of my woman. I know Apollo didn't get this side of her. My dick is about to tear through my fucking shorts.

"I *always* clean my plate, Wifey."

Her eyes widen with my words, and then she's making her way backwards over my torso. As soon as she reaches my shorts, she starts pulling them down my legs roughly.

I lift my hips to help her, watching as my cock springs free, slapping against my shirt and leaving a second wet patch of pre-cum behind. Now it matches my shorts.

Sabine hums happily, reaching out to wrap a cool hand around the length of it. "Mmm, Hermes. I see you've got a Goldilocks dick. My favorite."

My lips part as she gives it a few lazy pumps.

"Not too long, not too thick. Juuuust right."

My cock has gotten a lot of compliments in his time, but fuck if hearing her words of praise don't just suck *all* the remaining blood down south.

I'm putty in her hands and I don't think I have the willpower to stop her so I can fish out a condom. Not with the tantalizing promise of slipping inside her raw *right there* in front of me.

She makes the decision for me when she climbs back up and positions herself over the weeping head. I watch, speechless, as she eases herself down with an obscene moan until I bottom out.

Or was that me?

I can't tell, because I think I might have blacked out there from the sheer pleasure of entering her for the first time.

"Fuck, fuck, *fuck!*" I grit out, grabbing her hips and holding her down. Her cunt has a death grip on my cock.

I've imagined this exact scene and a thousand fucking others. Always in a what-could-have-been moment when I was younger and horny as hell.

Jerking off to the ghost of the girl we all loved.

But she's no longer a ghost.

...Unless I really have died?

I don't fucking care at this point.

It's torture.

It's bliss.

Sabine's already working her way up to another orgasm, strangling the life out of my shaft as her pussy tightens rhythmically.

"Fuck, yes," she breathes. Then she slides her fingers in between us, splitting them around the base of my cock, and using her thumb on her clit while she does.

I don't know if it's hearing her curse, knowing that I'm the reason for that little slip of control, or if it's the feel of her fingers rubbing alongside my dick. Either way, I'm fucking doomed.

"Wifey, baby, Sabine, I'm gonna come. Can I please come inside you?" My voice sounds strained, taut with the effort of holding off my orgasm, and I don't even care how desperate I sound.

Because I do feel desperate.

Desperate to fill this cunt, and desperate to bear witness to the resulting creampie as it oozes out when we're done.

"*Please*," I pant.

My chest feels like it's been pulled tight like a rubber band. Sabine's voice is filled with the same urgency.

"Yes, *fuck yes*, be a good boy and fill me up."

Here lies Lake 'Hermes' Ezekiel Miller.

Her words leave my spine feeling like a downed live wire and my balls are in my fucking throat. I dig my nails into her flesh for leverage and slam her down, grinding her clit against the hard muscle of my pelvis.

Then my jaw locks and my vision goes white and I'm painting the inside of her with wave after fucking wave of cum. It's endless.

When I finally regain my senses, Sabine is staring up at the ceiling, chest heaving. I realize that we didn't even bother to get fully undressed and I chuckle. She looks back down at me and the smile she grants me feels like I've won the fucking lottery.

I tap her on the thigh and she starts to rise in response. "Wait," I say, helping her ease off me. "I need to see it as it drips out of you."

She flicks her gaze down, slowing her movements. As my cock finally slips out of her, a rush of our combined fluids follows in its wake, coating her thighs and spilling onto my abdomen.

I close my eyes, letting out an agonized sound. "*So fucking hot.* Why is that so hot?" I whisper brokenly.

But I know the answer.

I've never fucked anyone raw before. Never had the pleasure of witnessing my release gush from the hole I'd just freshly filled.

Christ, this better not awaken anything in me.

Too late.

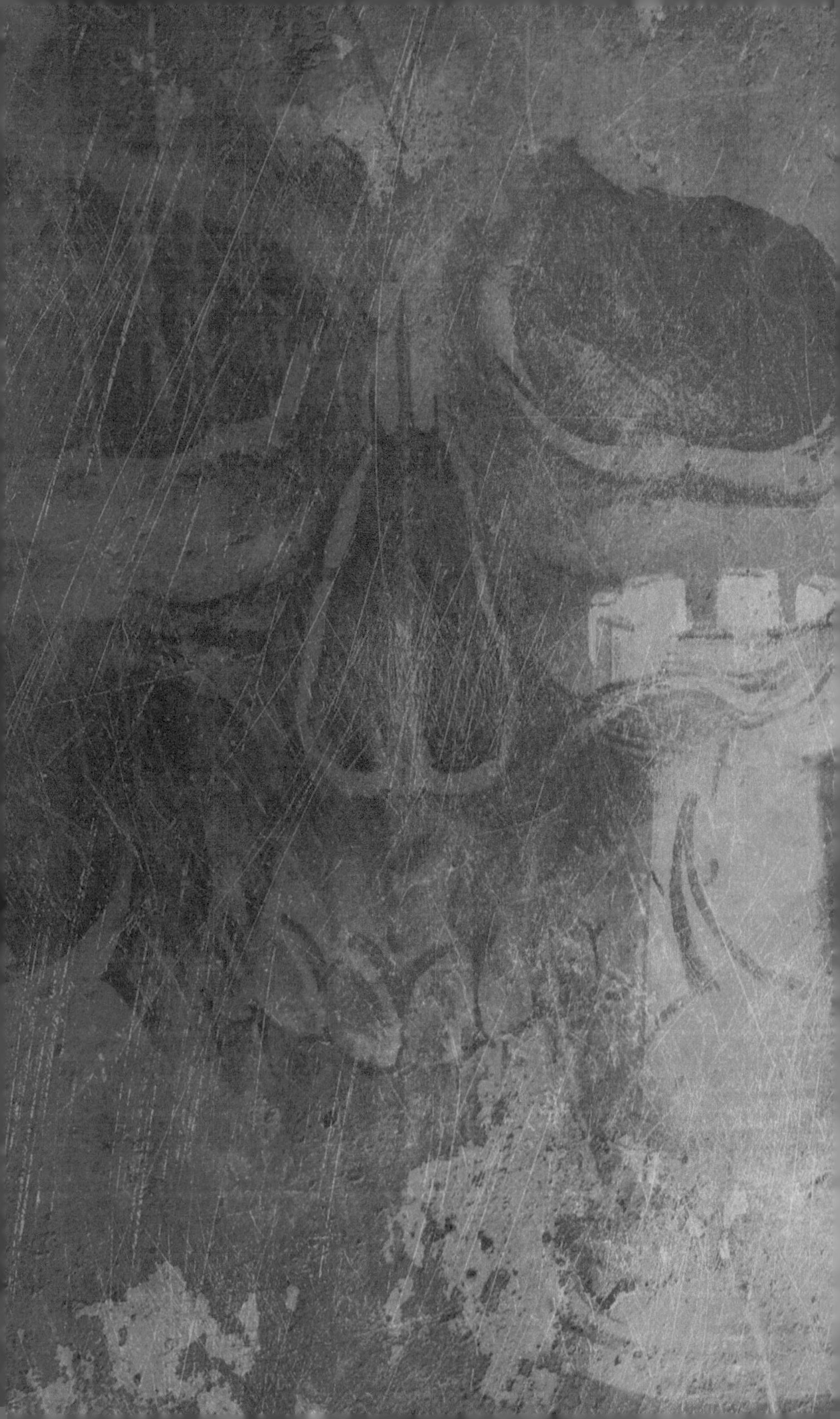

CHAPTER XXIV

SABINE

I GUESS when I was sorting out my daily planner this morning, I must have conveniently forgotten to pencil *Get Your Brains Fucked Out By A Rox Boy* onto the agenda.

Fuck. Who am I kidding? *Nothing* about this day has followed any sort of cohesive outline.

When I woke up, I'd been just about ready to take a kitchen knife and start peeling my skin off. I hadn't gotten high *or* laid all week and my emergency stash of gin was doing nothing to cut through the mess in my brain. Everything felt tight and hot and itchy. The irritation ran everywhere; from the top of my scalp down to the ends of my fingers and toes.

Hence the impromptu trip to Axel's room, timed so I knew he'd be busy skipping the Kraken's game to go down to the Pier with his crew of shithead friends.

I was still deciding whether I wanted to turn Axel, or whether I would send him down the same dead-end path as Sloane and her Irish lackeys. I think maybe he'd enjoy life as a Gray Man a little *too* much—if I'm honest—and I couldn't have that.

When I'd gotten there, I'd allowed myself exactly ten minutes to ferret around in all the obvious places, managing to come away with two Ziplock bags—one filled with the pre-rolled joints, and another bag similar to the one I'd tried to buy from him last weekend. This one had been a mixture of diazepam and what I think may be temazepam? It was a shit load of benzos regardless, and it felt like a sweet victory *fuck you*.

And after the disaster of my week, any small win helped take the sting out.

Not only did I spend several days staving off what was almost a full body system detox with nothing but alcohol and Tylenol, but I also didn't manage to enlist any new recruits.

It puts me a full week behind on the schedule I'd set for myself in order to achieve my numbers, but I had honestly needed to lay low until the heat around Zoe's death had died off a little. Word had also finally gotten around that there'd been a gang-related shootout outside the Guardhouse during the Welcome Back party.

Everyone had been just a little too spooked for me to safely approach without drawing too much attention.

So yeah, not gonna lie—I desperately needed these few stolen moments here with Miller.

The problem is that now there's an ugly sort of feeling growing inside my chest, worsening the longer I'm around him. Almost as if my heart and lungs were experiencing vertigo. Almost like the bizarre feeling of ownership I felt when Dominic reminded me that Sebastian wanted to meet them tomorrow night.

Perhaps what's really needed here is for me to start putting back some of the distance between us. I do need to remember they're supposed to be a mission, after all.

I rise up on shaky Bambi legs, and start freeing the skirt that's been gathered and stuffed into the waistband haphazardly. We both stink like sex and I'm going to have to do a complete walk of shame back to the dorms at this rate.

Hermes follows me up from the cushions, sliding his shorts back into place against his lithely muscled thighs. I watch as he tucks himself away and I can't help but lament the loss.

He really does have the perfect dick.

And I *really* did want to get him and Dio in a room together...*Or Hermes and Apollo.* Their gorgeous cocks would be a match made in heaven. Dickmatizing.

But I just know shit's about to turn *real* awkward if I let things like *emotions* start trying to muscle their way into what's supposed to be a harmless bit of fun. I just need to feel him out about tomorrow night first, and then I can make the split.

He stretches his arms above his head and his tank rides up. "I think I need to be hosed off. Up for a little skinny dipping?"

I snort, trying to keep my focus on straightening out my wrinkled pleats, and not on the sneak peek of those bronzed, toned abs. "Tempting..."

It *is* tempting, but this could be my chance to catch him off guard while he's still firmly in that post-jizz haze.

Worst case scenario, I can just try reading his body language again. It really wasn't difficult to recognize the craving for reassurance whenever he thought I was rejecting him. To push past all that bravado and to tap into his submissive streak. It was obvious that he needed those moments of surrender and I was more than happy to help give him that. If anyone understands, it's me. It's my usual *modus operandi*, after all.

And I can admit that it had been an excellent way to kill two anxiety birds with one stone. Unfortunately it may just be the key to killing whatever *this is* before it goes any further.

"—But I actually have a hair appointment to get to," I hedge, before adding, just as casually, "Need it ready for The Symposium tomorrow night."

Hermes's spine straightens and then he winces as soon as he realizes that my shrewd gaze has caught it.

I'll take that *as a resounding yes.*

The three of them heard me mention the Treaty in the alley during the failed contact with Morelli and his partner. They'd *have* to have concluded by now that they weren't the only ones with a toe dipped in the seedy waters of the Underworld.

Everybody's got secrets, Sabine.

Apollo did his best to deflect in the car, but I guess it was only a matter of time. Our paths were on a direct collision course, and what better crash site than the biggest event on the Underworld's calendar?

"You guys going then? I bet all four of you would

look pornographic in a tux." Not even a little lie there. If they show up to this thing in any sort of formal wear, my horny bitch spank bank will be set *for life*.

I see when his shoulders slump and he realizes that our collective layers of subterfuge were indeed starting to meet in the middle. "Yeah. We'll be there," he mutters tersely, looking away.

Then his gorgeous hazel eyes flick to mine. I see that open sort of vulnerability there again, just like each of the times he thought I was about to push him away.

Oh no.

Oh no.

I don't know him well enough to understand the origin of that fear, but I do know one thing—he's about to hand me his destruction on a silver platter.

"Who do you need to show up with? Maybe we can make a date out of it once we're there," he says, a crooked grin slipping through.

He just looks so...*hopeful* right now. The air in my lungs suddenly feels poisonous.

This is it.

"A date. With *you*?" I do my best to inject just enough incredulity into my tone, and that weird dizziness in my chest intensifies.

"No, not just me. All of us, together. Like it's supposed to be."

He steps towards me, hands out and reaching for my waist like he wants to pull me in. I cut him off with my best cutting, derisive laugh and he falters, mid-stride.

"The fuck? What kind of weird fucking fairytale are the four of you living in?" I spit, pushing out a lot more venom into it this time.

Hermes's mouth instantly turns down and his eyebrows clash together violently. "Wifey, I told you to stop fighting it. We're inevitable." His voice turns hoarse, sharp and pained. I feel it like a slice across my skin. *"Why don't you remember us?"*

"I've told you multiple times—I'm not your fucking *wife*, and there is no *we*. No *us*." I bend down and snatch up my shoes, making sure my phone's still in my skirt.

There's no way I can stay and face the devastation I'm wreaking on Hermes's already fragile mental state. I had no idea he—they?—was so far gone with this fantastical idea of us. I'd just thought it was all part of his larger than life personality. Charming the pants off the shiny new girl and everything.

No, I have to get out of here. The oxygen's all gone.

I pull out my cell to start sending a message to Dio while moving back towards the busted out doorway. I'm going to have to get him to come and make an emergency extraction.

One last parting shot.

"I mean, thanks for the orgasms and all, but you didn't think this was anything more than sex, did you?"

The last thing I hear before I leap over the railing is a *thud* that sounds suspiciously like Hermes's knees hitting the floor.

BY THE TIME Dionysus gets me back to campus, the sun is starting to set, and the ground is freezing beneath my feet. I hadn't bothered to put my socks or shoes back on—not with my feet all covered in sand.

The crisp bite of the approaching fall against my legs only serves to further remind me that I've once again found myself making my way back to my room at night, no underwear and thighs covered in dry cum.

The whole thing feels like a weird déjà vu moment.

Only I won't be coming home to masturbate furiously to Apollo's O face for an hour and a half like I did last time.

No, this time my lady parts are as solemn as the cavity in my chest.

Dio walks me all the way to Briarthorn, dropping me off right outside my door with a burning kiss to the neck and an accompanying slap to the ass. But not even that playfulness is enough to cheer me up.

I feel weirdly, oddly, foreignly, confusingly…*adrift*. And I don't know how to even begin approaching it.

I'm literally not emotionally equipped to face what just went down in that ramshackle beach house. What I just did.

"Why don't you remember us?"

I'm halfway through unlocking the three deadbolts on my front door, when my *spidey senses* send the hairs on my arms standing up. An answering flare of adrenaline shoots off an internal alarm and I tense.

Someone's in my fucking dorm room.

My sullen mood clears like storm clouds parting, leaving my mind in survival mode and racing. Waiting for any kind of movement.

Did the Aces find out I was in the alley that night? What syndicate did the Northerners belong to? Has Dominic changed his mind about me and come back to clean up the problem once and for all?

Considering my best course of action, I make the decision to stand my ground, rather than flee. I've never been one to run from a good fight, and they obviously already know where I live.

It's best if I can draw them out now and get ahead of the threat.

Besides, it's not like I don't deserve to face a little pain right now.

I finish with the last lock, before attempting to arrange the keys in my hand into some kind of fist-loaded weapon. It's the best I've got—I have nothing else on me except my phone and my shoes, which only have a short kitten heel.

Taking a steadying breath, I shove against the door, right near the hinge so that it swings back slowly. The interior of the apartment is pitch black, all the lights still off, just as I had left them.

Keeping my feet firmly on the hallway side of the threshold, I reach my empty hand around the doorframe and hit the switch for the lights.

Warm pendant lamps flicker to life across the living room and the kitchen areas, revealing the intruder that has very much made himself at home on one of my couches. There's a glass of water and a small stack of paper on the coffee table in front of him.

"*Jax*," I breathe out, before stumbling forward like a drunkard. The door swings shut behind me and the keys drop to the floor, forgotten. It's been two months since I've laid eyes on him. I feel about three foot tall right now, but I'm just so fucking overwhelmingly glad to see him.

"Sabe," he says in an equally relieved voice, rising from the couch and striding to meet me. He catches me up in a crushing hug.

My entire face is pushed into the warm embrace of his chest and the comforting, familiar scent of his cologne wraps around me, tugging together the fraying threads of my composure.

I pull back and take stock of him, almost afraid to believe he's really here. Both his hair and beard are much longer than he usually keeps them, giving a slightly wild and untamed edge to his already strong features.

His normally achingly bright blue eyes look dull. Defeated.

In short, he looks ragged.

"What's happened?" I croak. "Who died?"

I was just with Dio. "Is Knox okay?"

Jax shushes me, pulling me in for one more strangling hug before he turns to lead me back over to the couch.

"No one's dead. But I'm afraid that might be about to

change." His voice is raspy and grave, and it instantly has my hackles rising. "I believe my days are numbered."

"What are you talking about?" I hiss out. "Did the Herald announce a hit?" My brain feels like pure chaos right now, and I can sense the beginnings of a killer headache worming its way in from the base of my skull.

Sebastian has made no secret of his displeasure for Jax's organizational leadership style, but he's *obsessed* with his bloodline. There is no fucking way he would hand over the keys to his kingdom to *anyone* but Jackson.

There's just no way.

A sharp tang of copper blooms in my mouth and I realize that I've bitten down on my tongue.

Instead of answering me, Jax leans over and picks up the stack of papers. As he hands them to me, I see his Adam's apple bob harshly as he swallows.

My hands shake as I take them. Perplexed, I flick my eyes down, and as soon as my gaze connects with the top of the first page of the document my lungs seize.

DNA Paternity Report - Lexington Diagnostics.

I force myself to keep reading, all while spots begin to form in my vision. I can't tell if Jax is speaking because I can't hear anything except the thunder of blood in my ears.

The report is dated **November 28, 2005**. In the first allele column it lists the **Mother (Not Tested)** as one **Rosaline Bridgette Porter-Sinclair**. The next column lists the **Child** as **Tristan Marcus**

Sinclair. Apollo would have been just over fifteen months old when this test was carried out. But why?

And then I see it as my eyes slide to the third and final column. Instead of Martin Sinclair's name as I had expected, it lists the **Alleged Father** being tested as **Sebastian Norris Grayson.**

All the air leaves my lungs in a violent rush as I read the final portion of the results.

The alleged father cannot be excluded as the biological father of the tested child. Based on analysis of STR loci listed above, the probability of paternity is 99.99999999%.

Tristan Sinclair is Sebastian Grayson's son.

Apollo is Jax's brother.

And he just turned eighteen.

My vision blurs and bile rushes up my throat. Now it all finally starts to make sense.

They must belong to us by the end of the year, or do not return to Lexington expecting a warm welcome home.

All the times he reminded of a younger Jax, I thought it was just something in the way they both dominated the room. But it was more than that.

It was biological.

As I manage to pull in a single shaky breath, Jax's voice manages to finally cut through my rising terror. "Sabine?"

My head snaps up and I lock eyes with him. I understand now why he looked so tired. So haunted.

"You see now, don't you? The Gray Man already has his replacement heir."

**The Pantheon will continue in
Carry Your Debt**

*Did you enjoy this book? Please consider leaving a review
on Amazon and/or Goodreads!*

ABOUT THE AUTHOR

E.J. Campbell is an Aussie who loves caffeine and books, and spends most of her time living in Romancelandia. She chiefly enjoys reading reverse harem romances, especially when they're dark and dirty, contemporary, or fantastical.

She's a firm believer that every kink is sacred, and that romance novels are a beautiful way to let the average reader explore them, safely and unfettered.

Forget Me Twice is her debut novel, the first in her new *Pantheon* series.

Visit
ejcampbellauthor.com/stalk-me
for social links & newsletter sign-up

FIND & JOIN MY FACEBOOK GROUP
THE PANTHEON: E.J. CAMPBELL READER'S GROUP

hello@ejcampbellauthor.com

instagram.com / ejcampbellauthor
facebook.com / ejcampbellauthor
tiktok.com / @ejcampbellauthor
goodreads.com / ejcampbell
amazon.com / author / ejcampbell
pinterest.com / ejcampbellauthor

BOOKS BY E.J.

Imperium in Imperio
A SHARED CRIMINAL UNDERWORLD UNIVERSE

THE PANTHEON

(Reverse Harem Series)

I. Forget Me Twice

II. Carry Your Debt

III. Might Die Young

BLOODY LOVE NOTES

(Serial Killer Whychoose/Poly Duet)

I. The Bodies Between Us (*Coming soon*)

II. TLWB (*Coming soon*)